FAMILY AFFAIRS

SANDRA KITT

A SIGNET BOOK

SIGNET
Published by the Penguin Group
Penguin Putnam Inc., 375 Hudson Street,
New York, New York 10014, U.S.A.
Penguin Books Ltd, 27 Wrights Lane,
London W8 5TZ, England
Penguin Books Australia Ltd, Ringwood,
Victoria, Australia
Penguin Books Canada Ltd, 10 Alcorn Avenue,
Toronto, Ontario, Canada M4V 3B2
Penguin Books (N.Z.) Ltd, 182–190 Wairau Road,
Auckland 10, New Zealand

Penguin Books Ltd, Registered Offices:
Harmondsworth, Middlesex, England

First published by Signet, an imprint of Dutton NAL,
a member of Penguin Putnam Inc.

First Printing, May 1999
10 9 8 7 6 5 4 3 2 1

Dedicated with love and gratitude
to my mother, Ann, and to my late father, Archie,
and especially to my late maternal grandmother,
Lottie Wright.

With loving appreciation to:
Alan and Nenette Harvey
Sioux Taylor
Chuck and Barbara Belensky
Rob and Carol Wilson
d Meyerson and Pat Bowling
Branca Nicholson
Helmut and Francie Wimmer
Clyté Spiedel and Paul Keown

All of whom, in many ways,
have made me a part of their families.

Finally . . .
sincere thanks, as always,
to J. P.

Acknowledgments

I am in debt to the staff of the Genetics and Sickle Cell Center of Harlem Hospital in New York for aiding my research.

And to Ginger Davis of Brooklyn, New York . . . teacher, mother, survivor . . . for her personal insights.

PROLOGUE

"I have to go," Gayla whispered.

"Yeah, I know. Can't you stay a little longer? There's plenty of time . . ."

"No, I can't." But she didn't move.

He pulled her closer, until she could feel his chest hair brushing against her cheek, his hand gliding down her back. His closeness was still a novelty, and his touch made her skin tingle. It made her feel excited and bold and guilty . . . and damned.

"Gay . . . let's do it again."

"No."

She could hear that odd depth in his voice and had learned, in just a few weeks, to tell that he wanted her. Gayla hoped that she would always hear that because then she would be sure that Graham Whelan really cared about her.

Finally, when he didn't plead further, she reluctantly rolled away from him, sliding from beneath the sheet and swinging her legs out to the floor. She felt sticky with the summer heat and the other residue on their bodies from making love. Yet even as she sat up, all that had made their moments together special was already fading away into reality. Now all she could think of was getting back quickly and quietly.

Suddenly he hooked her around the waist with his arm, making her gasp in surprise . . . and satisfaction. He didn't want to let her go. She giggled when he pulled her down and onto her back again. He held her still with the weight of his leg.

"Graham . . ." she whined, halfheartedly fending off his attempts to kiss her and lay atop her body. "Stop it. You're going to get me in trouble."

"Nobody's gonna find out. Come on, Gay . . ."

His hand fumbled over her breasts, settling into gently squeezing and rubbing her nipples. He pressed kisses on her face, found her mouth and urged her to open hers and kiss him back, the way he'd taught her to. Gayla sighed and let the wet and slow dancing of their tongues seduce her once again into a state of limp willingness. He kissed so differently from Kadin or Brody. Better. But they were just boys. What Graham did to her exposed her totally, combined a brief pain with a sweet pleasure that throbbed deliciously throughout her body. It quelled the fear that she would pay for what she was doing.

She wanted to stay, but knew she couldn't take the chance. Gayla prevented Graham from positioning himself between her legs, thwarting his attempt to enter her. But she offered no resistance when instead he pressed his hand between her legs and stroked her. She was still wet, and initiated enough to welcome this intimacy which would culminate in shattering bliss. Gayla felt herself slipping into a sensual lassitude, a giddiness of the forbidden before her awareness of the time and the place intruded. Gayla pushed his hand away and closed her legs. "No . . . stop."

"Gay . . ."

"We can't," she whined in regret.

"You want to, don't you?"

She hesitated. "Yeah."

She loved that Graham wanted her. That he wanted to touch her body and kiss her. But Gayla was beginning to sense that letting Graham make love to her was a different thing. It was serious. It meant that he loved her, didn't it?

"What if your mother finds out?" She could see him shrug in the dark, but not the expression on his face.

"So what if she does?"

"Are you crazy?" Gayla's voice squeaked out, and she pushed impatiently against his chest. "Your folks will have a fit. They could say I'm trying to ruin your life. They could blame me for—"

"Don't worry about it. Dad's too focused on his own writing and stuff to notice anything. And Mom's not the kind of person to criticize. Besides, she really likes you a lot."

"Not *that* much," Gayla muttered. "I . . . I don't think we should do this anymore. And if my mother ever . . ."

He rolled toward her, shaking her gently. "Hey,

I'm not a kid anymore. I live my own life. My folks can't tell me who to love."

Gayla sighed and let her body relax. She was right. He did love her.

In the dark Graham's hand touched and explored her face. He levered himself onto his elbow and leaned in to kiss her. "I thought about you the whole damned semester. I was hoping Sylvia would bring you here for the summer." He kissed her again, his hand now gliding down her torso and stomach, an enticing lead-in to wanting more from her.

Gayla broke the contact of their lips. "Do you think I'm pretty?" she asked quietly.

"You're beautiful, Gayla. I've never known anyone like you."

She gnawed the inside of her lower lip. "Am I prettier than . . . Nancy Lynn Straitham?"

He stopped his seduction. "Nancy? It's not the same thing. You're so different from Nancy."

She tried to see his face, but it was shadowed. His skin looked flat and pale gray in the dim light, except for the dark island of hair in the center of his chest. "Why? Because she's got blonde hair? What do you mean, it's not the same thing?"

"I mean . . . she's nice and she's pretty, but Nancy's like every girl I went to high school with. Her folks are just like mine. They have everything and just accept it. Nancy is like those women in that movie . . . *The Stepford Wives*. Pretty, but empty. But you're different because you get such a kick out of everything. You're not afraid to try things. But you're also beautiful . . . so sweet and innocent. It knocks me out."

Gayla smiled at his words. "I think you're the handsomest man I've ever known."

"Oh, yeah?" He chuckled quietly. "How many men have you known?"

She couldn't answer, of course. There were no others. As far as she was concerned there never would be again. No one could ever make her feel as special as Graham. "I just meant that . . ."

"I'm only teasing. I'm glad I was the first with you. That's pretty special. But I know you're going to have to beat the guys back with a stick."

"No, I won't. I'm always going to . . . to . . . love you," she defended awkwardly.

"Sure you will."

"I will. Don't you believe me?" she asked.

"It's not that I don't believe you. It's just that . . . things can change. I say I love you and you say you love me. But I could go away. You're still in high school. You'll meet someone else."

"I won't. I know I won't . . ." He laughed lightly, and she hastily put her hand over his mouth. "Sssshh! You're going to wake someone up!"

He stopped laughing and pulled her hand away. "I told you I don't care, Gayla. I feel so good when I'm with you. I want everyone to know what you mean to me. We could get married someday."

Gayla held her breath. She wished she could tell from his voice if Graham was serious. She felt the tremulous jump of her heartbeat with both fear and joy. The zigzag of confusion. "You lie. You'd *never* ask me to marry you. You'd *never* tell your parents you want to."

Graham responded by setting his hands on her hips, and as he lay back on the pillows, he brought Gayla down on top of him. "Never say never . . ." he whispered.

She resisted, wary of the risk of staying any longer in his room. But his pronouncement made Gayla feel bold and careless. The feel of his knowing hands made her feel so soft and hot. Already her skin was damp with anticipation. Her mind purposefully blanked out other considerations, the world beyond the closed door of Graham's room, the magical isolation of the Green Mountains of the Vermont woods, the next day when they'd all have to go back to pretending that *this* was not supposed to happen.

A sudden shard of doom pierced Gayla's chest. She closed her eyes to block it out, and concentrated on the exciting novelty of her body awakened, for the first time, to physical pleasure. Real stuff. Grown-up doings. She made a sound of surrender.

But it was shut off abruptly when Gayla thought she heard something beyond the closed door of the room. She stopped moving, and when Graham tried to urge her on, Gayla wiggled away from him.

"Did you hear that? Someone's in the hallway. I have to get out of here . . ."

Gayla heard his groan of frustration as he reached for her, but she was already scrambling off the bed and reaching blindly for her T-shirt and panties.

"Come on, Gay. There's no one out there. It's two-thirty in the morning, for Christ's sake. Everyone is sleeping."

She ignored him this time, her heart beating with another instinct, all sensation of her desire gone in the need to protect herself . . . both of them . . . from detection. She pulled on her underpants, almost tripping as she forced her leg into the skimpy garment. Gayla grabbed a shirt, not even sure it was hers, and tiptoed to the door and crouched, listening, for sounds on the other side. There was nothing. For a moment she felt that perhaps Graham was right and she was being skittish. But she was going to leave anyway.

She turned her head and saw Graham languishing in the bed with the sheet tangled around his calves and ankles. For a moment she was angry with him. Why wasn't he trying to protect her? Why didn't he care that they could be caught? Why didn't Graham understand that she would pay a much higher price than he would if they were found together?

"Gayla . . ." He got out of bed finally, and walked to meet her at the door.

She watched him. Through her annoyance Gayla was again fascinated by his pale, naked body. The first time she'd seen all of him, Gayla had been shocked speechless. Especially by the rigid power of his penis and the silken tangle of dark hair around the base of it. Gayla said nothing as Graham calmly approached her. He pulled her into his arms, but she was stiff suddenly, with an animal's sense of danger.

"It doesn't matter what happens. I love you."

She believed him. Graham had been telling her that since she was seven years old. But was it a different love now than when they were younger and he responded to her adoration with gentle tolerance? Was it really a different kind of love than what he felt for his sister, Sarah?

She looked beseechingly into his face. "Graham . . . I have to go . . ." she pleaded on a whisper.

"Okay," he said reluctantly. "But I want to see you tomorrow. Can you get away?"

"I don't know. I don't think so . . ."

"All right. Then tomorrow night. Come back here tomorrow."

"Maybe. I have to see . . ."

He kissed her and quietly opened the door.

Gayla slipped out into the hallway, and the door clicked closed behind her. She felt foolish and exposed, sneaking about in the night in someone else's house . . . nearly naked. She hastily pulled the T-shirt on. She stood perfectly still for a moment, but could only hear alien night sounds. Not sirens or car horns or alarms, but crickets and an occasional frog; katydids and the twigs and leaves of the underbrush rustling as rodents and small animals made nocturnal hunts. The first summer she'd spent in Vermont she'd been afraid to go to sleep at night. At first it felt like she was living in a jungle.

The room Graham used was on the second floor of the old house. It was between a bathroom and a large linen closet, separating it from another room at the end of the corridor that was his sister Sarah's. And he had it to himself because his brother Reilly was away with friends in Canada. A wing had been added on the back of the house which provided a private master suite for Graham's parents. That lessened Gayla's fear that they would become aware of what was going on. But she wasn't willing to risk it any longer.

Gayla carefully tiptoed down the hallway, but with every step she was sure the squeaking floorboards announced her presence. She hurried down the stairs. She glanced at the closed door next to the pantry before turning to the left and the entrance into the living and family room, beyond which was the little den that was hers for the summer. When she rounded the corner into the living room Gayla realized that the side door of the house, leading to the backyard, was open. In the same instant she saw someone standing in the open door frame. A dark figure. Tall and slender. She started, her heart lurching.

A tiny orange ember briefly glowed and dimmed, indicating the lit end of a cigarette.

"Dak! What . . . what are you doing here?" Gayla hissed at the still form. Her guilt and embarrassment made her automatically defensive.

How long had he been awake? What had he heard? She got no answer as the figure in the doorway continued to smoke and stare at her.

"If someone sees you . . ."

"No one's going to see me unless I want them to.

Or if you say something," the male voice said insolently. "The way I see it, it's your ass that's in a sling. You just got busted," he said with derision. "If your mama finds out . . ." He let the thought hang.

Gayla felt a rush of panic at the implications. "You've been spying on me, watching . . ."

"And you been waxing the massa's son."

The disgust and censure in his voice . . . the truth . . . kept her silent. It made her angry all over again that she had to put up with someone like him. But she couldn't let on in any way that she'd been with Graham Whelan.

"I was right about you. Your mind lives in the gutter. All you know is how to be nasty. Why don't you get a life?" she responded tartly.

He drew on the cigarette. "Like these white folks? There's nothin' wrong with the life I got. At least I know what I am. At least I don't let nobody play me."

"At least I'm not a criminal," Gayla shot back.

Gayla froze as she heard yet another sound. The door of the room next to the pantry softly opened. Someone came into the hallway and headed toward the living room where she and Dak stood together in the dark.

Gayla was overcome with panic. There was no way she could make it to her bedroom without being seen. She looked at Dak for his reaction, but he had not moved, nor did he give any indication of doing so. Gayla glanced around. She couldn't think what to do.

"Who's in there?" came an imperious female voice. It held authority and fearlessness. "I said . . . who's there?"

Gayla tried to back into the shadows next to the fireplace. She felt stupid and childish, but she'd never be able to explain to her mother why she was standing in the Whelan living room in the middle of the night, dressed in nothing but a T-shirt . . . with Dak Kinney. Gayla glanced hastily around for an escape route, and settled for dropping to the floor, crouching behind the sofa. From the corner of it she could see both Dak and the entrance from the kitchen.

Dak pitched the butt of his cigarette out the door and exhaled the last of the smoke. Gayla couldn't help noticing a weariness in the gesture, like someone who was about to be caught at something he shouldn't have been doing. But *he* wasn't the one who had to worry.

Dak closed the door and walked back into the center of the room. He casually stood with his hands pushed into the front pockets of his jeans. His torso was bare, and Gayla could see the muscled roll of his shoulders. He had a young man's virility that reminded her of Graham. But somehow Dak Kinney's body seemed stronger and harder. Dangerous.

"David, is that you? Good Lord, boy . . . what are you doing in here? Didn't you hear me ask who it was?"

A woman appeared at the entrance to the living room. The sight of her mother made Gayla's stomach knot in apprehension. She felt hot and prickly all over. Too late it occurred to her that if she'd remained standing, she might have been able to bluff her way out; she, too, had heard sounds and had come from her room to find Dak awake. She had gone to the kitchen for something to drink. But now all she could hope for was not being found kneeling on the floor.

"I didn't want to wake nobody," Dak said in a gruff but quiet voice.

Gayla closed her eyes tightly and stiffened her body. She waited for him to tell on her to her mother.

"Boy, you should be in your own bed asleep. What are you doing up at this time of night?"

Gayla heard her mother sit down. She hazarded a peek around the edge of the sofa and saw her settling into the cherry-wood rocker. Dak's broad back was between them.

"I couldn't sleep."

The woman chuckled softly. "Don't tell me you're afraid of the dark. Maybe it's too quiet for you here. It sure isn't like being home in the city, is it?"

"No, ma'am."

Gayla listened. She was alert to the tension in Dak's responses. But she was also not surprised by the deference he paid her mother, addressing her as ma'am. She was the only person Gayla had ever heard Dak speak to with respect.

"Then what is it? You unhappy here? Mr. Whelan making you do things you don't like to do? You know I wasn't about to leave you by yourself in Manhattan. I couldn't risk that you wouldn't stay out of trouble. I'm sorry."

"That's all right. I didn't want to stay there, either. I just would have gotten into something. Messed up again."

"But you don't really like it here very much either, am I right?"

"I don't know. It's too quiet. Nothin' much to do."

"That was the idea," Sylvia Patton said wryly.

"At night there's all those sounds outside, but not like the city."

Gayla noticed that all the impudence had drained out of Dak's voice. His tone was still clipped and short, like he was still on guard. But he also sounded so . . . lonely.

"It takes some getting used to," Gayla's mother murmured. "It just about drove me out of my mind, the first time I stayed in this house. The thing is, you can hear yourself think. You don't have to keep looking over your shoulder. You have to work *real* hard to get tangled up with the cops here."

Dak snickered dubiously. "They'd find something if they had to. I just show up and they think I did something wrong. I bet there aren't a lot of folks like us up here. Anyone seeing me is gonna think I'm up to no good."

"Well, just don't you give them any reason to think so. I know you don't like it much out here in the country. Mitchell never liked it here, either," she said. "That child talked all kind of nonsense about things that could come out of the woods and eat him!" She chuckled again.

Dak shifted and hunched his shoulders. "It's not that I don't like it. It's just . . . I get jumpy, know what I'm saying? I need to be doing stuff, and seeing my friends."

"No, you don't," Sylvia said firmly. "You are never going to do anything with your life if you hang around with those no-account, so-called friends of yours. I'm telling you right now, I am *not* going to sit back and let you ruin your life. Your mother, God rest her soul, would never forgive me if I didn't look out for you. You're a smart young man. *Do* something for yourself. Think about your mama and make her memory proud."

Dak slowly lowered his tall lanky frame to a club chair, his knees spread and his forearms braced on his thighs. He dropped his head forward and through the sinewy valley between his shoulders Gayla could see her mother's face. Even in the dark of the room she could make out her body language, the tilt of the head that indicated sympathy.

"I don't belong here," Dak mumbled. "These people . . . I don't understand them. They're different from me . . ."

Gayla's mother snorted. "The only thing different about the Whelans is that they have money . . . and they're white. They have their problems like everyone else. They're not perfect, God knows. But they're decent, honest folks."

"I know they look down on me . . ."

"I don't believe that. Mr. Whelan gave you a job for the summer, didn't he? They welcomed you into their home. Mrs. Whelan says you have a good eye for details, and you're talented at building things. Graham is teaching you how to use all those power tools in the shed . . ."

Dak moved impatiently and sat up straight. Gayla braced herself. At the mention of Graham's name she felt almost naked. It instantly evoked the details of the physical intimacy she shared with Graham Whelan. Gayla shuddered with the knowledge of her own easy submission to him. She didn't want to think how disappointed her mother would be if she found out.

"Stop worrying about what other people think of you, David," Sylvia advised. "It's only important what you think about yourself. I thank God the court let me bring you home with me instead of putting you in that detention center. You don't need to be locked up just 'cause you got into a little trouble. You need someone to believe in you and love you." She leaned forward in the chair, and reached out to touch his shoulder. "That's what I'm here for, child. You need family around you. You don't need to be treated like a criminal, because you're not. I know you think my kids don't like you very much . . ."

"They think I'm just a punk."

"Hush! Don't talk like that. Mitchell . . . well . . . I think he's just a little bit scared of you. He's just a child and he's sensitive about things. Gayla is another story. Sometimes I think she has more brass than brains. That girl just throws herself into things without thinking. She's got more curiosity than's good for her. We *all* know what that did to the cat!"

Gayla grew uncomfortable, resentful that her mother would talk about her to the likes of Dak Kinney.

Her legs were beginning to go numb from their bent position, and the tingling pain was shooting to her feet. But she couldn't think of moving.

"She acts like she wants to be like them," he said.

"Gayla? Like who? What do you mean?" her mother asked carefully.

"She thinks she can fit right in. She act like nobody cares that she's from way uptown and black, or that her mother—" He stopped.

"Go on and say it. That I work for these people, too. There's nothing wrong with the work I do. It's honest. I earn good money and I don't owe anybody anything . . ."

"I'm sorry, Mrs. Patton. I didn't mean no disrespect..."

"The Whelans aren't better than you, or me and my kids." Sylvia sighed and shifted in her seat. "Now, I know what you mean about Gayla, and maybe you're right. I worry about her. She has all these ideas about what she wants to be and where she wants to go and what her life is going to be like. I suppose that's not a bad thing."

"No, ma'am," Dak said quietly.

"But I sure don't want her to think that it's going to be as easy for her as it is for the Whelans. It is *not* an even playing field out there. But you know, I wouldn't put it past Gay to get what she wants."

"No, ma'am."

"You too, David. I want you to have a good life and forget about what happened to your family. Don't live in the past, boy. Think about your future, when your probation is over."

"I got plans," he said mysteriously.

Gayla waited for a predictable revelation. She didn't think Dak Kinney was capable of very much beyond acting like a bully and getting into trouble. She wished her mother had let the judge at family court keep his ass in jail where he belonged.

"I think you better go on back to bed now, and try to sleep. You can see everybody gets up real early when we're out here in the country."

Gayla listened to the two people rising from their seats, and felt relief.

"Don't you worry, child. Everything is going to be fine. I'm not going to give up on you . . ."

Gayla looked again and saw her mother attempting to give Dak a hug. He was awkward in his response, as if he wasn't used to doing it. Her mother pulled away from Dak, patting his arm as she did so, and headed back toward her own room.

"Night, David."

Dak didn't answer.

Gayla waited a full minute after the door to her mother's room had closed before standing up. She grimaced and slowly straightened her cramped and aching legs. She tried to shake out the stiffness, watching Dak warily as he faced her. He said nothing, and his very silence humiliated her more, especially after what she'd heard between him and her mother.

She knew that somehow it was all up to her now. Ending the encounter and their standoff. She disliked him even more, as if it was Dak's fault that she had been put into such a compromising position earlier, that he had caught her in the middle of the night coming from someone else's room.

Gayla jumped when Dak took a few steps toward her. But then he bent to pick up a pack of cigarettes, extract one and light it. He ignored her. She didn't kid herself that Dak Kinney liked her very much, either. As if she cared. But it was more than that, Gayla sensed. She thought of how he'd caught her sneaking down the stairs, and realized that above all else, Dak Kinney had no respect for her.

The realization stung. Gayla hugged herself. She wanted to say something to him, but there was nothing to say. Despite everything, he hadn't said anything to her mother about her hiding behind the sofa . . . or about where she'd been for the past few hours. He'd saved her. What Dak Kinney knew made Gayla very uneasy.

She turned away and walked silently across the floor toward her room. She felt confused and upset and resentful. She felt a strange and unexpected regret. Gayla looked over her shoulder at Dak. He was a tall, slender dark shadow. He stood waiting.

She waited too, deliberately giving Dak a chance

to say something more if he chose . . . but he didn't. And she certainly wasn't going to give him the impression that she cared one way or the other what he thought about her. Nevertheless those extra moments made Gayla feel exposed to Dak in a new, unexpected way. He shared her secrets. He had divined her dreams and ridiculed her. She hated him for that.

Gayla decided finally that she didn't have to say anything. With a shrug of her shoulder she dismissed Dak Kinney, entered her room and closed the door on him.

CHAPTER ONE

"Morning, Teddy." Gayla looked at the wall clock and grimaced. "Or should I say, good afternoon. I bet everyone's waiting in my office," Gayla said as she swung through the open door and past the middle-aged security guard.

"Hello, Miss Patton. No, ma'am. The meeting is in the conference room. Mr. Coleman kinda took over when it was supposed to start at ten. I told him you'd called about being a little late."

"Mr. Coleman is here?" Gayla asked in surprise, then stopped short and frowned at the sounds coming from somewhere toward the back of the first floor. "What is that banging?" She stuck a finger in her ear.

"It's the installation. Some of the artists have arrived to put up their work. I know you like to check them in first and all that, but Mr. Coleman told them to go ahead. Hope that was okay with you."

It wasn't, Gayla thought in annoyance. But it was her own fault. She appreciated that Bill thought he was helping, but there were procedures to be followed. "I would have liked to have registered them first, Teddy, and made sure all the work meets the requirements of the exhibit. And you surely know that the artists have to sign an agreement for insurance purposes . . ." Gayla realized that she was almost shouting to be heard over the racket.

"Well, I tried to tell Mr. Coleman that, but he's a board member."

"Mr. Coleman knows the process as well as I do," Gayla said, putting her tote and attaché on the floor and unbuttoning her coat.

"Yes, ma'am."

"I'm not blaming you, Teddy," she hastened to assure the guard.

"No, ma'am."

"This is *not* turning out to be a great day . . ." Gayla began but was again distracted by the sounds.

Teddy chuckled behind her. "Hard to believe that all that noise and all that stuff spread out back there is called art."

"It probably doesn't look like much right now, but it will come together. Maybe I should take a look."

"Mr. Coleman said I should let him know the minute you arrive. He said he had something important to discuss with you."

"I'll be right there," Gayla said, detouring in the direction of the activity.

She entered the first gallery and immediately saw three artists organizing their works according to a plan which had been previously approved and worked out by herself and Marc Sterling, the exhibit designer. For a moment Gayla allowed herself to be drawn to the large, vibrant canvases, sculptures and other constructed pieces waiting to be hung. There was no loud noise here, only conversation among the artists, and a small boom box playing soft jazz for company.

Gayla nodded a greeting and moved on to the next salon. She glanced only perfunctorily at the framed work leaning against the walls. Usually she enjoyed taking her time to examine the individual entries, or to spend a few minutes chatting with the artists. But Gayla, curious about what sounded to be heavy construction rather than the simple hanging of work on a clean white wall, continued to the last space.

She entered the main salon and stared at the scene before her. A man was leaning over a makeshift worktable of two sawhorses and a wooden plank. Wearing work goggles, he was using an electric saw to cut off a measured length of a board. Another man, also wearing goggles, was kneeling on the floor hammering the pieces of wood together to form open frames. Some had already been finished and were piled on the floor. What also caught Gayla's attention were several boxes filled with what looked like plaster body parts. Heads and hands were sticking out of the pile.

"What is this?" Gayla asked in a stunned voice. "What's going on?"

At first both men ignored her. Finally the man on the floor glanced over his shoulder at her. He was wearing a white breathing filter and all Gayla could see of his face was a close-cut beard on his jaw and cheeks. He didn't say a word, but silently regarded her through the goggles.

The buzzing whine of the electric saw was beginning to irritate her, as did the continued lack of acknowledgment from either man. Then the one kneeling on the floor slowly stood up and reached to remove his goggles.

"Gayla . . ."

She turned at the sound of her name and faced Bill Coleman. In his white business shirt and conservative tie he was a little out of place in the chaos of the pre-opening setup. He looked every bit the lawyer he was, rather than someone who had once dabbled in printmaking and fancied himself a painter before realizing he had no real talent for either.

"Bill, who are these men?"

"Teddy called me and said you were down here. Didn't he tell you I had to talk to you?" Bill reached for her arm and firmly guided Gayla away from the scene in the gallery.

"Yes, he did, but . . ."

He glanced at his watch as he urged her back to the front of the building. "I didn't think I'd be filling in for you at a meeting this morning. I just stopped by to give you some information. I have to get back to my office . . ."

"Bill . . ."

"I'll explain. Let's go upstairs."

They reached the security desk, where Teddy handed Gayla her bags. She held off asking any more questions in his presence but once on the elevator for the short ride to the third floor of the small narrow building, Gayla faced Bill.

"Bill—" she tried again.

"Me first," he interrupted, holding up his hand for her attention. "Are you all right?"

Gayla smiled at his thoughtfulness. At six foot three inches Bill Coleman was thin and rangy, a bit scholarly-looking, but his self-assured voice always commanded attention. Gayla had learned it was a trait within Bill which made him an effective lawyer; people didn't get away with ignoring him, but neither was there a reason to be intimidated by him.

"Yes, I'm okay. I misjudged my time this morning and got backed up on all my appointments."

"Did Allison mess you up?"

"No, I can't blame it on Allison this time," Gayla said, suddenly hesitating.

Bill frowned and took hold of her arm, squeezing through her winter coat. He studied her expression. "Did you have a bad night?" he asked quietly.

She nodded. "Thank God for Tylenol."

"So why didn't you call me?"

Gayla sighed patiently. "There's nothing you can do. You know that."

He bent to stare into her eyes as the elevator slowed to a stop. "I could have just been there with you."

Gayla shook her head as Bill held the door open to let her exit ahead of him. "I don't like anyone watching me when I'm having an episode. Sickle cell is something I have to live with. I try not to burden anyone else with it."

He grunted. "Your pride again."

"No, it's not," Gayla defended as they walked to an open doorway. Low conversation could be heard from within. "It's the pain. It's all I can think about or feel. And I'm hardly at my best. I appreciate your concern, Bill, but sympathy just doesn't help."

"How was Allison?"

"Asleep, so she wasn't even aware. I try to keep it from her if I can. She gets very scared and upset."

"It's understandable." He leaned toward her and said quietly, "You know I'm here for you, Gayla. I'm good in an emergency."

"I know. Thanks." Then she stopped short and glared suspiciously at him. "But you still haven't explained what's going on in gallery three."

He nodded as they entered the room. "I will . . . Look who I found," Bill announced to the three people sitting at a cluttered conference table.

"Sorry I'm late. Did you all get my message?" Gayla asked.

"Something about a missed doctor appointment, and the buses and trains running late."

"Close," Gayla murmured dryly as she shrugged out of her coat, placed it in Bill's outstretched hand, and took her place at the table. She nodded a greeting to the other occupants.

The conference room door was closed behind her, blocking out the loud sounds of activity coming from the first floor.

"I forgot to pick up a prescription from the pharmacy, and Allison missed the school bus." She opened the leather attaché and quickly assembled her notes and papers in front of her.

"So you had to take her, right?" Margaret Donahue guessed.

"No, I didn't," Gayla said. "I put her into a cab." She scanned through several notebook pages, and accepted an agenda from Bill, seated to her right. She nodded when Bill used his pen to point out where they were on the list.

"You haven't missed much," he said. "Do you want some coffee?"

Gayla smiled briefly at him. "Thanks, I'll get it as soon as I get organized here."

He squeezed her arm. "No problem." He got up and left the room.

Margaret, seated to Gayla's left, chortled. "My mother would have made me walk."

"It crossed my mind, but it's a bit too far. Anyway, she had some test she had to take. As annoyed as I sometimes get with Allison, I wouldn't risk her missing anything at school. I'm going to make her pay me the fare back out of her allowance."

"I don't remember getting any allowance, either," Margaret further commented.

"Look, I appreciate your patience with me and Allison this morning, but don't let her take over the meeting in absentia, okay? What did I miss?" She accepted the mug of coffee from Bill and he sat down again. "Wasn't Keith supposed to be here with a final proof of the program from the printer?"

"He's with the printer even as we speak. Some mix-up," Bill said.

"Actually it worked out. We had to make some changes anyway in the copy," Margaret added.

"I don't like the sound of that," Gayla said, referring to a list. "The exhibit opens in less than a week, and there seems to be a lot of things that aren't settled yet. Do we have the caterer confirmed for the reception?"

"I spoke with them last night. Everything is fine," Margaret said.

"What about the quartet? Marc, you're taking care of that." Gayle raised her brows at the young man lounging on the other side of the table.

He leaned forward. "I'm on it."

"I've never heard of this group. What's it called? The Moody something-or-other?" Shauna Bickford, the gallery manager, asked.

"Mood Indigo. After the Duke Ellington number," Bill said.

"My brother's in the group," Marc informed them.

"Besides, we can't afford the groups you've heard of, Shauna," Margaret said. "This is a fund-raiser, remember?"

"If someone can get me a price listing from the artists for their work and some promo cards, I can have my office do a mailing to collectors and dealers. People who are going to spend money," Bill offered.

"Good," Shauna said. "We have no more money for another mailing."

Gayla turned to regard Bill Coleman with a smile. "Thank you. But you've already gotten your office to handle all the contracts and registration forms and the insurance . . . That's a lot of resources, Bill. One of these days . . ."

"I'm going to get fired? Not with the kind of billing I bring in. I'm a partner, remember? I have my own reasons for committing to your organization," he said quietly to her.

Gayla noisily shuffled papers, cringing at Bill's comment. It struck her as almost personal, and she wondered if anyone else noticed.

"He's scoping out the next Romare Bearden," Marc filled in.

"Not only that," Margaret continued. "There are a lot of businesses and corporations in this city that spend money on artwork for offices, conference rooms and reception areas. Why shouldn't talented black artists get in on the action?"

"That's one of the reasons I'm here. To see that the wealth gets spread around," Bill added.

"I wish we had more support like you," Gayla said, glad the conversation had veered back to safe ground. "Did the press releases go out?" she asked.

"Yes, and I talked to a photographer at the *Amsterdam News*, who said he would try to make it to the opening night," Marc informed them.

"That's good, but I was hoping for some of the

bigger papers to turn out," Gayla lamented. "It's so hard to get the media here for our shows."

"That's 'cause nobody's ever heard of the artists," Marc pointed out.

"Well, they have to start somewhere. I don't see MoMA or the Whitney giving many of our artists a chance," Gayla said.

"At one time nobody had ever heard of Romare Bearden, either. I think we have a good lineup for this show, even though we're down one artist."

Gayla became instantly alert at Shauna's comment. She frowned. "What do you mean, we lost one artist?"

Shauna raised her brows and looked at Bill. "Did you tell her what happened?"

"No, he didn't," Gayla answered, turning to him.

Bill calmly leaned back in his chair and crossed an ankle on the opposite knee.

"What happened? Which artist backed out?"

"The Trinidadian artist who was going to do murals and recreate a marketplace in gallery three. His mother and a sister were killed in a street accident sometime yesterday morning and he's had to return home."

"Oh, my God," Gayla said sympathetically at the news of the tragedy. "I'm so sorry to hear that. Of course his family matters come first."

"You were in Albany so Shauna and Margaret tracked me down," Bill said.

"I told him we'd be glad to schedule him for a

later show, when he's had a chance to recover from the loss," Shauna said.

"Good." Gayla turned to Marc. "Make sure we send condolences from the staff . . ."

"Bet." Marc nodded.

"So is this where you explain that all that noise, and two men I don't recognize in gallery three, and boxes of plaster heads has something to do with the artist we lost?"

"Pretty much," Bill said. "You know that gallery three is the largest room. When we lost our Caribbean entry to the show we lost what was probably going to be the biggest part of the exhibit, the culmination. It was hard finding a last-minute replacement to fill that space."

Gayla was waiting for the punch line. "So, who is the replacement artist? What kind of work are we getting? Is it any good?"

"The work is a combination of sculpture, construction with found objects . . ." Bill began.

Gayla frowned. "What?"

"That's what I said," Margaret commented. "Sounded to me like someone had emptied out their closet."

"It's . . . innovative," Bill responded carefully. "It's very hard-edged. Political . . ."

"He means it's street art," Marc said with a sly smile.

"I don't like the sound of that. It means that there's no formal background or training," Gayla said to Bill.

"Well, he's a little short on that side, but I heard his stuff is interesting . . ."

Gayla tried to clarify. "So, you don't actually know this artist or anything about him?"

"That's sometimes how it is," Bill said reasonably. "I think you're getting yourself worked up before there's a reason to, Gayla."

"What's his name and how did you find him?"

"David Kinney. I've never heard of him."

"I'd never heard the name, either," Margaret said. "We've established a pretty good network of creative artists and pretty much everybody knows everybody else."

"I was with a colleague and friend yesterday afternoon. . . ."

"David . . . What was the name again?" Gayla requested, cutting into Bill's explanation.

"David Kinney . . . after I got the call about the artist dropping out of the show and knew we had a problem. I was going to call you with the bad news, but then this friend of mine said he thought he could help out."

Gayla stared speechlessly at Bill as he explained. But she was trying to decide what the chances were that either she had heard him wrong, or that he had the name wrong . . . or that there were possibly two people with the same name.

"Hey, the man didn't even want to do this show. I was told he doesn't seek out a lot of attention."

"David Kinney . . . is that . . . his full name?" Gayla asked.

Bill looked at her quizzically. "Yeah, that's it." He lifted a sheet of paper sticking out of a manila folder in front of him. "Wait a minute . . . it's David Alan Kinney, to be exact. Why? Have you heard of him?"

"Where did you find him?"

"You are *not* going to believe it," Shauna said with an incredulous shake of her head.

"I can tell you it wasn't from one of the colleges, or a studio," Margaret offered.

"Hey . . . don't forget that guy two years ago who was living on the streets on the Lower East Side. We did a whole show on his stuff," Marc reminded everyone. "The man was profiled in *Emerge* magazine a few months ago."

Gayla was still focusing on Bill Coleman for a response. "Bill?" she prompted.

"Upstate," Bill said.

"Near Ossining," Margaret added.

"You mean Attica," Marc corrected.

"Prison . . ." Gayla concluded in a flat voice. Yes, she knew exactly who he was.

"Thank you all for staying," Gayla said as everyone gathered their belongings at the meeting's conclusion. She stretched her back, and absently crossed her arms to rub her elbows.

"Don't worry, everything's going to be fine," Margaret said to her as she passed behind Gayla on her way out of the office. "I'll call the printer about the programs."

"I'm sorry the meeting took so long." Gayla apologized.

"You get no more work out of me until I get something to eat. It's way past lunch. Care to join me?" Marc asked Gayla as he stacked his files and tucked them under his arm.

"No, thanks. I have things to do. My daughter is meeting me here after school."

"Then I'll see you in an hour or so."

"Marc, thanks again for arranging the music. I appreciate that your brother's group has agreed to play."

"Yeah," Marc cackled. "But nobody asked me if he's any good."

Gayla laughed. "Do you play an instrument, too?" she asked him.

Marc shook his head. "No, but it's not as if my mother didn't try. I studied the piano for a couple of years, but I figured the world already had a Ray Charles and Bobby Short and Herbie Hancock."

"Didn't like the competition?" Gayla asked as they entered the elevator and it started down.

He shook his head. "Didn't like the piano. My goal is to be a set designer for theater and films. So, why work in a small not-for-profit gallery, you will ask? Because black folks with money are just like white folks with money . . . They like to buy things with it, like original art. At the last exhibit we did I met someone who is with the *Smokey Joe's Cafe* show. He was with this woman who works at the Public Theater."

"So you made a contact."

"Being talented helps a lot," Marc said as the elevator arrived on the first floor. "But who you know is even better. What happened yesterday is a good example. I'm telling you, if Bill Coleman hadn't gone ahead with this Kinney guy from upstate, would you have let him exhibit in this show?"

Gayla thought about it for a quick second. "No." She shook her head. But not for the reason Marc implied.

"How come you don't ever try to show your own work?" Marc asked Gayla as the elevator reached the first floor and they headed toward the front of the gallery.

Gayla shrugged dismissively. "I don't consider myself an artist."

"Hey . . . a lot of people say they're artists who have no talent. I've seen your work. Sounds to me like maybe *you're* the one worried about competition."

"I have a daughter to support in the style to which she's become accustomed . . ." Marc laughed. "There's a lot to be said for the regular paycheck and health benefits."

"You're just scared," Marc scoffed.

"Absolutely."

"I'm going to suggest a staff show, or maybe one with work from our permanent collection. Then you'll get to strut your stuff, girl."

Gayla grinned as Marc continued on to the exit, waving an airy goodbye. Teddy looked at Gayla.

"Ms. Patton, one of the artists said she had to talk to you."

"Oh-oh. I hear a complaint coming on," Gayla said wryly. She was aware, too, that the awful banging of that morning had stopped. She wondered if the two men were still there. She wondered if one of them really was . . .

"Here she is now," Teddy informed Gayla, interrupting her thoughts.

She blinked at the approaching young artist, whose expression clearly registered annoyance. Gayla smiled brightly at her, immediately forestalling any temperamental displays of ego.

"I'm so glad you agreed to participate in this show," Gayla complimented her.

The artist returned the smile, her features visibly softening. "Thank you. But there is one problem. The space I was given is smaller than anyone else's."

Gayla nodded and sighed inwardly. "Why don't we go to my office," she suggested. She cast one curious glance in the direction of the third gallery before giving her attention back to the woman.

Between the unplanned meeting and phone interruptions it was more than an hour before Gayla returned to the first floor. She was sorry, now, that she hadn't asked Marc to at least bring her back a salad. More questions to be answered from a few other people on staff, a UPS package to sign for, an unexpected drop-in visitor . . . the day was almost over.

Gayla returned to the first floor, saying good night to some of the artists.

"I'm waiting for my daughter to arrive. Call me when she comes in."

Teddy nodded.

"I'll just take a quick walk through the gallery," Gayla added.

"You go right ahead," he said.

Gayla waited until he was sitting behind his desk at the front door. And then she sighed, feeling as though she'd been holding her breath the entire afternoon. It was quiet now, all activity suspended for the day. There were still ladders opened with tape and tools resting on the rungs, waiting for the mounting work to continue the next day. There was no music playing or conversation as most of the artists had left as well. But the lights in the third gallery were still on. Gayla began walking down the corridor in that direction. Earlier she had felt a sense of disbelief . . . and a sense of invasion. Like she'd come all this way from being a headstrong girl, growing up and having a child of her own, developing a career . . . but never actually getting away from the past at all.

Gayla's footsteps echoed softly as she walked down the hallway and into gallery three. The first thing she noticed was that some of the pine frames had already been hung on the wall, although they were empty. Others were suspended by thin catgut from a white beam just below the ceiling. Whatever this contribution to the exhibit was going to be it wasn't finished yet, either. And then Gayla realized she was not alone. She wasn't surprised.

She turned to her right . . . and he was there. Squatting down on his haunches, knees spread with his back braced against the wall. He was wearing black jeans and a black turtleneck sweater. Chalky patches of white dusted his clothes, and the white breathing filter and goggles he'd had on earlier hung around his neck from their straps. He stared openly at Gayla, not moving. His utter stillness reminded Gayla that there had always been something predatory about him; he would wait, biding his time . . . and then attack.

"Dak . . ." she said.

She stayed where she was. Slowly, he pushed himself up until he stood straight. She could see that he was still slender, but the large hands had gotten bigger, more adult with thick wrists. Nor was his face one of a boy anymore. The short beard covered most of it, adding style and maturity. The eyes had not changed, however. They were still direct . . . seeing more than she thought David Alan Kinney had a right to. One more thing had not changed. She still did not trust him.

He knew she would come back.

As well as he knew that it wasn't curiosity that had drawn her back, but disbelief. The waiting had been worth it to see Gayla's expression. Stunned. And confused. What was he doing there? As if he didn't have the right.

He'd had all afternoon to get over not surprise— nothing surprised him anymore—but his reaction when she'd first walked in on him. Two things had immediately come to mind. The first was recalling the time when Gayla Patton had told him he was little more than a lowlife hood. The second had been the time he'd come upon her crying.

To be honest, Gayla looked good. She had a figure now and wasn't just skinny. She had grown into her own style, knowing what clothes most flattered her. She was wearing a knit charcoal gray dress and a red scarf wrapped loosely around her throat. The dress was calf length and worn with black suede boots. A red barette at an angle over her short, feathered hairdo. Very little jewelry, silver ear studs and a necklace of similar rounded beads. No rings. She'd always made a point of not looking like everyone else. He remembered she used to be fresh and smart-mouthed . . . like himself. She used to give as good as she could take.

Gayla stepped toward him to take charge.

"My mother never told me you were back in the city." She didn't bother with a greeting. It wouldn't have been sincere.

"Your mother doesn't know."

She raised a brow, kept her attention on the worn and dusty clothing as if they held more significance than the man who wore them. "Is there any reason why she doesn't?"

He hesitated. He had a notion to be honest with her, and then decided not to. She might hold it against him. He shrugged. "Didn't have a chance. Between moving and this show . . ."

"When did you suddenly become an artist?" Gayla cut in.

He slowly put his hands into the front pockets of his jeans. The stance gave him an air of masculine indifference. He narrowed his gaze on Gayla, assessing the question.

"What difference does it make when? It's what I am now."

"Among other things," she said tartly.

He nodded. "Among other things."

"Who was that other man I saw here this morning?"

"Someone I paid to help me out. A local student who was recommended. I had a lot of work to do to get here at the last minute."

"I thought you were living upstate. You moved pretty fast to get here."

He pursed his mouth, hesitating long enough to quell his annoyance at her dismissive tone. He shrugged. "There wasn't much to move. I brought what I needed."

She glanced quickly at him, unsure if he was being reticent or very honest.

Gayla turned away, eyeing the disarray of his equipment and work. She walked slowly around a set of sawhorses, gingerly picking up one thing and then another spread out haphazardly on the plank of wood which served as a workbench. "So, which of this is the art?" Between her index finger and thumb she held up a child's stuffed teddy bear. One of the button eyes was missing, and one of the arms hung by threads, nearly severed from the body of the toy.

He took his time answering. "All of it."

Gayla sighed and put the toy down. "Look, I don't know how you managed to—"

"Get myself into your show? Didn't Bill Coleman tell you how it happened? He came to me. I was very happy minding my own business until I got a phone call yesterday."

"Bill is a trustee of the gallery. He's not an artist, an arts administrator or a curator."

He relaxed back against the wall, bending a knee and carelessly placing a boot on the pristine white wall. "Don't you trust his judgment?"

"It's not that," Gayla said patiently.

He smiled slowly. "I know. It's me."

She opened her mouth to respond and couldn't. He was right. Nothing had changed.

"So, if you didn't want to be here, why did you say yes?"

Doubt flickered in his eyes but he quickly recovered. There were a number of reasons, none of which he was willing to share with Gayla Patton, and all of which he was sure she'd ridicule. But the most compelling? He was afraid not to; that's how he knew he had to.

She didn't wait for an answer. Impatiently Gayla glanced at her watch. "The gallery is closing soon. You have to leave. Tomorrow you can . . ."

"Then you're going to let me stay in the show?"

"It's too late now to do anything else."

He chuckled softly. "But you sure would if you could."

She ignored the sarcasm. "I suggest you go through the normal channels and be processed like the other artists."

With a swift and easy motion he pushed away from the wall. He took his hands out of his pockets and crossed them over his chest. But the effect was the same. He looked solid and grounded . . . and unintimidated by her.

"In case Bill Coleman didn't tell you, I didn't want to be here. You and your gallery aren't doing me any favors. I don't need your approval for my work or anything else I'm doing."

"Well, that's a good thing, since I haven't seen anything that would rate."

"That's because you'd already made up your mind. The moment you knew I was involved. Right?"

Again she couldn't think of an adequate response. Not that she didn't have one, but Gayla could feel the truculent streak in her that insisted on going tit for tat.

"There was no reason for me to think that you have any talent. Why should I have thought of you for this show? Where did you take classes? Where have you exhibited before? My mother never told me you were interested in art."

"Probably because she knew what you would say." There was no rancor in his words. It was just a statement of fact.

"Then there was no way for me to know, was there?"

"Sure there was," he said easily, walking slowly toward her.

She held her ground, watching him approach, sensing all the old stuff about him that put her on the alert. He didn't stop until he was just three feet away. Gayla could now see closely the way his facial hair lay smooth and neat against his cheek and jaw, the edges finely shaped and trimmed with a razor. His eyes were sharp and probing as he looked down at her.

"You could have asked me."

She noticed the way his jaw flexed. Was he angry or just nervous? "If I cared."

As they stood silently staring each other down, it was several seconds before either of them registered the footsteps. Someone entered the gallery behind Gayla and broke the chill of the standoff.

"Hi, Mom. Teddy said you were back here . . ."

The young girl stopped in mid-sentence as she saw the second person in the room.

Gayla turned and scolded her. "Didn't I tell you you are not to call Mr. Stewart by his first name? It's disrespectful."

The girl was not chastened. She kept her gaze on the man. "Teddy said I could."

"*I'm* telling you you can't. Where are your schoolbooks?"

"I left them at Ted . . . at Mr. Stewart's desk."

The girl came to stand next to Gayla but her attention was still riveted on the man. He was staring back, both fascinated and surprised.

Gayla tugged on the collar of the girl's coat to re-align the neckline. "This is my daughter, Allison," she said without having been asked.

His eyes briefly shifted to Gayla, and he registered the touch of defiance, the unmistakable note of pride in the announcement.

Allison suddenly lowered her gaze and turned half away from him. "Hi," she mumbled.

"This is Dak Kinney. He's one of the artists in the show next week."

That got the girl's attention. She blinked at him. "Dak?" she questioned skeptically. "That's not a real name."

"Allison, I—"

"No, it's not," he interrupted Gayla.

"What does it mean?"

"My full name is David Alan Kinney. Nice to meet you, Allison." He made an awkward gesture, as if to hold out his hand to the girl, and then changed his mind.

"Why did my mother call you Dak?"

Gayla could see the questions were making him uncomfortable, but she did nothing to help him.

"It's a street name," he said reluctantly. "Made up of the initials."

"Like those names that guys spray-paint on walls? You know; to mark their territory and stuff like that?" Allison asked with a tone of derision. "Do you belong to a gang?"

"I'm too old for a gang."

"But did you ever belong to one?" she persisted.

Gayla gave David a warning look as she broke in to address her daughter. "Allison, I think you've asked enough questions."

He ignored her. "I used to. When I was about your age."

Allison pulled away from her mother and began to wander around the room. "Dak is a stupid name," she said.

Gayla wasn't expecting that, but before she could react, he spoke first.

"Yeah, I guess it is pretty stupid. That's why no one calls me that. I'm not a kid anymore."

"Come on, Allison. We have to go . . ." Gayla reached out to the girl, who was busy inspecting things on the workbench in pretty much the same manner she had a moment before.

"What's this for?" Allison asked, holding up the teddy bear carelessly.

Instinctively Gayla started to instruct her daughter to be careful with the fragile toy, but David was already approaching her to lift it out of her hand.

"It's part of a piece that's going to be in the show."

"Are you an artist?" Allison asked.

He glanced at Gayla, keeping his expression blank. "I think you'd better ask your mother. She's the judge."

Gayla addressed her daughter. "I haven't seen his work before. He's new."

"My mother's an artist," Allison said, tilting her head and boasting coyly. "If she wanted to, she could make a lot of money selling her work."

"Really? What does she do?"

Allison shrugged. "All kinds of things. She made my grandmother a bowl out of clay. She made me a quilt when I was a baby. And she made this . . ." Allison dug into the neck of her coat, inside a crewneck sweater to extract a silver pendant. But she didn't really intend that he see it closely. The object twisted and swung before Allison abruptly scooped it into her hand and dropped it back into her clothing.

"Your mother's a Renaissance woman," he said.

"What's that?" Allison asked, ignoring her mother's beckoning hand.

A small smile broadened his lips through the thin beard. "Someone who knows everything."

"Come on . . . Let's go, Allison," Gayla said. She headed toward the gallery opening. Allison didn't follow. "Allison," she urged, her impatience growing at Allison's lack of obedience. But she didn't want to create a scene in front of David.

He spoke up as if he hadn't noticed Gayla's attempt to leave. "Are you going to be an artist, too?"

Allison looked as though the idea had not occurred to her before now. Finally she shook her head but didn't enlighten him with any other options.

Gayla reached out to Allison. "Go find Mr. Stewart. Tell him we're ready to leave. Mr. Kinney is leaving, too."

"Okay," Allison said obediently. Without a look or word in his direction she left the gallery.

The chill descended again.

"Congratulations," he said quietly.

"On what?" Gayla asked.

"On Allison."

Gayla narrowed her eyes, scanning his features for signs of sarcasm. "Thank you," she said shortly.

"She's very pretty."

Gayla was pleased. She accepted the compliment with a nod.

"When did you get married?"

She looked sharply at him, but the question was not unreasonable. Gayla tightened her lips.

"I'm not married," she responded, but saw no satisfaction at her admission, only mild curiosity. "I've never been married," she added. She turned to leave the gallery.

"Wait a minute. There's something you ought to know."

"What is it?" Gayla asked impatiently. She was anxious to get away.

"I used to be very young and dumb once. Dak was a kid I made up when I wanted to show people how down and bad I was. Dak was somebody who was rough and angry all the time." He was standing right over her now to make his point. "But he grew up. And like the Bible says, I put childish things aside. My name is David Alan Kinney. Period. Remember it."

Gayla had no answer ready. None that would have served her well. So she silently conceded the point to him, and walked away, refusing to acknowledge what he'd said.

CHAPTER TWO

"I like the work of the fiber artist."

"Nia Murdoch. She's really a weaver. And she sidelines designing costumes," Gayla said.

Bill nodded thoughtfully. "Putting her in the middle gallery avoids bunching together the big pieces by the male artists."

"You should see this piece she did called *The Sea of Galilee*. A great wall hanging. I'd love to have a spring coat made out of it."

Bill laughed. "That's like saying you'd like to use the *Unicorn Tapestry* as a tablecloth."

"That's not a bad idea, either," Gayla said brightly, making Bill laugh again. "Functional art."

"I don't think the Met would be too happy with that."

"On the other hand, woven Indian baskets are now collected as great craft, as well as eighteenth- and nineteenth-century quilts our grandmothers made for beds."

"Nana said when I get married, she was going to give me the quilt her mother made for her when she was a little girl. How come I have to wait? Why can't I have it now? Besides, I don't want to get married."

"Thank you, Allison," Gayla said dryly. "Eat your dinner."

Allison dutifully picked up her fork as her mother turned once again to Bill Coleman.

"I'm not so sure about the work in the third gallery," he said. "It looked a little slapdash to me. Like just a lot of stuff this man found and decided to call art. Weird stuff, I might add."

Gayla raised her fork at him. "Do you know how often I've heard that about experimental artists and their work?"

"Experimental doesn't mean it's art. Neither does having the right degree or background."

"Hey, you're the one who's always telling the board we have to give more opportunity to emerging artists and cutting-edge work. This last . . . *artist* . . . I guess fits the criteria."

Bill shrugged skeptically.

"How did you say you found him again?" Gayla asked cautiously.

Bill drank from his water glass, and lifted the final portion of his roll from his bread plate. "A friend of mine. He's an associate with another firm. He has a country house upstate and knows a lot of artists and craftspeople there. He's seen some of this guy's work at a local show. He said it was interesting stuff."

"Uh-oh. When something is 'interesting,' that means that no one wants to admit it's really bad," Allison murmured.

Gayla ignored the comment.

"Well, my friend did say it was kind of . . . controversial."

"That's even worse. What do you know about him?" Gayla asked carefully, wondering just how much Bill had actually found out.

Bill chuckled. "Sorry, but I forgot to ask for references. Did you also want family and medical history? His high school diploma? Fingerprints? What is this? Why the interrogation?"

Gayla shook her head and shrugged. "I'm not interrogating you."

"Gay . . . what's the big deal? I don't know much about any of the artists that come through Jump Street Gallery, except for their work. That should speak for them."

"I just like to be careful. You know, we're liable during these shows."

"For what? In case one of the frames is stolen? In case one of the guests gets mugged while standing in front of a painting?" he teased.

"Something like that," Gayla said stubbornly, even though she knew she was coming across as needlessly judgmental.

"Look, we'll get some information on him before the show. But if we can't, I don't think we should just take him out because you haven't seen his birth certificate. You'll look paranoid. And you could get sued."

She looked shocked. "Why would I get sued?"

"You and the gallery. For breach of contract.

You're the one who reminded me of liability. It goes both ways."

Gayla chortled. "I don't think someone from his background would try anything like that."

Bill glanced at her with a frown. "What do you know about his background? You just got through complaining about the lack of information."

She quickly covered herself. "That . . . that's what I mean."

Bill nodded after a moment and returned to eating. "My friend only said that David Kinney had an interesting history."

"Really?" Gayla inquired.

"Ummmmmm. But he didn't say how come." He again glanced at Gayla. "You haven't even met the man yet."

"Yes, she did. So did I," Allison piped up.

"Oh, yeah? When?" Bill asked.

"This afternoon. He's got a funny name. Dak. He says it's a gang name."

"Really?" Bill asked, his interest piqued.

"He didn't look dangerous or anything," Allison continued. "But I don't think he can be trusted. He had these weird dark eyes and he kept staring at me, and his beard made him look sinister."

"Sinister, eh? Seems you found out quite a lot about him," he observed to Gayla with a smile.

Gayla decided that the best thing was just to ignore her daughter's observations. She knew, however, that Bill was curious about the brief encounter. Looking back on it, she remembered the immediate tension inside her upon recognizing David Kinney, and the way he'd stared at her had made her feel both vulnerable and resentful.

"When we finished the meeting and I was waiting for Allison. I . . . happened to walk through the galleries and Da . . . Mr. Kinney was still there."

"Dak? Is that what he calls himself?" Bill inquired.

"Well, no. He—" Gayla began.

"He said it was his initials," Allison volunteered again.

"Allison," Gayla said in warning to her daughter. Allison retreated back behind her book. "His name is David Alan Kinney, and that's what he wants to be called. He said so."

"So you talked with him, eh? Why didn't you just ask him what else you wanted to know?"

Gayla shifted in her chair. "There really wasn't time. It was late, and Allison arrived shortly after I ran into him . . ."

"Well, I hope you learned enough to be comfortable that the brother is not a rapist or ax murderer," Bill said, joking.

Gayla experienced a curious twist of her stomach muscles. She knew no such thing.

Bill pointed at her plate. "You didn't eat very much. But I'm not surprised. There's nothing there but vegetables and potatoes."

"It was plenty," Gayla said.

"Can I have your potatoes?" Allison asked.

Gayla handed her her plate.

"I can't see how being a vegetarian is supposed to

help you. It doesn't look like a healthy diet," Bill commented quietly.

"It's not a diet. It's a balance of certain foods that keep my body fueled in the way it needs to keep me out of trouble." Gayla spoke softly so as not to have her daughter pick up on their conversation, and she raised her brows at Bill as a silent signal to get off the subject.

"Got it." He nodded. "Sorry. They're predicting rain on the night of the opening. How many invitations did we send out?"

Gayla sipped from her water glass and stared off into space, mentally counting before responding. "Well, there's the gallery mailing list of members and former guests. Plus staff names and contacts, the press, some local art schools and colleges. I'd say about fifteen hundred."

Bill nodded. He wiped his mouth and laid his napkin next to his plate. "Under normal conditions about three hundred people would make it. If it rains you may only see about one hundred guests. Maybe a little more."

"I know," Gayla said. "But even under the best of circumstances sometimes we put together a show, make sure there's a variety of work and no one shows up. Worse, no one buys anything."

"So, you're just figuring that out?" Bill asked with a grin.

Gayla leaned forward, resting her folded arms on the edge of the table. "No. But it's still frustrating.

That's why my mother didn't want me to become an artist."

"That's your mother. Why didn't *you* want to be one?" Bill asked.

"You know why. We've talked about this before. Being a creative artist and trying to support yourself is hard."

"People do it and become successful and make money all the time."

"Mostly after they're dead," Allison tossed in.

Both Bill and Gayla looked at Allison. She was slightly slouched in her chair, reading a paperback book. Gayla exchanged glances with Bill whose eyes were filled with amusement.

"Allison, please put the book down and finish your dinner."

"I *am* finished," she responded.

"No, you're not. You've eaten the sweet potatoes and left everything else."

Allison restrained herself from making a face. She peered over the top of the book into her plate and, looking as if it had just been announced that she would be force-fed, she took her fork and began moving the greens and baked chicken around on the plate.

"Stop playing with it and eat," Gayla instructed patiently, watching and waiting for further signs of impertinence from her daughter.

Allison finally condescended to nibble a piece of meat before putting her fork down and sighing. "I'm full."

"The greens?" Gayla pointedly reminded her.

Allison frowned at her mother. "I don't like greens. It's old-time country food like Nana eats."

Gayla could only stare at Allison. She knew that if she looked at Bill she'd find him trying to hide his laughter.

"I tell you what," Bill spoke up. "I'll have the waiter give you a doggy bag and you can deal with it at home."

Allison started to protest, but a quick glance at her mother's expression made her retreat behind her book once more.

"Do you want coffee?" Bill asked Gayla.

"Please," she sighed.

Gayla gave up on the issue of her daughter's eating habits and tried to pick up the trail of the earlier conversation with Bill. Yet that led her back to David Kinney, and she didn't want to go there. She smiled warmly at Bill, with a certain amount of intimacy that she knew would please him. For that moment it made him the center of her universe.

She watched as he signaled the waiter and ordered their coffee. Gayla enjoyed the refinement with which Bill conducted conversation, gave orders and responded to her—and her daughter—with his complete attention. As they drank their coffee, she tried to imagine that the scenario was normal. That their relationship was grounded in commitment, equality . . . and love.

Gayla was surprised at the sudden twisting of her insides again, and tried to shake it off. But instead she was filled with a sense of falsehood. Something wasn't right, and it made her oddly afraid. She again smiled at Bill, giving him all she had, but the magic she strained for was elusive. Finally Gayla gave up.

The coffee was served, and as Bill launched into an anecdote of a recent case in his office, Gayla found that her attention was drifting. She went over a list of things that had to get done, both at home and at work. She needed to speak with her mother about David.

He was back.

"Bill, I really have to get home. It's late and I know Allison has homework," Gayla said, looking at the time.

"You're right. I have to review a contract tonight, and I have an early morning appointment at my office. What are you doing next Friday?" he asked as he gestured to the waiter for the check.

"Nothing that I know of. Are you asking me for a date?"

"Can I come, too?" Allison asked eagerly.

"Allison, don't be fresh. He wasn't talking to you."

Bill laughed softly at Allison. "I don't think so. I want to take your mother to a black-tie affair. It's only for adults. But I'll make it up to you."

"Can I have anything I want?" Allison tested, with a beguiling smile calculated to melt resistance.

"Don't you dare try to bargain with—" Gayla began.

"That depends. If it costs under fifty dollars, is not

farther than fifteen miles from the center of Manhattan and doesn't require assembly and batteries."

Allison giggled in delight.

"Bill . . ."

"Do you need to make a pit stop before I take you home?" Bill directed the question to Allison.

She thought about it, her face scrunched up like a child's. She nodded, pushing her chair back and getting up. Gayla waited until Allison was out of sight before she turned in disapproval.

"Bill, I wish you wouldn't do that." Her voice was low but firm.

"Do what?"

"You know what I mean. I know you like Allison, and I'm glad that you two get along so well. But please don't override my instructions to her. I want Allison to listen to me. She gets a little beside herself sometimes and I don't like it."

"Come on," Bill began, trying to quietly coax Gayla out of her sternness. "You're overreacting. Besides, I know when Allison is trying to wrap me around her finger."

"And she succeeds a *lot*. But the point is I don't want there to be any confusion about who's in charge. It's me, not Allison."

Bill's expression became serious. He leaned back in his chair and, with his elbows on the chair arms, rested his mouth and chin against his clasped fists as he intently regarded her.

"You think I'm trying to act like her father, is that it?" he questioned quietly.

Gayla lowered her gaze, struggling to soften her annoyance. "You indulge her too much."

He was silent for a long moment, during which Gayla knew he was still regarding her closely. "I would love to be her father. You know that."

Gayla shifted, nervously. "Bill, look . . ."

"Making me back off is not the answer to your problem."

She met his gaze squarely, frowning at him. "There is no problem. Allison is very clever and she'll try to manipulate anyone to get what she wants. You play right into her hands."

"Maybe I don't mind."

"But I do. She needs boundaries, and a reminder to show respect. I know you think I'm hard on her sometimes, but if you had children of your own you'd understand."

As soon as the words were out of her mouth, Gayla regretted them. She could sense more than see that she had made her point, even though Bill's expression remained calm and thoughtful.

"I'm working on it," he responded. "And I'm looking forward to the experience."

Gayla was spared any further comment when Allison returned to the table, ready to leave. She let her daughter and Bill conduct the bantering, silly conversation as he drove them home to their apartment near Columbia University. During the ride Gayla searched for a way to apologize to Bill for being snappish with him. But she also knew that her mood was tied to having met David Kinney earlier. Her uneasiness and irritation she'd transferred to Bill, yet it could really have been shared by both men but for different reasons.

Allison led the way into their pre–World War II building on 119th Street and raced ahead to get the mail as Bill and Gayla waited silently for the elevator. When Gayla looked up into his lean face, she saw only understanding and warmth in his eyes. He was rarely annoyed, let alone angry, with her. She wished he would be. Gayla wished sometimes that they could just go at it, and she didn't have to worry if she was going to hurt his feelings.

She absently rubbed her elbows. They were beginning to ache in the joints and she made a mental note to take some Tylenol for the pain before going to bed. Solicitously, Bill reached out to place his hand on her shoulder and squeezed. Gayla knew he was trying to smooth things over.

"Bill, I'm sorry."

"What for? You're probably right that I overdo things with Allison."

"I should be glad you're so fond of my daughter."

"Yeah, you should be," he agreed.

Gayla grinned and relaxed. He never held a grudge, either.

"Mommy, there's a letter from the mayor's office. Maybe he's going to put you on one of his committees," Allison suggested brightly.

"I seriously doubt it," Gayla said, accepting the handful of envelopes and glossy junk mail. A quick glance identified a letter postmarked from Alaska.

She pursed her lips and put it at the bottom of the pile. She wanted to read that one last.

When they arrived at the seventh floor, Allison rushed ahead to unlock the apartment door. She stretched on tiptoe as Bill bent down so that she could kiss him on the cheek.

"Night, Bill. Thanks for taking us to dinner."

"My pleasure. Good night."

Allison entered the apartment, leaving her mother and Bill in the hallway.

"I'll say good night here," Bill murmured, stepping closer to Gayla.

"Why don't you come in for a minute, at least?" Gayla said automatically.

Bill shook his head. He took hold of her arms so they faced each other. "Not tonight. Will you come with me to this thing I have to go to?"

Gayla nodded. "All right."

"Wear something that's going to make me lust after your body," he teased with a soft chuckle.

Gayla playfully pushed his chest and grinned. She blinked at him, seeing the intent consideration that he saved for the moments when they were alone. Which wasn't often enough, Bill had said more than once, but he was not a complainer. She, however, was content to let their relationship meander. She liked that he wanted her. She liked that he wasn't physically aggressive with her. But there was also a perverse impatience at times with Bill, because he was so unfailingly polite. So . . . straight.

Gayla could count on Bill being the complete

gentleman. There were no surprises. She thought of all those years alone when Allison was a toddler, then a small child, when her evenings and weekends were spent only with her daughter. This was better. To have someone she could count on. But he went home at night. Or no later than the next morning. Bill Coleman's devotion was a godsend, Gayla admitted. She was grateful.

She brushed her hand against his cheek affectionately. It always surprised Gayla that Bill's skin was so soft. She felt a burst of coyness which rose above her normal pragmatic caution. A need to reward Bill for his steadfast attention.

"I'll send Allison to my mother's for the weekend," Gayla suggested. The words brightened his eyes with pleasure.

"An offer I have no intention of refusing. I'd settle for even one night. I'll have to make it up to Allison, though."

"I wouldn't if I were you. She'll make you pay far beyond what the evening is worth."

Bill shook his head and growled in the back of his throat. "It'll be worth anything her little heart desires."

He pulled her forward and bent to cover Gayla's mouth with his. The good-night kiss was gentle and slow. Gayla knew how to let her tongue roll with his, when to withdraw so that he would pursue. She knew when to let Bill take command, to deepen the fusion of their lips, and when to tilt her pelvis provocatively against him. She let him gently end the kiss, his breath warm on her skin.

Bill moved his mouth to the corner of hers and then to her closed eyes. Gayla leaned into his body. For a moment she felt the utter safety of being within Bill Coleman's embrace. This was a man who was strong and constant. She trusted him. She'd resisted his attraction and pursuit for months before giving in to the gentle persuasion that was charming as well as seductive. Their affair so far was tasteful, satisfying and discreet . . . Allison's presence and awareness notwithstanding. Gayla was not unmindful of how lucky she was to be the object of his desires.

And yet as he whispered good night and headed back toward the elevator, Gayla entered her apartment feeling disturbed. She kept asking herself if Bill Coleman could be the man of her dreams. But Gayla suspected that if she had to ask, then perhaps he wasn't.

CHAPTER THREE

"Allison, you have ten minutes before the bus gets here, and you haven't finished your breakfast," Gayla called out from the kitchen, where she was sipping from a cup of coffee.

"I'm coming," Allison responded from her room.

"Don't forget Bill is coming over tonight, so please don't count on taking over the living room sofa and TV."

Allison rushed into the kitchen. She struggled to get her arms through the sleeves of a pullover sweatshirt. In her teeth was clamped a spiral-bound yellow notebook. She dropped a canvas knapsack on the floor with a solid thump. She blindly handed the notebook to her mother.

"Here's my homework."

Gayla accepted the book and began leafing through until she found the current assignment. "The oatmeal's ready. And don't put more than one teaspoon of sugar in it."

Allison glanced at her mother with a frown. "How come you're wearing my fleece sweater?"

Gayla pushed up the sleeves on the oversized top. "It was handy. You left it in the living room."

Allison was thoughtfully silent for moment. "Did you get cold?"

"I was, but I'm fine now. There was no pain at all," Gayla added, hoping to prevent any more questions about her health. But Allison was not so easily put off.

"Is it going to get worse?" Allison asked quietly, staring at her mother.

Gayla smiled and shook her head. "I don't think so, hon. This is the way it's been for a long time. And it's not so bad, is it?"

"Well . . . what if you have to go to the hospital or something?"

Gayla kept her smile in place, trying to allay Allison's fears. "You can't remember the last time that happened. You and I both understand that sometimes I get pain in my joints and sometimes I get tired. But I've never missed one of your school programs, or broken a promise to take you shopping."

That elicited a weak smile from Allison who seemed only mildly mollified. "I just wish you didn't have that sickle cell at all. How come Nana and I don't have it?"

Seeing the potential for too much revelation, Gayla avoided a direct response. "You should be glad you don't. Isn't it enough that you've already had appendicitis *and* your tonsils out?"

That made Allison roll her eyes as she went to the stove to peer into an aluminum pot and stir the contents with a wooden spoon. "You made the oatmeal too thick again."

"We can fix that real fast. Cook it yourself," Gayla said sweetly.

"That's okay, I don't mind," Allison said, ladling the oatmeal and taking the bowl to the table. She sat at a place setting where there was already a glass of orange juice, milk and a small dish of raisins which she liberally sprinkled into the oatmeal along with only one spoon of brown sugar, as instructed by her mother. "Can I go ice-skating this Saturday with Denise and Carol?" she asked as she began to eat breakfast.

"You have a dentist appointment on Saturday."

"Can't I go afterward?"

"You're not going anywhere until you clean up your room. From the way it looked last night, that could take the rest of the weekend. There's a mistake on your math page. Look it over again before you leave this morning." Gayla folded back the pages of the notebook, laying it on the table next to Allison. "Wasn't there a report or something you had to turn in?"

"It's due next Monday."

"Another reason why you may not get to go skating. Knowing you, you'll wait until Sunday evening to get started." Gayla scanned her daughter's school outfit for anything inappropriate or outrageous. What Allison wore made her sigh in resignation, but it was acceptable. Concessions had to be made, after all, to her age and the current fashion dictates of her school crowd.

Gayla smiled lovingly. She reached out and smoothed her hand gently down Allison's hair. It was just below her shoulders and rather thick, with strands that were more corkscrew than curly. The roots were a honey-blonde that grew out into brown hair which looked light against Allison's brown skin.

"Are you going to comb this back?" Gayle asked, fingering her soft hair.

Silently Allison held up her hand, showing the rubber band that circled her wrist. Gayla tugged it off and efficiently gathered the girl's hair into a bushy ponytail and pulled it through the band. Allison tilted her face up to her mother.

"Are you and Bill going to talk mushy stuff tonight? 'Cause if you are, I'm going to stay in my room."

"Don't be cute. We have to talk about some final details for the art show." Gayla looked at the wall clock. "You have five minutes. Hurry up."

Allison took her time with the cereal. "Is it only business or is it a date?"

Gayla looked exasperated. "You know full well the difference. I go out with Bill because I enjoy his company."

Allison seemed satisfied. "Then it's not serious."

Gayla was careful in answering. "Not really."

"Good."

"What do you mean, good? I thought you liked Bill."

"Yeah, I do. But you know as well as I do, Mom, that when women start going out with men they get silly."

Gayla was tempted to smile at the assessment. "Have you ever seen me silly?"

"Well, maybe not silly. But you start to worry about what to wear, and where he's going to take you and what to do with me."

"So that's really the issue, right? You feel neglected."

Allison slowly stood up from the table, taking the nearly empty bowl to the sink. "Not exactly," she said. "But everything gets different."

"Allison, I can assure you that Bill and I are just really good friends. He's a nice man, and a very smart one. And he's been very good to both of us."

"Yeah, but does *he* know you're just really good friends?"

Gayla shook her head at Allison. "You know something? I don't think that's any of your business." She pointed at the notebook and Allison bent over the pages, looking for the equation which needed correcting.

"Yes, it is," Allison responded boldly. She quickly made an erasure and penciled in a new set of numbers, and then closed the notebook. "Why can't I say how I feel about it? You're my mother, and I have to watch out for you. You might not be able to see that some guy is a dog . . ."

Gayla laughed despite herself. She watched Allison gather the rest of her things for school. "I appreciate your concern, Allison, but I think I can tell the difference between a man who's running a game and a man who's sincere."

Allison kissed her mother on the cheek, and they walked together to the apartment door. "Like that man last night. He's not your type, and I don't think you can trust artists anyway."

Gayla gaped at her daughter, not sure what question to ask first. "Why is that?"

"I don't know. Female tuition."

"Intuition . . ."

"Yeah. I don't think you can trust a man who wears a beard. And what was he doing with a teddy bear? Weird."

Gayla watched as Allison walked out the door and headed for the elevator. "You don't have a thing to worry about."

The neighborhood had not changed all that much. It didn't really look any better than the last time he'd been through, it seemed to David's way of thinking.

His old building was gone. Along with it had disappeared the Mount Zion AME Church of Christ, a storefront house of worship on the first floor from which came creaky piano hymns on Saturday night and most of Sunday afternoon. Gone, too, was the hole-in-the-wall variety store that had stocked every kind of nickel and dime candy treat he'd loved as a child. The store also sold an assortment of hair oils, cigarettes, Pampers, detergent, instant coffee . . . anything someone was likely to need to save the seven-block walk to the local supermarket. In its place was a red-brick high-rise, sleek and clean and graffiti-free. A more desirable place to live than what had been before it . . . but without an ounce of character or soul.

Locking his car, David stood at the bottom of the steep rise of 145th Street and Amsterdam Avenue to survey the community he'd started out from. Everything was familiar, and yet it all felt different. He shouldn't have been surprised. And in a way, he was glad. He had come to the neighborhood propelled by two thoughts. One was the memory of a Friday night domestic disturbance—as the police report would later call it—which had forever changed his life. The second thing was the desire to see Sylvia Patton.

Looking up and down the street, he didn't see a single person he recognized or who seemed to know him. David began to feel that perhaps the past was fading after all. He might yet return to visit it without succumbing to the memories that still made him feel overheated and scared. He began slowly walking up the incline of the street toward Convent Avenue and Hamilton Terrace. He'd always hated walking away from St. Nicholas Place because eventually he always had to return to the bottom of the hill. He slowed his steps as he neared the corner. To his left was the church where he'd gone to Sunday school and whose doctrines he'd abandoned at thirteen for more interesting lessons in the streets. But it was also the church that had conducted the services for his mother, and where he wished he could have stayed afterward because he didn't know where else he would go to live. With his grandfather in South Carolina? With an aunt he'd never met in St. Louis?

At the corner, the world changed.

Gone suddenly were the dilapidated tenements and row houses, the garish and unattractive stores and shops of the avenue below, replaced by a series of streets of quiet, solid residential buildings and brownstones. A century old, many of them were still stately and elegant, unmarred by the urban decay and chaos which existed only one block either east or west. Up here were trees and narrow streets, landmarks and a college campus stretching a half-mile south.

His mother had always wanted to live on the Hill.

David hitched up his knapsack into a more comfortable position, hanging by one strap from his shoulder. He was still not used to carrying one, but had discovered useful advantages beyond transporting newspapers, a notebook or bottled water. The bag made him fit in. Normal citizens leading upstanding lives used them. There was no reason for anyone to single him out for suspicious attitude, dress or intent. He had no concealed weapons, or contraband. He put his hands into the pockets of his casual black slacks and began walking leisurely south on Convent Avenue. A quick look around assured him that no one was paying any particular attention to him. There were several middle-aged men and women. A smattering of students on their way to or from classes on the campus. No one was loitering in front of buildings or otherwise gathered aimlessly.

David forced himself to relax. His attention was drawn to the wonderful details of the brownstone buildings on either side of the street. He tried to imagine what it would be like, living peacefully . . . sanely . . . in the heart of Harlem.

He reached a sand-colored brick building right on the edge of the college campus and entered the foyer. Reading the long listing of resident names, David rang the bell for S. Patton and waited for a response. There was none. He tried again. When there was still no answer he checked his watch and considered whether to wait a few more minutes or leave. While he was trying to decide the front door of the building opened behind him, and two young white women came in, chatting about something at work.

Reflexively, David stood aside as they neared the door and one reached into her purse for keys. He automatically turned away so as not to draw attention to himself.

"When I told my supervisor about it, the only thing he said was to not make an issue of it. Excuse me, do you want to come in?"

A few seconds passed before David realized that the question was directed toward him. He turned in surprise and quickly appraised the young women, but didn't respond.

The woman smiled and pushed the door open as her companion went on through. "I said, do you want to come in?"

She was quite open and comfortable in asking. She

wasn't threatened by him. He came down on the side of caution. "That's okay. I'm waiting for someone."

She shrugged. "Fine." She let the door go and continued into the lobby.

David's gaze followed her. Too late he realized he should have thanked her. He sighed. *I'll get the hang of this*, he thought wryly. He wasn't used to not being held suspect. But what were two young white women doing uptown? A lot of things *had* changed since he'd left the city, David concluded. But he wasn't convinced yet that it was a safe place for him to be.

He walked out of the building considering his options. He checked his watch again. He really had to get back to the gallery and finish hanging his work. When he looked up he saw a woman coming round the far corner of the apartment building, pulling a shopping cart half-full with plastic bags of supermarket items. It wasn't until the woman smiled and waved her arm to get his attention that David recognized Sylvia Patton. He'd forgotten that in the almost seven years since he'd last seen her, she would have changed along with everything else.

The first thing he noticed was that her hair was stylishly shorter, and all salt and pepper. Her face had a soft roundness of age and no makeup except for a little lipstick. What he had remembered as freckles were gone, somehow flattened and blended—maybe also with age—into the caramel-toned skin. But there was that smile showing near-perfect teeth, and the laugh which was rich and throaty. Sylvia

Patton had an honest laugh, he thought, because she used it sparingly. It made David feel special to hear it. But as she approached, David also saw the way Sylvia's eyes narrowed and scoped him out closely. In that moment he could see the physical attributes that made Gayla her mother's child. But he had not seen much of it in Allison, the grandchild.

"David! Oh, I'm so glad you didn't leave . . ."

Unexpectedly, he felt a smile begin to pull at the corners of his mouth. Sylvia was excited to see him. He was relieved. It was safe to be here and, more than anything else, he could be himself.

David hurried forward to greet her and help with the laden cart.

"Sylvia, hey. Here, let me take that for you . . ."

"Oh, forget that thing. Look at you! It's so good to see you!"

He was not prepared when Sylvia reached out and hugged him tightly. As he bent forward to accommodate her shorter height, he felt the weight of his knapsack pulled from his shoulder. It slid to the joint of his elbow, swinging heavily against her. Sylvia didn't seem to care. David could feel the softness of her black wool coat, and he could smell her skin. He felt himself lost for a moment in the overwhelming warmth of Sylvia Patton's welcome. Her hand patted his back, as only someone who was a parent could. *There, there . . . everything is all right.* It made him feel so young, so needy. Like when he used to hold onto his mother. That had stopped abruptly when he was nine years old.

"It's . . . good to see you, too, Sylvia," David responded with a hint of reserve. It had been a long time since anyone had been this glad to see him. Gayla had not even bothered to say hello.

Sylvia Patton pushed him away so she could see into his face properly. Her eyes were bright, reflecting her joy. But her brows drew together as her gaze took in every detail. She reached to rub her palm on the hair-layered cheek and jaw. She checked out the functional black attire. Nothing fancy and nothing fashionable. He didn't want to be noticed.

Sylvia shook her head. "Well . . . you made it," she whispered.

David grinned wryly and shrugged. "Barely."

She squeezed his arms, feeling along the length. "But you're so thin."

"You just haven't seen me in a long time."

She hit him playfully on his chest. "It's not as if I didn't want to. Why haven't you answered my letters? I got so worried about you. And of course I imagined the worst."

"I'm okay," David assured her with offhand calm. He stepped back, spread his arms and turned around. "See. In one piece."

Sylvia's gaze softened and she sighed. "Praise the Lord for that."

"I don't know if He had all that much to do with it," he said cynically.

"More than you give Him credit for. Let's go upstairs. I just picked up a few things, in case you're hungry . . ."

David laughed as he viewed the packages in her shopping cart. "Man, I'd have to stay with you a week to eat all of this."

Sylvia held the door to the building as David lifted the cart and carried it up the front steps into the entrance. "At least you'd be back home where you belong."

Home, David repeated to himself. He thought of all the places he'd lived in for the past fifteen years. He had never considered any of them home. Maybe when his parents were alive and there were four people occupying the same space. David only remembered of that time, however, that he and his older brother Spencer would sit in the dark of their bedroom listening to the almost nightly fights between their mother and stepfather. He used to think that everyone's home was like his. A battlefield of screaming and yelling. He couldn't remember many times when they were all together that didn't have the background sound effects of furniture being knocked over or broken. The sounds of slaps and punches. David remembered the countless times Spencer threatened to kill the motherfucka and once actually trying to. But Spencer was gone, too. Spencer, only three years older but who had been fearless and had protected him from the drunken abuse of their stepfather. But Spencer's anger had been self-destructive, leading him into a too short life of street crime and the wrong people. He'd been found stabbed in the hallway of a building across the street from where they'd lived. No one had ever been found or brought to trial for his murder.

David knew that but for Sylvia Patton's intervention he might have ended up the same way.

David clenched his teeth and took a deep breath to vanquish the memory which, even now, caused his body to tense in anger and helplessness. He let Sylvia chatter and carry the conversation on the elevator ride to her fifth-floor apartment. He nodded and gave monosyllabic answers to her questions. She had so many that, for now, there was no need for him to respond. Once inside the roomy four-room apartment, David unloaded the groceries onto the kitchen table as Sylvia put things away and began to assemble something to eat.

From the moment David walked through the door, he was plummeted into the past. He remembered the first time he'd come to Sylvia Patton's home and she'd told him that he would be living with her from now on. She had talked with Social Services. She had met with a judge. It had been settled in family court.

"Gayla called me. She told me you were back in the city."

"I was hoping to call you first."

"Why didn't you?" Sylvia asked.

David could hear the disappointment in her voice that he hadn't. "Because I wanted to get settled first. I didn't want to come to you asking for help, or needing a place to stay."

She shook her head. "Don't you know that as long

as there is breath in my body you have a place to live?"

"I appreciate that, Sylvia. You know I do. But a man needs his pride. This time I wanted to come to you and not have to ask for anything."

"So, where have you been? What have you been up to? Or should I ask?" Sylvia drawled.

"I was upstate," David said. She shot him a frown. "Working on a farm."

"A farm? By choice?"

"Pretty much. I didn't have anything else to do at the time. That was about six years ago."

"What in heaven's name do you know about farming?"

"Not a damn thing. But I needed work, and I was offered a job. I had room and board. I learned a lot. Worked on building a few houses. This is going to make you laugh but . . . I liked it 'cause it was quiet." Sylvia did laugh. "Then . . . I started fooling around with woodwork and carpentry."

Sylvia smiled wistfully. "Emily Whelan always used to say you were clever with your hands. She still has that table you made that year in Vermont. So you decided to become a craftsman?"

"Not exactly. I didn't give much thought to what I was doing being art. Someone saw some of my stuff and I started selling. Upstate they called it arts and crafts.

"I have a temporary sublet. I'm going to be in the city for a while till I decide what to do next."

She slowly looked over her shoulder at him, her gaze skeptical.

"Here?"

"Not uptown. I got a place on Fifteenth Street off Seventh Avenue."

"That's a little better, I guess. But I hope you don't plan to take up with that old crowd of yours."

David didn't answer. Some of them were dead. Some in jail, some he'd lost touch with. Sylvia was right. He didn't need to have that kind of profile.

"Gayla said you're going to be in the show at her gallery. How did she find you?"

"She didn't. I heard about the show from someone else. I didn't even know Gayla was in any way involved until I got down here."

Sylvia glanced at him. "You've seen her?"

He nodded. "Yeah, I've seen her."

Sylvia gave some dishes and silverware to David and pointed for him to set the table. "And?"

"And nothing's changed. Why should it?" He returned her steady gaze. "I met Allison."

A thoughtful smile touched Sylvia's countenance. "Were you surprised?"

"Not really."

"What do you think of her?"

David thought carefully. "She's . . . something else. Pretty. Seems to be smart. Probably a little spoiled."

"And she can be a little fresh. I have to remind her sometimes she's not grown up yet," Sylvia said dryly, turning from the stove with a pot in one hand

and a serving spoon in the other. She looked squarely at him. "Is that *all* you think?"

He shrugged. "What do you want me to say, Sylvia? I'm not in a position to judge anybody. Gayla would tell me up front it's like the pot calling the kettle black. I take it things didn't work out like she wanted?"

Sylvia began serving rice onto the plates. "No, they sure didn't. I tried to warn her but that girl can be stubborn. Now she's paying the price."

"Maybe it was a little high, but she's got a beautiful daughter. You have a grandchild."

Sylvia brightened. "Lord, yes. Ali is a blessing."

He watched as she followed with a ladle of heated chicken gumbo over the rice. From the refrigerator Sylvia took out a small bowl of already prepared salad. The last item was a chilled bottle of white wine, a pinot grigio.

David laughed to himself when he saw the bottle. He took it from her and found the corkscrew in the utility drawer. He expertly extracted the cork and poured glasses for them both.

"I remember when you thought Boone's Farm and pink Champale were the *thing*," Sylvia said.

"I remember when Gayla used to laugh at me because I drank them. What did she call it?"

"Bilge," Sylvia pronounced, imitating her daughter and chuckling. "But you got her back. You asked her what that meant and she didn't know."

David shook his head as they sat down at the table.

"Didn't make any difference. She still thought I was low-class."

"Well, I remember that you had a few choice adjectives for her, too."

They faced each other across the small round table. The steam of the hot food wafted into the air between them. David saw the light of affection and caring in Sylvia's face. She saw a young man who had been through too much in his life. Who'd walked on the wild side and been too close to the edge for her taste.

"I don't think I'd be here if it wasn't for you," David admitted.

"And the good Lord," she said. "You can't forget Him."

"No, ma'am," David responded.

But he wasn't just humoring her. He reached out across the table. Sylvia grabbed hold of his hands. She closed her eyes and murmured a prayer of thanks for him, for their food.

The doorbell rang when they were almost through. A key turned in the door as someone let themselves in. Sylvia, listened, her head cocked to the side.

"Mitchell?"

"Yeah, it's me," a male voice answered.

"I'm in here. I have company."

David folded his arms on the edge of the table, as if they gave him an anchor. Sylvia went back to eating, but David stared at the kitchen door until a young man appeared and slowly walked in.

"Look who's here," she said.

Mitchell Patton stopped behind his mother and

openly scrutinized David. The look was filled with caution and curiosity, but David could also detect an arrogance. It hadn't existed when they had first met, unlike his sister, Gayla. Mitchell had kept to himself, out of his way, David knew, because he had been afraid of him. He'd only been a child. But David had quickly figured out that Mitchell had a lot to be afraid of. He hadn't played on that.

It was clear that Mitch had made peace with himself—not about identity, but orientation, life style. It was a matter of survival. In that, David considered, they had a lot in common. Mitchell's weapons were style and presence and ego, and the irrefutable fact that Sylvia was *his* mother. David knew this stemmed from Mitchell wanting to remind him that he was in on a pass, that he wasn't welcome and never had been.

The difference now was that David had no desire to fight back, no need to. Besides, anything he did to Mitchell Patton in retaliation would hurt Sylvia. He never wanted to do that.

It was nevertheless dispiriting to David to realize that both Gayla and Mitchell Patton continued to see him as unworthy of their mother's regard.

"Dak . . . I heard you were back," Mitchell said.

David half stood up and reached out a hand to Mitchell. For a moment he didn't think Sylvia's son was going to accept, but he finally did shake the offered hand.

"It's David. News travels fast," David murmured.

"Only bad news. You know how that goes."

"Mitchell." Sylvia frowned at her son in disapproval. "Do you want something to eat? There's food left."

"No, thanks. I'm not staying. I came by to pick up some clothes I left here."

"And to check me out?" David boldly asked.

"That's right."

"Now, you two stop it. I'm not going to have it."

"It's okay," David said, staring at Mitchell. "I don't mind. In a way, he has a right."

Mitchell didn't have a response to that and backed off. "Are you staying here?" he asked instead.

"No. I have a place downtown." David looked at his watch. "As a matter of fact I have to go soon."

"Not on my account," Mitchell baited.

"Absolutely not," David answered. "I have things to do."

"David, you just got here," Sylvia complained.

"I'll be around. We'll get together again." He stood up and started to clear the table.

"I'll get my things," Mitchell said and left them.

"Thanks for lunch, Sylvia. When I get my act together, I want to take you to dinner," David said.

"There's no need for that. You know I love to cook, and it's more comfortable here."

David smiled and bent to kiss her cheek. "I appreciate what you're trying to do, Sylvia, but I think I can afford to buy you dinner."

"And don't mind Mitchell," she whispered to him.

"I can handle Mitchell. You don't have to worry."

"I don't want any trouble between you two . . ."

"Sylvia . . ." David began soothingly, sensing her agitation. "I never said or did anything to Mitchell because he's gay. Yeah, I had some attitude about it when I was sixteen. I was also stupid and had my own troubles. He doesn't have to worry about what I think. Besides . . ." he said mischievously.

Sylvia narrowed her gaze on him. "You are not going to tell me you have friends who are."

"Some of my best friends."

Sylvia scoffed and affectionately shoved him. "You're a mess!"

David and Mitchell left the apartment together, but in silence. David saw a young man who was slender and good-looking, dressed with style and care in the manner of someone for whom appearance means a lot. Mitchell was an adolescent when he'd last seen him, small and scared and furtive and resentful. He'd been ambivalent about himself. *But so was I*, David reminded himself. And it was for the same reason that Mitchell had turned his dislike on him. Neither had known enough to know better.

Once they boarded the elevator, however, the smaller space made it seem silly to ignore one another. After a moment Mitchell again looked David over.

"What's the matter? Surprised to see me alive?"

Mitchell shrugged. "I heard you were sent upstate for a few years."

"Right where I belonged, right?"

Mitchell stared straight ahead. "It ain't no spa."

"I survived."

"You on parole?"

"Nope. I was let go because I wasn't supposed to be there to begin with."

"Right." Mitchell nodded, clearly skeptical.

David turned the tables. "What about yourself?"

Mitchell looked down at the floor. "You don't care a fat rat's ass how I am. I'm just a limp-wrist fag. Ask me if I care."

"Look, I know how you feel about me, Mitchell. Maybe you were right. I was an asshole. There was a lot I didn't know or want to know. I made some mistakes and I paid for them. But I'm not blaming anybody, either. So don't dump your shit on me."

Mitchell continued to look down. "I came out when I was fifteen. I got tired of getting jumped in school. Once I told everybody, it stopped. It wasn't fun anymore to pick on me."

"And Sylvia?"

"She doesn't talk about it. So I don't talk about it."

The elevator reached the first floor, and they exited the building together.

"How long you going to hang around?" Mitchell asked.

David put his hands in the pockets of his slacks again. He squinted against the afternoon sun, low in the sky, and thought about all the things he'd like to do . . . he needed to do now that he was back. "A while."

"I didn't think we'd ever see you again," Mitchell confessed.

"And you didn't particularly want to."

"That's right." Mitchell began backing away.

David shrugged. "Look, I'm not interested in giving you a hard time, so why don't we not dig up the past and pretend like we're meeting for the first time?"

Mitchell considered that. He nodded. "It doesn't matter. I don't think we move in the same circles anyway. I have to go . . ."

"I have a car. Can I drop you off?" he asked.

Without waiting for an answer David turned to retrace the way back to his parked car. Mitchell fell into step next to him. Other than giving David his destination there was no conversation until they were headed downtown.

"You know, I still don't like you," Mitchell announced at a stoplight.

"That's cool," David said calmly. "You'll get over it."

CHAPTER FOUR

"Why don't you wear this?" Allison asked as she pulled from the closet a bolero-length sequined evening jacket in shades of blue.

Distracted as she considered two other outfits already laid across her bed, Gayla frowned at her daughter's choice.

"Ummmmm . . . I don't think so. Too showy. Too formal."

"Yeah, but you could wear it with those silky pants you bought on sale," Allison enthused. She held the sparkling top in front of her chest and pivoted back and forth in front of the full-length mirror inside the closet door.

"Allison, move out of the way, please." Gayla gave the suggestion only a passing glance. She reached past Allison with a hanger draped with a long blue outfit.

"Oooooh, that's pretty. What's wrong with that?" Allison asked, watching the garment disappear into the closet.

"It's a jumpsuit."

"It's so cool."

"I'll be zipping myself in and out of it all night," Gayla muttered. "Every time I go to the bathroom, I'll have to take it off."

"Go to the bathroom before you leave home. That's what you always tell me when we're going out someplace." Allison held up the sequined jacket and ran her hand over the tiny metal and beaded attachments. "You have all this great stuff you never wear. Can I have this? I like it."

That got Gayla's attention, and she chuckled, looking incredulously at her daughter. "No, you can't have it. It's too old for you, too big and it was too expensive."

"It's not too big," Allison countered, and she demonstrated by laying the sleeve of the jacket along the length of her arm. "See?"

The jacket was too sophisticated for a thirteen-year-old, but she noticed the ease and confidence with which her daughter made a case for herself. Even if it was really ridiculous, if it was something Allison wanted she just plunged ahead, trying to persuade everyone else otherwise. *Just like her father*, the thought came unbidden to Gayla. She was momentarily stunned at the unexpected flashback and quickly swept it aside.

Something else drew Gayla's attention and made her stop in her consideration of an outfit to wear. It was the picture she and Allison made in the mirror as they stood next to each other. Gayla had accepted that there wasn't much of herself physically present in her daughter. Except for the shape of her face, a bit of her mouth and certain body mannerisms. The sound and tone of her voice, perhaps. People sometimes confused them on the phone.

Despite having her father's features, Allison had never shown a lot of interest in who he was and Gayla had never volunteered very much. While she was grateful for not having to evade the truth of the circumstances of her daughter's conception and birth, Allison's lack of curiosity had always been a surprise to her. She'd supposed that Allison was so confident in the love of her mother, uncle and grandmother that she had no sense that she was missing anything important.

Gayla also noticed that her daughter was now as tall as she was. In another year Allison would be taller. She was certainly going to be beautiful, as had been apparent since she was three months old. Gayla was, however, pleased that Allison seemed to put no store in her beauty. She was blissfully uninterested in capitalizing on her looks by wanting to be a model, as was frequently suggested to her.

"Can I have the jumpsuit?" Allison boldly asked her mother.

Gayla took the hanger from her daughter. "I'm trying to get dressed, Allison, and you are in the way . . ."

The telephone rang, immediately grabbing Allison's attention. "I got it."

Gayla shook her head. The only other things that got her daughter's attention as effectively were the prospects of shopping for clothes or going out to eat. The apartment buzzer also sounded. She looked at the clock on the nightstand and gasped at the time.

"Oh, my God . . . Allison, if that's the car service, tell him I'm on my way down."

Allison was already answering the phone.

"Hello? Hi-Miss-Donahue-I-gotta-answer-the-door-here's-my-mother," Allison got out in one breath. She scrambled across her mother's bed, pushed the cordless receiver into her hand and dashed out of the room.

"Hi, Margaret. I'm still getting dressed, and . . ."

"I just wanted to warn you," Margaret began.

Gayla frowned. "Warn me? About what? Did something happen?"

"Well, not exactly. Did you do a walk-through of the exhibit yesterday?"

"No, I didn't. I was overscheduled with meetings and had to leave early. I didn't think I had to. I know what each of the artists had submitted for the show."

"Except for that last-minute replacement, Kinney."

"Did he drop out, too?" Gayla asked apprehensively.

"Oh, no. He got his work in, but . . . I don't know what to say. It's different."

Gayla had visions of disaster. Something ugly, incompetent or just awful came to mind as well. She had seen the layout on paper for David's work in the exhibit. She had even witnessed some of the installation, but had not thought it necessary to see the entire finished gallery with all the work in place.

Nothing she'd seen had led Gayla to believe there would be a problem.

"Is it going to embarrass us? Will we get negative press?" Gayla frowned. "It's nothing that could get us sued, is it?"

"The answer is maybe, maybe and probably not . . ."

"Mom, it's the car service," Allison said, coming back into the room. She wandered over to her mother's dresser and began poking through the jewelry box.

In the middle of two pressing decisions Gayla pulled herself together. She spoke into the phone. "I'll be there in half an hour," she announced and hung up. She turned to Allison as now the doorbell rang. Gayla sighed in exasperation.

"That must be Mrs. Perry," she murmured, opening bureau drawers and pulling out fresh panty hose and an evening purse. She went to the closet and bent over in search of the right pair of shoes. "Allison, go let her in."

"I don't need a baby-sitter," Allison scoffed in complaint.

"Did you finish your homework?"

"No," Allison reluctantly admitted.

"Did you find that overdue library book?"

"I'm looking for it," Allison defended.

"Did you—"

"I get the point," Allison sighed.

"If you can't do the things you're supposed to,

you're going to be twenty before you can be without a sitter. Now, I'm running late . . ."

"I know. Unless I'm bleeding or the house is on fire, don't bother you. I told the driver you're on your way down." The doorbell rang again, and Allison sighed in resignation. "Okay, I'll let her in."

"Thanks, hon. I'm glad I can count on you," Gayla said.

"You owe me," Allison called out.

Gayla chuckled again at Allison's impertinent response, knowing that her daughter was going to actually try and hold her to some mythical obligation.

Gayla began pulling on the panty hose, feeling anxious and annoyed. It seemed ridiculous that this current art show was turning into a nightmare of mishaps. She had been valiantly trying not to let the fact that Dak Kinney was involved get on her nerves. In the middle of chaos he was a highly questionable substitute, and Gayla had concluded that nothing had changed. From the first time she'd met him, until the latest call from Margaret, Dak had been and still was nothing but trouble.

Gayla smiled at Teddy as he greeted her. He was a bit more formal and uncomfortable this evening. He wore a dark blue suit. The only one he owned, by his own account, and which served multiple duty for church, funerals and the quarterly exhibit openings. Teddy informed Gayla that most of the artists and some of the staff were gathered in the front gallery. The musicians had arrived and were setting up their instruments.

She could hear voices and laughter but made no attempt to join them. In another half hour the guests would be arriving. Gayla decided instead to bypass the gathering and headed down the corridor toward the last gallery room. Even as Gayla approached she could detect the reflective glow of lights from the room, yellow and red. And there was a noise. Almost unintelligible human voices coming through electronic static. Expecting the worse, she entered the room.

There was nothing half-finished about it now. The entire room had been transformed into not so much an exhibit as a stage setting for a happening. Gayla felt herself not just a viewer on the scene; the moment she walked into the gallery she became part of it.

A banner just inside the entrance featured a blown-up headline of an actual newspaper: URBAN JUNGLE. All throughout the gallery were similar banners for specific areas of artwork with titles such as THE PROJ-ECTS, HOOP DREAMS, DRIVE-BY SHOOTING and THIS WAY OUT. The yellow and red glow came from replicas of the roof lights of police squad cars; two long glowing bars were mounted inside a pair of plain pine frames. Two more wooden frames just in front of the lights had plaster molded grilles, like the bumper and hood of a police cruiser. Scratchy human voices were emu-lating a patrol car squawk box. The frames, with their stylized contents, were like police cars and had been

positioned on either side of the entrance, like sentinels, keeping the natives in, Gayla thought.

She stood transfixed. The pine frames of varying
sizes created shadow boxes, each holding details of
life in a black community. Some frames held dôc-
tored photographs or drawings. Others contained
found objects, or plaster representations of things like
shopping carts, basketballs, newspapers . . . and body
parts. On the floor of the gallery a path was laid out
through the hanging frames, using the footprints
from a pair of sports shoes.

Gayla followed the path with her head turning left
and right. She tried to absorb all the vignettes and
captured moments cleverly created in the frames.
Some contents were very simple, like a series of three
mailboxes of the kind used in project buildings. They
were all made of white plaster, and constructed to
look like they'd been broken into. The caption
attached under the frame said, FIRST OF THE MONTH,
an allusion, Gayla understood, to the arrival and
sometimes theft of welfare checks. In a plaster card-
board box that had its four flaps partially twisted
closed was something more complicated. There was
just enough of an opening to invite a look-see, and
when she did so she gasped and pressed a hand to
her mouth. Inside the box was a brown rubber baby
doll, wrapped in towels. It seemed horrifyingly real,
and deadly still. The caption title was AFTER-BIRTH.

Gayla closed her eyes, shaken, because she knew
that some babies really were quickly disposed of like
garbage. On a far corner wall was a splattering of

brownish-red paint. It had been allowed to drip to the floor. Like blood. She didn't want to go closer and find out where the blood was supposed to be flowing from. Gayla stared, dumbfounded. She felt surrounded and overwhelmed by the silent white plaster artifacts and the cold stark facts of black life caught in each piece. She was not aware of the audible sound which came from the back of her throat. Shock? Recognition? The power of suggestion?

"Don't worry. There's a soluble gesso on the walls. The paint won't stain."

She felt herself start at the voice, but calmly turned around to face the owner. She held her tongue for the moment, for two reasons. Gayla was trying to recover from the power of those few moments alone in Dak's universe.

Dak was looking past Gayla to the gallery. She took the opportunity to assess him. She was sure that this was the closest she'd ever been to Dak Kinney without instantly feeling anger and resentment. And for the first time she could see beyond all of her past feelings about him and just see the man. She'd never before thought of Dak as adult.

His eyes were intense, taking in everything. His firm, wide mouth was no longer petulant and tight. His back and shoulders were straight, instead of a slouch to his spine that suggested indifference. Dak Kinney was a man with a past, filled with the kind of trouble that eats up young black men and spits them out, mangled or destroyed. But he was a survivor.

She'd never thought of him that way before. That Dak could have gone through the kind of youthful encounters and experiences guaranteed to kill, but that he had come out on this end, whole. She wondered what she would see or learn if the film of Dak Kinney's life was played in rerun.

The thin beard on his face emphasized his mouth and nose, sculpted to a mature masculine edge. It came as a surprise to Gayla that she would now consider Dak good-looking, in a dangerous and magnetic way. In the way of someone who had a lot of strength and mystery about him. What *had* he been doing all those years? Who had taught him to use his eyes . . . and his hands . . . so effectively?

"Is this from experience?" she asked tartly.

He nodded, not offended by her question. "And a lot of nightmares," he added quietly.

An odd statement, Gayla considered. The yellow and red chase lights cast an eerie reflection on his face and made his eyes bright and weary. For a brief instant Gayla knew herself privy to much more than what met the eye.

As if aware that he'd revealed too much, Dak squared his shoulders, pursed his mouth and crossed his arms over his chest. He shook his head. "But you wouldn't know about that."

She raised her brows. "Are you asking or telling me?"

"Telling you," Dak responded.

"How would you know what I know? What makes

you think I don't know about crime and police brutality in our communities?"

He glanced at her, his eyes narrowed. A slow, knowing smile transformed his mouth and gave the contours of his face sharp angles. "*Our* communities? You didn't hang out in the street. You wouldn't have had anything to do with the brothers trying to get over, or the sisters competing. You didn't get locked in 'cause you weren't around most of the time."

The inference that she had no time for what went on in Harlem struck a nerve. But Gayla quickly assessed that was Dak's intention. "I lived all my life in the same neighborhood, with pretty much the same people you did," she said.

"Yeah," Dak drawled, his voice amused. "But not my block or my building. You never claimed the community as yours or stayed around long enough to make a difference. You were too busy trying to find a way out and downtown. You missed it."

Gayla stiffened at the criticism. "You mean stuff like this?" She nodded toward the open gallery. The repetitive flashing lights were beginning to irritate her. "I wouldn't be so proud of it if I were you. What's wrong with wanting to live someplace safe and clean? What's so noble about having seen someone shot dead, or being collared by the police, or spending time on Rikers? I don't need to see the crack vials to know they're sold on the corner to folks."

Dak turned to her. "Okay. But that's all in your head. You still don't *feel* what it was like. You didn't go through it and experience it. You're just glad it wasn't you. You were above it," he said.

"Yes, I was. I'm not going to apologize for it, either."

"I'm not surprised," he said smoothly.

She narrowed her gaze on him. "You think I was too conceited to care. You're saying I was full of it."

He grinned in an indulgent manner, as if she'd answered her own accusations.

"The life you've . . . you've . . . *created* here doesn't make this art," Gayla declared in mild annoyance, waving her arm to include all of the exhibit.

Dak's gaze followed her gesture. He shrugged and shook his head slightly. "That's not your judgment to make, thank goodness." He looked at her. "And you miss the point. But then, you always did."

They stared at one another. Any thawing that might have begun between them as they stood alone was cut short. The gauntlet had been thrown down again.

"Go on. Say what's on your mind," Dak quietly invited Gayla.

She wouldn't take the bait. "Guests are going to be arriving any minute . . ."

"Say it."

"And you're going to have to deal with them, not me."

"You wouldn't give me a break even if I said I was a born-again Christian."

"I might not believe you, but you *are* getting a break. You're here, aren't you?"

"I wouldn't have been if you'd known sooner. You still think I'm a punk. Right?"

There was no anger in his voice, no powerful spewing of words that warned he wanted to strike out, destroy something . . . take someone out. *That* was different, too, Gayla conceded.

"The only question tonight is, are you an artist? We'll find out. This is one time and place you can't just get over."

Voices in the corridor and other galleries grew louder. The jazz combo started playing.

"Gay . . . we need you up front." Bill Coleman's voice suddenly cut into the room.

Gayla and Dak both turned to watch him.

Bill's eyes looked from Gayla to David and then quickly swept around the gallery. "Well, you sure do know how to make an impression," he said, bringing his attention back to Dak. "The show hasn't officially opened yet, and people are already talking about your work. You're creating quite a stir."

"Yeah . . . but is it art?" Dak drawled.

"That depends on the impact your work makes on the viewer, and whether they're willing to write a check for any of it."

Gayla smiled at Bill. "I wasn't expecting you until later. I'm glad you're here."

"Well . . ." Bill began carefully. His smile encompassed both Gayla and David. Casually he put one hand into the pocket of his trousers and used the other to smooth his expensive and conservative tie. "I thought it was a good idea for at least one member of the board to be here on time." He took hold of Gayla's arm. "Come on up front. Everyone's going to want to say hello . . ."

David watched them walk away. He didn't follow. He didn't think that Bill Coleman's invitation included him . . . and he wasn't ready to face a lot of strangers just yet. He listened as Gayla and Bill's banter was absorbed into the other sounds. Left alone, David began to feel more than just isolated. He had the suspicion that he was way out of his league. Gayla's digging at him notwithstanding, he wasn't sure his work was art, either. Other people had declared that. Other people had encouraged him, and he did what he did because, otherwise, he wasn't at all sure what else he had to turn to as an outlet for his frustrations, and all those visions of destruction dancing in his head.

He turned around and looked at his work, trying futilely to see what other people would see. Perhaps his work was too personal, too angry. Perhaps reality wasn't what people wanted to see at all, but bright colors and shapes that held their attention, didn't hurt and made them feel good.

Matt Nelson had told him once that after what he'd been through, after all he'd witnessed, that this was the easy part. But David knew the truth, that this moment was no different than when he'd hung out in the streets as a young blood.

He was still scared.

* * *

"I heard that this is his first major exhibit. Who represents him? What gallery is he signed with?"

Gayla tried to keep her expression interested, her responses enthusiastic and her smile fixed. She was forced to speak loudly in order to be heard above the din. She was also feeling warm in the crowded gathering. Gayla held a glass of wine in her hand. She had been trying to sip from it for the past hour but conversation had been so continuous that the wine had grown flat. In her peripheral vision she was aware of a small group of visitors surrounding Dak, asking him questions and commenting on his work.

"Well, he's not known here in New York City. He was a last-minute selection for this show. We, er, really didn't know too much about his work, but Bill Coleman recommended him."

"What's his name again?"

"Dak Kin . . . I mean, *David* Kinney."

The woman scrunched up her face. "What is that? Dak?"

"I'm sorry, Priscilla. It's David Alan Kinney."

"I didn't see anything about him in the program," the woman said, shifting her position as someone inadvertently jostled her.

"Like I said, he was chosen at the last minute. What do you think of his work?"

The woman shook her head. "It's . . . amazing. He sure put a lot of hours into all those pieces. It's too real. Besides, I'm not sure I'd spend any of my money to have a plaster head of a police officer in my living room. And did you see that box with the . . . the—"

"Yes, I saw it," Gayla interrupted. She didn't want to hear anyone else's description of it.

The woman's mouth opened in astonishment. She placed her hand over her ample bosom and struggled for words. "I . . . I couldn't believe it. Well, honey, when I looked into that box and saw that child . . ."

"You mean the doll . . ."

"It scared me half to death. I thought it was real."

"I think that's what the artist intended."

Gayla casually glanced around. She located Dak in the crowd and saw that his expression was tight and closed as he continued to be engaged in conversation. His arms were crossed over his chest, the hands tucked under his armpits.

"You know, I could hardly have anything that looked like a dead baby in my house, either."

Gayla brought her attention back to the stout journalist and grimaced. "No, but you'll never forget it, and you'll talk about it for the rest of the week."

"That's true. It's very visual. It's exactly the kind of thing that works in a traveling show. You should talk to the folks at the downtown Whitney. I understand that they're putting something together for a five-city national tour. Do you see the way Barbara Rich just has so much to talk to him about? Ever since her divorce the woman has been *dangerous.*"

"Have you seen the paintings in the second gallery?" Gayla cut in. She'd noticed that Barbara, the owner of two bookstores, was not the only woman who'd found reason to hang around the third gallery and the artist.

Priscilla frowned. "I've been through the whole show. Now, let me think . . . Were those the abstract portraits by a woman?"

Gayla smiled patiently. "No. Those were Winston Jefferies' paintings. Nia Murdoch is the weaver."

"That's right. I'm going to pay her to do a coat for me. Now *that* I'd spend money on."

"As long as you also say something positive about the show, Priscilla," Gayla said, trying to end the conversation and ease away.

"Oh, I'll put something together. Now, I'm not sure about all that stuff in the last gallery, but the artist, Mr. Dak? Boyfriend is *seriously* cute."

Gayla grinned as the talkative writer for a local community weekly found someone else to say hello to.

She took a quick glance at her watch. Another half hour before the reception would be over, but there were a lot of visitors who didn't seem inclined to leave. A brief appraisal showed Gayla that most of the activity was still centered around the third gallery and David Alan Kinney's installation. At least for tonight his work had created the most excitement and comments. Many guests had already gone through it twice. Everyone seemed to be enjoying the event. Except for Dak.

A few minutes earlier she'd spotted him talking to a styles editor from one of the largest New York weeklies for the black community. The editor was not known for subtlety or tact. But neither was Dak, as Gayla remembered. She'd given them ten minutes together before sensing that the editor was growing aggressive in his questions and Dak was growing impatient. Gayla wasn't sure what to expect from him if he decided he'd had enough. She did know what would have happened fifteen years ago.

But now she couldn't see Dak anywhere. He was no longer standing in the gallery, available to talk about his work. Surrounded by women. Gayla looked around, trying to see over the heads of the milling crowd. She was worrying too much.

"How are you holding up?"

Gayla turned to smile at Bill. "I'm fine."

"Quite a turnout."

"You won't hear me complain," she said. "The show we had last September had a fraction of this crowd for the entire duration of the exhibit."

' "You look tired," Bill said solicitously, gazing down into her face.

She nodded. "I'm getting there. My tolerance for this kind of thing is about an hour."

"It's almost over. Want to go somewhere quiet for some coffee afterward?" he asked.

"I think I'll go on home. I have a baby-sitter with Allison tonight."

"I'm sure she didn't like that." Bill raised his brows. He looked up and all around him. "Congratulations. I'd say this was a big success. That Kinney guy has been the center of attention all evening. Or at least his work has. He seems to have disappeared . . . I had some people I wanted to introduce him to . . ."

"Gayla!"

Both Gayla and Bill turned. She saw a couple trying to make their way through the throng of people. An older white couple who were smiling broadly as they forced their way toward her.

"My goodness . . . look at you!" the woman exclaimed.

"Hello, Gayla. It's so good to see you!"

Gayla's recognition of the couple rushed through her body, bringing in its wake a jumbled wave of emotions. Among them was surprise and gladness, and many wonderful memories. But another sensation equally as strong was panic. She stared at their approach as if they were ghosts, and it was several seconds before Gayla could summon up a smile.

"Hi," she said weakly. The woman reached her first and opened her arms to wrap around Gayla with easy familiarity and obvious affection. Gayla held her arm out so as not to spill her wine.

"Oh, Gay! My God, it's been years. I'm so happy to see you," the woman said excitedly.

"I think we really caught you by surprise," the man said with more reserve, but his brief hug was equally warm.

"Yes . . . yes, you did. What are you doing here? How did you know where to find me?"

The couple exchanged glances. "Sylvia," they both said.

"Well, this . . . this is fantastic," Gayla said, trying to overcome her mixed emotions. Trying to match their warmth. She turned to Bill, who was standing patiently next to her, a witness to the reunion. "This is Bill Coleman. Bill is an attorney and is one of our board members. This is Emily and Paul Whelan."

Hellos were politely said all around, and then Bill turned to Gayla. "I'm going to see if we can start winding things down. Nice to meet you both," Bill said, and left.

Gayla wished she could have thought of a reason for him to stay. But the couple gave her no time to think. Their presence had plunged her back to her childhood and the circumstances which had led to the Whelans and the Pattons crossing paths. She used to think of them as celebrities, because *she* was so pretty and blonde, and *he* was so tall and handsome, and they seemed to have everything.

"It's so nice to see you both," Gayla said. "It's been . . . so many years."

"Yes, but we've been keeping up with your activities through your mother," Paul informed her.

"Although I have to say Sylvia hasn't given us an awful lot to go on," Emily Whelan complained. "I was always asking her to have you call us. We wanted to know how you were doing and if you finally got into art, and . . . oh, so many things!"

"Well, I've been keeping up with you, too. You both look terrific," Gayla said.

"Just getting grayer and older," Emily smiled. "You've grown so pretty. I'm sorry we lost touch over the years."

"Well . . . you know . . . being away for college, and then finding a job and a place to live . . ."

"And having a baby," Paul said smoothly. "You're so much a part of our family that Em and I felt like *we'd* become grandparents, too, along with your mother."

"We would love to see your daughter. She must be about ten or eleven now," Emily said probingly.

Gayla had no chance to correct her as several people passed by and got her attention.

"We're leaving now, Gay. Interesting show. I'll call you next week."

"Thanks for coming. Good night . . ."

Emily reached out and grabbed Gayla's hand. "Don't you hate when they say it's 'interesting'? We saw Dak's work. It's very powerful, don't you think? I'm glad that he took my advice to develop his talent. And I'm so glad you're in a position to give him a chance to show his work."

"He's not the same young man we met when he was sixteen," Paul commented caustically. "He's a *new* Dak."

"Yes, he . . . his work . . . well, he's very—"

"Great show, Gayla," someone else interrupted as he headed out.

"Thanks, Omar. I'm glad you could come."

"I want to send over a photographer to take some pictures. Maybe I can get some coverage in the Sunday arts section."

He waved and was gone. Gayla turned back to the Whelans.

"Look, I can see that you're still working, and it's getting late. I'm starting a ten-city book tour next week, but when I return we really want to get together with you . . ."

"I want to hear all about what you've been doing. And you can fill us in on Dak," Emily Whelan added.

"Well, for starters he doesn't like being called Dak anymore," Gayla said.

"Why not?" Paul raised his brows. "It's a wonderful moniker for getting attention. If he wants to make a name for himself having a hook is how you do it."

Emily smiled patiently at her husband. "This is not like fiction, Paul. Your name sells books now. David's work is a strong enough point of view."

Paul shrugged. "You know we're still on Central Park West, but we have a house in Connecticut where I do a lot of my writing. I'm going to have Sylvia up to help me out on a new project soon." He reached into the opening of his outer coat and the inner pocket of his sports jacket. He took out a pen and began writing some information on the edge of his exhibit program. "Why don't you think about coming up for a weekend? Bring your daughter. What's her name again? Allison?"

"Yes, Allison," Gayla said, accepting the phone number he'd written. She stared at it and after a moment reached into her purse for one of her own business cards. "Here's my card . . ."

"Put your home phone on the back," Emily said, offering her husband's pen to Gayla. She took the wineglass.

Gayla obliged, although she felt reluctant. Not that she didn't like the Whelans or want to see them. But she was cautious of being pulled into their lives again. Of revealing too much of herself. But she gave them the card and remembered to ask the question she knew couldn't be avoided.

"How's everybody?" Gayla asked. "Mitchell said that Sarah is working somewhere downtown."

"Sarah is Sarah. She does her own thing," Paul informed Gayla in a stilted way. "She's working for a small film company as a gofer. Not exactly why we paid for her to go to Brown."

Gayla nodded. They offered no more information and she knew there was no way around the rest of her inquiry about the family members. "I . . . I heard about—"

"Excuse me, Gayla," Bill whispered close to her ear. "I told the musicians to stop playing. Maybe everyone will take the hint."

"Including us. We have to go. Keep in touch, dear," Emily said, briefly hugging Gayla again and giving her back her wineglass.

"It was good to see you both," Gayla called after them as they headed for the exit.

"You seem to know them very well," Bill observed.

Gayla sighed. "I do. They're like family. My mother has worked for them for more than twenty years," she murmured. "Now it's just occasional work for Paul Whelan. He's a writer."

"The name is familiar. Sylvia didn't come tonight? I don't remember seeing her."

"Here and gone," Gayla informed him. "She can't take the noise after a while, and her feet hurt from standing around. She's always after me to put in more chairs. I can't seem to make her understand that you don't put chairs in galleries."

Bill chuckled. "I'm going to try and hustle folks out of here so I can take you home."

Gayla nodded as Bill walked away. She helped by quietly whispering to guests as she passed through the exhibit that the reception was ending and the gallery was closing. She took a few moments to listen to visitors' comments, and say hello to some she was only seeing as they were about to leave. Gayla congratulated the artists on their opening as they also prepared to go home. Dak wasn't among them.

Teddy had already begun to turn out lights . . . another hint to stragglers. The clinking of glasses could be heard as the catering service packed up what remained of the refreshments. Gayla used the phone at Teddy's desk to call home and let Mrs. Perry know she'd be there within the hour. When she put the phone down, she sensed a presence. She glanced up and found Dak sitting on the steps that led up to the second-level administrative offices. It startled her to know that he was in a clear position to have watched her. Had he been listening in on her conversation?

It was hard to read what he was thinking, and Gayla realized then that Dak Kinney was always going to be someone on the outside looking in. It suddenly struck her that maybe he didn't have a choice. There were lots of times when lots of people had worked to keep him at arm's length.

There was something careful and deliberate about the way he silently stared down at her. Not hostile, which she'd certainly experienced before. But a waiting quality. Paul Whelan had called him the new Dak. What exactly had happened to the old one?

"We're closing." Gayla finally found her voice, only to realize how blunt and cold she sounded.

Dak didn't respond right away. He seemed reflective and quiet. He made a vague gesture with his hand. "Are you going to drink that?"

"What?" Gayla asked, confused.

Then she realized that she was still carrying the glass of wine. She held it out, and Dak stretched from his perch on an upper step to take it. He considered the contents briefly before drinking the entire glass in one great swallow. For a second Gayla was sure he would do something crass, like smack his lips in exaggeration. But instead Dak silently handed the empty glass back to her.

She accepted it. "Well, it was quite a night," she began awkwardly. His aloofness was unsettling. She was much more used to his strident attitude of toughness and invincibility. This thoughtful man was a total enigma, his quiet watchfulness throwing her off.

"You could say that," Dak murmured.

"I guess I should congratulate you."

"I don't need congratulations."

"I meant it as a compliment," Gayla stiffly defended herself.

Dak's gaze slowly rose to her face. He shook his

head. "No. What you meant was you can't believe anyone took my stuff seriously."

"You don't know that. Don't put words in my mouth."

"Okay. But you know I'm right," he said smoothly.

She shifted impatiently. "Look, I thought you'd be happy that so many people crowded into your show. Every time I passed by you were surrounded by half a dozen people. Holding court and . . ." Gayla stopped as a smile flickered in his eyes. Unmistakable and interested. "The whole point is to get attention and have your work noticed and praised."

"Is that right? That's not why I did it."

"Well?" she prompted when he didn't elaborate.

Dak leaned back, resting his elbows on the upper step behind his shoulders. "I did it for me. It was either this or maybe doing something else that would have kept me in trouble. You're right, you know. I did all that stuff so I could make it look like real life. My life. Then I can change it. Fix it. Make it better."

"You didn't enjoy tonight, did you? You gave people something to talk about."

"And you think I'm ungrateful."

"Yes."

"That's because you don't know the difference between pride and conceit. What I do, I do for myself. I don't really care what anyone else thinks. Not even you."

If Dak had been argumentative or nasty, if he'd been boastful instead of just truthful Gayla would not have let him get away with his smugness. But that's not what he was doing; he gave her no room to feel insulted. Gayla frowned at the man so calmly regarding her. He retreated somewhere behind a shield of awareness she couldn't penetrate, and didn't even know how. As if he knew something that she did not. It was so different from when they were both young and they resented each other, coming from different backgrounds and families. Now, if they weren't on equal ground they were certainly pretty close to it. Dak's attitude annoyed her. But she was also curious.

"I don't understand you," Gayla murmured.

"I know," Dak responded.

"Gayla?"

She turned around quickly at the sound of her name, and saw Bill approaching.

"I was looking for you. I don't see that we have to hang around any longer. Everything's taken care of and—"

Bill stopped when he realized that Gayla was not alone. He saw Dak and the familiar warmth in his voice for her instantly shifted to a more commanding tone. He held out his hand to Dak.

"You were well received, my man."

"Thanks," Dak said laconically, shaking the offered hand.

"I hope this leads to great things for you. I know you could use a break. Pete Hampton told me a little about your background."

"Yeah, I know Hampton. He has a place upstate. He's seen my work before."

Gayla heard the warmth in Bill's comments. But she also heard something else, and judging from the guarded expression on Dak's face, she knew he was aware of it, too. Condescension.

"If you need some help or advice, please don't hesitate to call on me. I might be able to hook you up with some people."

"I'll keep that in mind," Dak responded calmly.

"Ready?" Bill turned to Gayla, placing his hand possessively on her lower back to steer her away. He took the empty wineglass and placed it on the edge of Teddy's desk.

"I'll get your coat," Bill said, heading to a closet reserved for staff.

For another moment Gayla and Dak were alone again. There was no attempt to pick up the threads of their conversation, and no time to finish it in any case. The look they exchanged went a step beyond the Mexican standoff which had endured for fifteen years between them. Gayla wondered what would replace it, if anything.

"You better go. He's waiting," David quietly said to her.

Gayla nodded. She hesitated before finally, unexpectedly, saying, "Good night."

She didn't wait for his response.

David knew something was wrong the moment he stepped off the elevator. It was a kind of sixth sense only someone who'd been in trouble could pick up instinctively, because it frequently meant the difference between life and death. He stopped to let the noisy sounds of the departing elevator fade before walking to the metal door to his left and on the opposite wall. His footsteps were silent on the terrazzo floor.

With his key poised, he tilted his head and listened for sounds from within the apartment. He scanned the floor and frame around the door, running the pad of his thumb over the keyholes of the two locks. No roughness or metal filing dust. No evidence of forced entry. Finally, he inserted the key and unlocked the door. He thought for sure that would signal his arrival, and there would be the inevitable giveaway of some presence within. There was nothing. With the door unlocked, David entered slowly. He always left a muted safety light on, plugged into the baseboard next to the entrance. It was still on. But so was the light in the bathroom, its glow spreading on the hardwood floors of the hallway.

It was just too quiet, and that alone was a hint that there was a problem. But he was out of shape. Not soft, exactly, but he had let his guard down a little in the past few years and was not conditioned to do battle. He never thought he'd have to again.

Closing the door quietly behind him, David eased the straps of his knapsack from his shoulder and placed the bag on the floor. Then, very low, he heard the first sounds. He felt his adrenaline pump through him as he located its direction. It was coming from the front room. The repetitive deep cadence grew louder as David approached.

When he reached the open room, David walked to the sofa and saw the silhouetted outline of a pair of boots propped over the sofa arm. He bent over the sofa, bracing his feet and tightening his leg and thigh muscles. He raised the hand with the key, prepared to use it as a gouge, and with the other turned on the floor lamp.

The snoring stopped abruptly, and a prone body sprang up with surprising agility. David focused only fleetingly on the intruder's face before settling on the hunting knife with a serrated edge a mere inch from his chest.

"Fuck, Dak! You scared the shit out me, man," the intruder complained angrily as he lowered his weapon and let his body slowly uncoil. "Why didn't you say something first? Just about had a goddamn heart attack, man."

David's own heartbeat didn't slow down one bit. He felt a terrible pall grip him, as if he'd seen a bad apparition.

"Kel . . ." David uttered in a flat tone that hid his surprise and defeat.

He hadn't gotten away from his past after all.

CHAPTER FIVE

David unclenched his muscles, and the hand with his keys dropped heavily to his side. He stared at the stocky man. Kel's entire attitude toward being discovered in someone else's home was one of calm entitlement.

He yawned expansively, taking his time to stretch before sheathing the knife in the holster inside his right boot. When he stood up again, he engulfed David in a bear hug.

"It's good to see you, man. What's up?"

David was a beat late in returning the embrace. Kel pulled back and grabbed his hand in the familiar street greeting.

"Wondering who the hell was sleeping in my bed," David quickly improvised, keeping his voice even.

Kel yawned again, shaking his head. "Papa Bear, bro." He looked at his watch. "I been waiting all evening. Where've you been?"

"What are you doing here? How did you get in?" David asked.

Kelvin Earl Monroe sat down on the sofa, lounging back, making himself right at home. "You gotta be kidding me, man. I just called up a couple of the brothers, and one of them from upstate ran you to ground." He grinned broadly. "Been a long time, bro. Six . . . seven years. Ain't you glad to see me?"

David studied Kel for a moment and considered the question. His former running buddy was a big man who'd learned early how to use his size to intimidate people. To bogart his way past resistance to instant gratification, whether it was for advantage in a one on one at the hoops or with a woman in bed. Kel Monroe didn't compute what no meant.

David could still see the restless weariness in Kel, the amazing instinct he had for protecting himself. There were very few people he was loyal to or honest with. He was the consummate survivor; you either followed him or got the hell out of his way.

David scratched his chin. "Am I glad to see you? That depends."

He walked to the bathroom. From behind the door he'd heard a plaintive cry of indignation. When David opened the door, a gray-striped cat scurried out. Its belly was low to the floor as he caught the scent of the stranger. David bent and picked up the animal. He could feel the sinewy tension in its feline body. The motor-like purring idled low as the cat let himself be massaged behind his ears, butting his head into the familiar hand.

"Why'd you lock him in the bathroom, man? You

afraid or something?'' The cat relaxed against David's chest, but his claws were half-extended.

Kel made an indifferent gesture with his hand. ''How come you got a cat, Dak?'' he asked derisively, as if the animal was a disease.

''You first,'' David said, cradling the cat as he settled on the edge of a stool.

Kel shrugged. ''I don't trust 'em. Too damned sneaky.''

''You should talk,'' David murmured dryly. He gazed down at the animal who was regarding him with adoration through half-closed yellow eyes. He continued to stroke the cat, arched against his chest, its tail swishing the air. ''This place belongs to King Tut. I'm here on a pass.''

''King *who?*'' Kel asked.

With a final reassuring ruffling of fur David put the cat on the floor. The animal shook his head, glanced warily at Kel and, meowing once to express his opinion of the man, sauntered away to a bookcase, where he leaped onto the top shelf and lazily stretched out his body. Through narrowed eyes King Tut balefully eyed Kel seated across the room.

David settled more on the stool and stretched out his legs. He went back to his original question. ''How'd you get in?''

Kel cackled quietly. He sat with his knees spread and his arms stretched along the back of the sofa. ''Come on, man. There ain't no lock nowhere I can't jump.''

David shook his head. "Don't you know breaking and entering is against the law?"

"Yeah, right. I saw Deacon about a week ago, and he said he'd heard you were back. But he said he didn't think you necessarily wanted to let any of us know that. Said you didn't hang anymore. How come you dropped out? I been asking around, and nobody had heard a thing. I thought you'd bought the farm or was still locked down. Or maybe that bitch Terry had bagged your ass after all when she had that kid. Claiming it was yours and shit."

David crossed his arms over his chest and squirmed at the litany of possibilities, any one of which could have happened . . . but didn't. Terry was a different matter. David momentarily squeezed his eyes closed when he thought of the boy, Drew. He'd be about fifteen now.

Terry had said the boy was his, and David had been willing to believe her. Drew might have been the glue that would have cemented the on-again off-again relationship. He had been ready to put himself into having a real life and family. Four years was a long time to pursue a dream long-distance, though, and from the beginning Kel, and even Sylvia Patton to whom he'd confided, had told David that the child wasn't his. But was that because neither had ever trusted Terry . . . or because it was true? Simple math and calculating of time left ambiguity. David still wasn't sure what the truth was. And maybe it didn't matter. He was sure he was always going to think of Drew as his.

"Deacon said you were straight. That you haven't been into anything for something like ten, twelve years."

"I served my time and got out. And I was never going back, Kel. Not for *any* reason," he said significantly.

Kel shrugged and pursed his full lips. He stroked his thick mustache, grunting brutishly. It was a mannerism that fascinated women, and intimidated other men. "I know you didn't roll over on me, man. That was good lookin' out. But you're my main man. I got your back. You got mine, right?"

David clenched his jaw. He felt the tension begin to rise in his body again. Loyalty was one thing. Sacrifice was something else. He said nothing, wondering what kind of game Kel was running, looking for clues as to why Kel had so precipitously appeared in his life.

Then he noticed the leather three-quarter-length jacket Kel wore was a size or two too small. The sweater and pants were nondescript. Discount or sales items, maybe even secondhand. The shoes were new, but also not expensive. Kel wasn't wearing a hat, and David could see he needed a haircut.

"How long you been out?" David asked.

Kel averted his gaze. "Few weeks."

"How long this time?"

"Five to fifteen. But I got a break. Fuckin' pros lawyers kept evidence from my attorney. I got released on a technicality and time served. Three years."

David nodded. Of course he knew what was coming next and tried to think of a way to head it off at the pass. But Kel continued, preempting his line of defense.

"My mom passed while I was up last time."

David felt no mourning or loss from Kel. "Sorry to hear that."

"Cancer."

Broken heart. Disappointment, David mentally added.

"I heard you got into art," Kel said, casting a sideways look of disbelief at David.

"Yeah? Where did you hear that?"

"I heard it," was all Kel would say. "On the street. People said you were upstate in some hick town playing with finger paints and crayons," Kel cracked. "Oh, man . . . I said, my man *Dak?* Then Deacon said he saw your name in the paper for some show. David Alan Kinney. He said at first he didn't remember that's your real name." Kel looked squarely at David. "I thought you was just jiving about all that stuff."

"I remember you and Deacon dogging me about it."

"Man, you must be frontin' or something. You can't make no kind of money doing that."

David stared at Kel. "Maybe not. But it's enough for what I need. I'm out of the game, Kel. We were kids back then. If it wasn't for . . ."

"Yeah, yeah, I know. Sylvia what's-her-name. Sounds to me like you just lost heart."

"I just decided the short-term rewards weren't

worth risking my life on. It can't have a good ending."

"I'm not talking about no end."

"Okay, so what are your plans?" David asked alertly.

"I got some things lined up," Kel said evasively.

"Legal?"

Kel grinned boyishly. "Yeah. It's straight up."

David searched Kel's face for a hidden agenda. But he saw instead the ruggedly handsome face of the teen who had more confidence and balls and charisma than good sense. It amazed David how easily Kel always managed to land on his feet.

Which was what made David nervous.

Kel glanced around the room. "How long you been here, man? How come you didn't come back uptown?"

"Not long. I'm not sure what I'm going to do."

"What are the choices?"

"Come back to New York. Go back upstate."

"That ain't no choice. What's upstate?"

Peace. Anonymity. A second chance. "I like it up there," David said carefully.

Kel shook his head. "Too close to the joint. I got to be where things are happening." He looked speculatively at David, and gestured vaguely with his hand. "Look, Dak. I need a place to stay. Just for a few days. Maybe a week. Till I get myself set up."

David stared silently at him. It jolted him a bit to discover that his very first thought was not whether he wanted Kel to stay with him, but what if Matt, his former parole officer, current friend and advisor found out?

Or Gayla Patton.

That was the last thing David wanted. "This isn't my place, Kel."

"It's only for a little while, man. Come on . . ."

David narrowed his gaze. Tension and resentment wound tighter within him. But he couldn't seem to say the word no. "Kel . . ."

"Look, you won't even see me. I got my own plans, like I said. I'll be out of here during the day. I just need a place to crash at night. Shower . . . check on a couple of messages."

"I have things to do."

"Hey . . . it's me you're talkin' to, Dak. I'm cool."

"You can have the sofa," David finally consented, but uneasily. "I'm in the bedroom."

"Thanks, man," Kel said, smiling, as if the outcome was never in doubt. He took off his coat and carelessly tossed it over a still unpacked carton of David's belongings. He looked around. "This is a big place. You could really hook it up."

"Like I said, it's temporary. I needed a place when I got into this art show. It belongs to someone else."

"You seein' anyone?" Kel asked suddenly.

"Not at the moment." He looked closely at his friend. "Who are you on the run from this week?"

Kel shook his head. "Man, I'm not having nothing to do with it. I already got three kids. I gotta be careful. All them bitches out here want is someone to take care of them."

"Are you at least taking care of the kids?"

"Yeah . . ." Kel drawled with a charming smile.

David wasn't sure he believed him. He took off his coat. The cat, sensing the end of the conversation, jumped from the bookcase, arched his back in a stretch and quietly padded out of the room in the direction of the kitchen. Soon David could hear the crunch and chewing of dried cat food.

Kel reached for a tightly packed canvas duffel which had been stowed beside the sofa. He placed it heavily on the cushions and began to open it. "You got any money you can lend me?"

David wasn't surprised by the request. He reached into his pocket and pulled out all the bills. He unfolded and smoothed them, extracting two and handing them to Kel.

"Forty?" Kel asked.

"It's more than you came here with," David reminded him. "That's all I can spare right now."

"Man, we used to blow this in ten minutes on cabs and tips!"

"There's an extra sheet and blanket in that box," David said, indicating one of many that lay open and filled with his possessions.

Kel folded the bills and stuffed them into the pocket of his sweater. "What are you going to do about the cat?"

"I'm not going to do anything with the cat."

"Just don't leave him out here with me. I told you. I don't like cats."

David briefly considered Kel as he tossed him one

of the pillows from his own bed. "Forget the cat. He's going to be the least of your worries."

Allison slouched way down in her chair, sighed dramatically and closed her library book with a snap.

"Are you finished yet?" she asked when her mother didn't respond to her nonverbal hints.

"In a minute," Gayla murmured, picking up the phone to dial another number.

"You said that a half hour ago. We're never going to go downtown."

"We're leaving right now. Just let me make these two calls . . ."

"Okay, just two more. I'm going to count," Allison said.

Gayla glanced at her daughter, whose frown and pouty mouth showed her growing impatience with the delays in their Saturday plans. Any parental response she might have given was weakened by her guilt over using some of their time together for business.

"Why don't you go look through the gallery. You haven't seen the show yet. You usually like to do that."

"I don't feel like it."

"Okay. Then please sit still. I'm almost finished."

Allison, realizing the futility of complaining, opened her book and went back to reading.

Gayla waited through several rings on the line before the automated greeting played. She found herself caught up in the resonance of the male voice.

Years ago anger and arrogance were so palpable in everything David Kinney said. He was different now, but it annoyed Gayla that her response to him continued to be so . . . emotional. And unfair, Gayla reluctantly admitted.

"Dak . . . I'm sorry. David. This is Gayla Patton. Please give me a call at the gallery as soon as you can. My number is . . ."

As Gayla prepared to dial the next number there was a knock on her open door. Both she and Allison looked up as David suddenly appeared.

"I heard my name. Looking for me?" he asked, addressing Gayla.

"Oh . . ." she said at his unexpected arrival, fumbling to replace the phone in its cradle. The quiet, simple question made her feel oddly defenseless.

David didn't wait for her reply but transferred his attention to Allison. He inclined his head in a brief nod. "Good morning."

Allison haughtily averted her gaze back to the book. "Morning," she muttered indifferently.

Gayla frowned at her daughter's response, but turned to David. "Hi," she said. "I just left a message on your machine."

"What about?"

Allison sighed again and got up from her chair abruptly. "I can't concentrate. I'm going downstairs."

"Sorry. Did I interrupt something?" David asked her.

But Allison ignored him, grabbing her book, jacket

and fashionable purse-cum-knapsack, and squeezed past him out of the office.

"Allison . . ." Gayla began, surprised at her child's behavior, but Allison was gone. Instead Gayla turned to David with a shrug. "Sorry. I've been keeping her waiting for the past hour. We have plans for today."

"The delay didn't have anything to do with me, did it?" He took the chair just vacated by Allison.

"No, not at all. At least not entirely. I had some things to do here first. I . . ."

She stopped, and they looked at each other. For just an instant, both their guards were down. They weren't circling each other as if expecting an attack. There was no reason for either to act defensive because they weren't enemies anymore.

"I bet your daughter is going to blame me for the delay."

Gayla raised her brows. "Why? She's been fussing since we got here."

"Maybe so. But she'll want to blame someone because she had to wait."

"I think you're wrong," Gayla said protectively. "She has no reason at all to blame you. She doesn't even know you." When David said nothing, Gayla again noticed the lack of desire to engage in conflict. "What are you doing here?" she asked instead.

David shifted in his chair. "I stopped by with a friend. He heard about the show and wanted to see my work."

"Is he an artist, too?"

"No, he's not. He's into . . . other things. He's

downstairs now. Your weekend receptionist said you were here." He shrugged, shifting in his chair again. "I thought I'd stop up and say hello."

Gayla began fidgeting with papers on her desk. "Well, that was . . . that was, eh . . . it's actually good that you're here," she said, struggling for the right words. "I have some news for you. You've sold one of your pieces. Congratulations."

His expression was totally blank. After a moment David blinked and lowered his gaze to his lap, where his hands were clasped together.

"Did you hear what I just said? Your work sold. Aren't you—"

"I heard you," David said too sharply.

Gayla was taken aback. "I don't get it. I just told you someone wants to write you a check, and you act like—"

"It's not for sale."

Her mouth dropped open. She was incredulous. "Excuse me?"

"That work isn't for sale."

She made a helpless gesture with her hand. "Not for sale? Are you crazy? You haven't even asked who it is that wants to buy it. You don't even know what's being offered."

"Look, I hadn't planned on selling anything from the show."

"Are you telling me you don't need the money? Are you telling me you don't care, you just like showing your work?"

Gayla stopped, seeing signs of awkwardness and

uncertainty in his body language. "David, don't tell me you've never sold any of your work before. Or are you so attached that you can't give them up? That's pointless. Don't you know what this means?"

"What does it mean? Someone who doesn't know a thing about me thinks my work is good? They know what I'm trying say and they approve? Are you saying I should be grateful for that?"

Dak Kinney was back.

Gayla recoiled and glared at him. "Yes, you should be grateful, Dak. *You* of all people can't afford to let your pride get in the way."

His jaw began to clench reflexively, and he slowly stood up and looked down on Gayla. "My name is David."

Gayla stood up, too. "Okay, David." She felt heat infuse her face, a mixture of anger and embarrassment. "You should have checked your pride at the door. You're on exhibit, whether you like it or not, as much as your work. You're right. People don't know anything about you, so your work has to speak for you. What people see is work that moves them, makes them think. Whatever. It gets their attention. Don't tell me that's not what you wanted."

David said nothing. He slipped his hands into his pockets, and although his mouth was still tight he nodded at her briefly. "You're right," he said simply.

His capitulation made her back down as well. "I'm sorry."

"For what? For being right?" he asked wryly.

Gayla blinked at him. "You're the only artist so far who's made a sale. Aren't you happy about that?"

"But I lose control of my work."

"No. You get recognition."

"I'm selling my memories."

She shook her head slowly. "You're selling art," she said. "It happens to be art that tells stories."

The observation was not lost on David. "You think so," he stated rather than asked.

Gayla sighed. It was an admission she wasn't going to take back. She relaxed as the tension of their encounter receded. "Your work is powerful. Extraordinary. Anyone seeing it has an immediate reaction, David. It's alive with feeling . . . and important messages. Good or bad, no one is indifferent. You should read the comments in the guest book." She waved vaguely in that direction. "Look, I don't know if you really wanted all of this but . . ." She struggled for words, holding his gaze as she added earnestly, "Don't you understand? You've done what every creative person I know would kill for. You're getting noticed as an artist."

David nodded thoughtfully, clearly not having seen it that way before. "Which piece sold?" he asked hesitantly.

Gayla smiled to herself in surprise. She found his quiet question . . . charming. "The three-panel piece. *Father, Son and Holy Ghost.* A doctor from New Jersey called in his offer yesterday."

David liked that piece. Three frame boxes, two of equal size with a taller one in between. Each box was backed with a montage of black-and-white or color photographs with found objects superimposed. The first box had a picture of a liquor store in the background, with an empty pint bottle of cheap wine inside a brown paper bag placed in the foreground. The right-hand box had a photo of a police precinct, in front of which were a pair of handcuffs and a handful of spent and unspent cartridges from a Walter PPK. And the center box showed a church. In its foreground lay a New Testament, and a page from a yearbook with the faces of black boys circled, accompanied with notices of their obituaries.

David frowned and absently rubbed his hair-covered jaw. "That piece is . . ."

"Personal?" Gayla filled in smoothly. "They're all personal. That's what makes them work. They're from your heart. From life. Are you even curious about the offer?"

"What was it?"

"Thirty-five hundred dollars."

He stared blankly. "Thirty-five hundred dollars . . ."

"Well, I guess I could have gotten more. You didn't give me a price list, and I . . ."

"Thirty-five hundred dollars?" he repeated.

"Are you going to complain?"

"Complain?" He chuckled. "I wouldn't have bet anyone would give three hundred and fifty dollars for it."

"Are you serious?"

David shrugged. "Like I said. I didn't expect to be

selling anything. How'd you come up with that figure?"

Gayla again went back to fiddling with things on her desk, lowering her gaze. "Well . . . I estimated what I thought it was worth based on . . . a lot of things. And then I added five hundred dollars. And the gallery gets a commission."

"What things?" he asked.

"Execution. Concept. Impact. I didn't go overboard. I want to keep the good doctor interested. He saw something else he wanted as well, but I hedged a bit on his offer."

"Why'd you do that?"

"I wanted to build up his curiosity and desire. I created the impression that there was other interest in your work. I told him you were getting a lot of bids, and we were considering a couple of things and . . ."

David suddenly burst out laughing, and Gayla stopped. She didn't think she'd ever heard him laugh before, let alone seen him smile. He had an utterly handsome face when he smiled. His laugh was a deep stomach-rippling bark. And he had beautiful teeth.

"Thirty-five hundred dollars . . ." he said yet again. "Is it worth it?"

Gayla sighed. She liked that he was asking, as if her opinion counted. There was no getting around it. "Yes."

David's expression turned reflective. Perhaps even sad as he stared off into space. Gayla didn't doubt that he was thinking of his mother. Maybe even that terrible day when he was nine years old and lost her, long before he had a chance to make her proud of him. Long before he was old enough to be on his own without her love and belief in him. Long before he'd nearly self-destructed.

"Not bad at all for a guy from up the river who didn't have any prospects," he murmured.

"Not bad at all," Gayla agreed softly.

"Can we go now?" a petulant voice said behind David.

He moved aside to reveal Allison, who stood with impatience spread across her pretty face.

Gayla looked at her watch, grimaced and stepped from behind her desk. "Yes. I'm sorry, sweetie. We're on our way right now. I was just telling Da . . . Mr. Kinney about his first sale. Isn't that exciting?"

Allison rolled her eyes. "What's the big deal? I could do some of those boxes. I bet you can't draw."

"Allison!" Gayla said in shock.

"A little bit," David answered calmly. "I guess I could use some lessons. Can you draw?"

Allison blushed but held her ground. "I won a contest with a drawing I did when I was twelve. I got five hundred dollars from the borough president's office."

"What's the matter with you? You don't talk to people that way. Apologize right now," Gayla insisted.

"She was just voicing her opinion. Let it go, Gayla."

"I'm sorry, but she knows better than that." She glared at her daughter. "I'm waiting."

Allison seemed to remember that she was not going to get over on her mother. "Okay, I'm sorry," she said quietly.

"Thank you. Put on your coat and wait for me by the door. I want to close up my office."

Without another word Allison turned and left.

"There are times when I think people without kids have the right idea . . ." Gayla mumbled.

And then she stopped herself and glanced furtively at David. He was watching her, and he knew Gayla was waiting for him to make the obvious comment, ask the obvious question. He remained silent, and she spoke first.

"Do . . . do you have kids?"

David appreciated her ability to cut to the heart of the matter. He looked thoughtful but shrugged. "Not that I know of."

"Oh," she responded, not expecting quite that degree of honesty. "Kids are . . . challenging," she murmured.

"Your daughter is going to be quite a woman someday," David commented.

Gayla looked at him, suspecting he meant more. What was he going to ask her about Allison? What did he already know? She was sorry she'd asked if he had kids. "Thank you."

She dropped a pen and some floppy disks into her purse during the ensuing silence.

"You said you never married."

Again, it was a statement, not a question. She shook her head but didn't look at him.

"No, I didn't."

"Didn't want to? Or . . . it just didn't work out?"

She felt herself closing down, pulling back as the defenses went up again between them. She didn't respond.

"You don't want to go there."

Gayla nodded in agreement. "That's right. I don't want to go there."

David jingled the coins in his pockets as he watched her put on her sporty wool car coat. Every now and then he caught glimpses of the girl he remembered. He suspected that, as with him, many of her dreams had not materialized. Except Gayla had Allison. Living proof that she had been in love at one time, and that someone loved her.

It was the one thing David envied her.

"I want you to know I wasn't bothered by what Allison said to me. She wasn't being rude, Gay."

"I don't mind her having an opinion, but . . . I didn't like the way she spoke to you. It was disrespectful. I'm really surprised that she—"

"Don't make an issue out of it. As I remember it, guts is a family trait."

Gayla smiled at his comment.

When Gayla and David caught up with her at the gallery entrance, Allison turned her back to stare out the glass doors to the people passing by on the street rather than face them. Gayla handed two Express Mail envelopes to the receptionist for pickup, and continued with a brief conversation about minor problems and concerns with visitors.

David took that moment to approach Allison. It was a sunny Saturday, and the brightness of the day reflected through the window lit up the color in her hair. Distinctly blonde mixed with the brown strands, and making her skin a honey-gold hue. She was lighter than Gayla. She was going to be taller. There was very little of the Pattons in her physical appearance. David wondered how Allison felt about all that. And what Gayla had told her.

"Did you mean what you said?" he asked, standing just a bit behind her.

She spared him a glance and went back to squinting out the window. "What?"

"When you said you were sorry, did you mean it?"

She shrugged. "Yeah."

"I don't think so."

She blinked and turned her head further away.

"I think you just said you were for your mother's sake. I can't tell you how to deal with her, but when you're talking about me I'd prefer the truth."

She turned and looked at him closely for a second, her face a study of many youthful emotions. He remembered that he had frequently acted purely on instinct when he was about her age. It sometimes went against what other people wanted from him . . . but he had been true to himself, and honest.

Allison unconsciously gnawed her lip, as if considering the consequences of her answer. She glanced furtively at her mother, just ten feet away, and returned her gaze to David.

"This is between you and me," he said, as unthreatening as he knew how.

Allison turned back to the window. "No, I wasn't sorry about what I said," she whispered in a small voice.

David smiled to himself in appreciation. *Definitely her mother's child*, he thought. "That's cool. I can handle it. But I don't trust people who don't say what they mean."

Confused by his acceptance, Allison turned away without saying anything more.

"Allison, let's see if we can still have a good time today," Gayla said as she joined her daughter. Allison responded by going through the door to wait on the sidewalk. Gayla sighed in exasperation at her child's behavior and addressed David. "The piece you sold will stay in the show until it closes at the end of May. Can you hold out that long for your check?"

He nodded. "I'll manage."

She buttoned her taupe coat and pulled bright orange chenille gloves from the pockets. "Well . . . you should call my mother and tell her the good news. She'll be really pleased for you."

"You mean you won't mind?" he asked.

Gayla let a bit of the past animosity show through her smile. "No, I don't mind. I was taught to share and play nice with the other kids." David managed a small smile. "It's a good thing we grow up, isn't it?"

He shook his head. "I can't believe I'm really hearing you say that. Fifteen years ago you were sure I'd end up dead."

"True," she conceded readily. And then looked closely at him with an uncertainty she'd been trying to understand since he'd turned up at the gallery. "But I'm glad you didn't. It would have been a waste. My mother, at least, always knew that."

With that, Gayla turned away, exiting the gallery. He watched as she put an arm around Allison's shoulder, kissed the side of her face and whispered something that brought a smile to her daughter's face. Allison put an arm around her mother's waist, and together they went down the block.

"What you watching, man?"

David turned to Kel. "Nothing."

Kel came to stand next to him, following his gaze out the window. He pointed. "I saw her. She was just standing over there. You know her?"

David thought about it. "She runs this gallery. She and her daughter stopped by before heading off downtown for the day."

"Lookin' good." Kel nodded in approval. "How come you didn't introduce me?"

"She's not your type. What did you think of the work?"

Kel shrugged. "It's all right. Weird stuff, man. Is that what they taught you upstate?"

David shook his head. He wasn't inclined to share with Kel what he had done. It would be lost on Kel's sensibilities. And besides . . . it was private. There had to be one part of his life and experience, David decided, that didn't also belong to anyone else.

"I took some classes. Worked with some carpenters and contractors."

"So you nailed some boards together and they call that art? Maaannn . . . that looks like shit I was about to throw out."

David grinned. "It would be . . . if you had anything to throw out."

Kel broke into laughter.

That was also okay. And Kel didn't need to know that someone was willing to pay money for what he did.

CHAPTER SIX

"Thanks for coming, Sylvia."

"That's okay," Sylvia Patton said, slamming the car door shut as she settled in the passenger seat of Emily Whelan's champagne-colored Toyota Camry and reached for the seat belt. "As long as we're back by four o'clock."

Emily hesitated. "I know it seems silly. It's not as if I haven't made the trip by myself before, but . . ."

"It's the weather," Sylvia said knowledgeably. "I wish it weren't raining. It makes you feel even worse having to go. Sadder, I think."

"You're probably right. We'll be back on time. Paul and I have plans, too." She watched in the side mirror for an opportunity to pull into traffic. "We're supposed to meet Sarah for a preview of some independent film."

"Yes, she called to invite me, too. I didn't remember that Sarah wanted to be an actress."

Emily sighed. "I don't know what Sarah wants. I don't think she does, either. But I want to understand and just be supportive. Not be so hard, like with Reilly . . ."

She merged slowly into traffic, turning on 67th Street to head east across Central Park. The windshield wipers made irritatingly squeaky friction sounds against the glass window.

"My granddaughter is coming over for the weekend."

"Are you baby-sitting?"

Sylvia sighed. "That's what I do. Not that I really mind, but trying to keep up with Allison can wear you out."

"I don't suppose you remembered to bring a photo of her for me to see."

Sylvia tsk'd, murmured distractedly to herself as she made a show of rummaging through her purse. "I sure didn't. You know, I don't carry around pictures in my wallet. I'm sorry."

"Don't worry about it. I told Gay that I was dying to meet Allison and we've promised to try and set up a time to get together. Maybe we can do some kind of reunion."

"Well, I don't know about that," Sylvia said quietly.

Emily seemed to concentrate on the traffic and her driving. She frowned through the rain-splattered window and took a long time to respond. "That's not such a good idea, is it?" she said softly. "It wouldn't be much of a reunion without Reilly."

"Just don't call it a reunion. Especially a family reunion," Sylvia advised.

"No, you're right."

Sylvia looked at Emily's profile. She still favored

her hair, once blonde but now an interesting ash color, pulled back into a ponytail. She never wore makeup, not even lipstick, but her skin was surprisingly taut and fresh for a woman approaching sixty. Sylvia used to think that Emily Whelan's blind optimism contributed to her youthful appearance. It was only after working for her and her husband Paul for some twenty-five years that she came to see her positive outlook as a strength that had made her adaptable to misfortunes and the capriciousness of marriage to a man who was a major literary star.

"Mr. Paul isn't coming with us?"

"Sylvia, you know as well as I do that *Mr.* Paul isn't sentimental. He said he had an important meeting with his agent. And we've told you you don't have to call him Mr. Paul."

Sylvia sighed impatiently. "You can't tell me Mr. Paul has put Reilly out of his mind. He'll never admit it, but I think what happened was hard on him. He failed that boy, and he knows it."

"Maybe he does have a guilty conscience. He was just awful when he found out Reilly was gay. As if it reflected on him."

"I can understand that Mr. Paul was . . . disappointed," Sylvia said quietly.

"Honestly, Sylvia, if you hadn't been around all those years for me and the kids . . ."

"You and your family would have managed. You would have found someone else to be a housekeeper."

"Manager." Emily reached out and patted her hand. "It wouldn't have been the same."

"You've been good to me and my kids, too. Maybe I didn't lose Mitchell because of Reilly. I know it's a terrible thing to say."

"Yes . . ." Emily murmured thinly, as if any mention of her second son just wore her out.

They crossed the 59th Street Bridge into Queens and onto the Long Island Expressway. Emily broke the reverie first, returning quickly to the present and the good things which had come of their past.

"I am just so pleased about David. I *know* you are."

Sylvia beamed. "Yes, I am. That child sure had a rough time of it. But he's going to be fine now. Just fine."

"And Gayla, too."

Sylvia frowned at Emily. "What do you mean?"

"Look how well everything turned out. She's doing a terrific job with that gallery, and you've said she's a good mother." Emily hazarded another glance at Sylvia. "It's kind of a relief, don't you think? Especially since they didn't seem to like each other very much. On the other hand, I've always wondered . . ."

"About what?"

"Well . . ." Emily drawled carefully. "Of course Paul and I were so surprised, and upset I admit, to hear that Gayla had had a . . . a baby. It was just her freshman year and I thought she would drop out of school. That would have been a shame because she's so talented and I wanted to see her really get somewhere with her work. You must have been beside yourself."

"No, I wasn't happy about it," Sylvia admitted just as carefully, wondering where Emily was headed.

"When you told us about the baby I thought David Kinney might be the father."

Sylvia's head snapped around as she stared at Emily Whelan. "What in the world makes you say that?"

Emily shrugged. "It makes sense. She could have gotten pregnant sometime that last summer we were all together. Graham had announced he was getting married and Gay was about to leave for college. Gay and David had been kind of thrown together a lot. And despite the little arguments between them, I . . . well, Sarah told me that she'd seen them together once and Gay was crying."

Sylvia was too stunned at this revelation to even pretend surprise. She wondered suddenly what else went on that she hadn't been aware of. How much did Emily actually know?

"Gayla and Mitchell had always been resentful of David coming into our family. I'm not surprised there was tension, but . . ."

"The timing is perfect, you know."

Sylvia sighed and turned her attention to the road again. "Yes, I know. But . . . I don't think it's my business to tell you about Gayla and the father of her child, Emily. She was scared when she found out she was pregnant. Didn't tell me until she was more than six months along."

"I do think it's David . . ." Emily said firmly.

Sylvia frowned. "Why do you care? To my knowledge there has never been any complaints or questions from Allison about her father."

"I found it odd that you never told us about Allison until she was almost two years old. And, unfortunately, when you did David was serving time. Your granddaughter may not say anything about her father but that doesn't mean she doesn't think about it."

"Then we'll just have to wait until she does say something. Or Gayla does."

The conversation annoyed Sylvia, and she fell into a silence that didn't encourage more talk. At least not about Allison. Or Gayla's relationship with David. She couldn't even credit the idea of there having been anything between them. But she couldn't help trying to recreate the events of that last summer.

She'd always enjoyed working for the Whelans but had worried about the blurring of the lines of demarcation between her family and Emily's. It was a fact of life that they were white and privileged. It had not been a fact that they were somehow better. The similarities had not been a surprise to Sylvia either, but the differences had been instilled by history and tradition. She'd wanted her children to keep them in mind, particularly Gayla.

She had failed.

Emily had her own thoughts to occupy her as well. After a moment Sylvia came to see that perhaps all the questions about Gay's life were just a distraction. A smoke screen between other issues like the loss of Emily and Paul's middle child. The worry over Sarah's haphazard life. The Whelan's good fortunes had not spared them disappointment and personal tragedy. The silence was then understandable to Sylvia as the car finally turned into the entrance between ornate heavy wrought-iron gates, opening to pristine stretches of grass and trees carefully planted to offer a sense of order and serenity. The sloping crescents and knolls encouraged reflection . . . and prayer. The silence felt safe and holy.

Sylvia let the mission of the moment supplant her personal concerns. Emily drove even more slowly, as if reluctantly, until they reached a discreetly marked pathway, requiring that they stop and park the car. Sylvia glanced at Emily but saw only a peaceful calm as she stepped out of the car. Sylvia followed suit. This place was about redemption and peace.

Although Emily Whelan didn't bother with any head covering, Sylvia opened her umbrella and trailed a distance behind the woman who moved briskly and with purpose down the walkway and unerringly toward a granite marker set in a site on the grass. She watched as Emily had her moment of privacy and silence. Her job was to lend support and company.

Sylvia had promised herself she wouldn't do this; she wouldn't allow herself to drift into the past and sift through memories of Reilly Whelan. She wasn't going to listen to Emily Whelan talk to her son as if he would answer. She wasn't going to grieve over someone else's child. But Sylvia had her own memories and her own regrets. And much to be thankful for. It might have been Mitchell, too, but for the grace of God . . .

Grieving, in her own way, was exactly what she did.

Sylvia stopped momentarily in her word processing when she heard the apartment door buzzer. Paul Whelan was somewhere in the apartment, but she quickly got up to answer so he wouldn't be disturbed from his own work. She tried to remember if Paul or Emily had been expecting anyone. However, the doorman had not called to announce a visitor.

Sylvia opened the door to a tall man in khakis, Dock-Siders and a yellow anorak jacket. He was wiping his feet on the outside mat and stuffing his cap into the jacket pocket. He looked and was dressed like most of the other white thirtysomething males who lived in the building, and in fact had grown up there.

"Well, look who's here," Sylvia said with a mixture of pleasure and caution.

"Hey, Sylvia." The man chuckled in genuine surprise and pleasure.

She allowed him to swallow her in a warm and crushing hug as she patted Graham Whelan affectionately on his back. "Boy, don't squeeze me too hard. You trying to kill me?"

He laughed, ignoring the warning and rocking with Sylvia for a moment. "How's my best girl?"

"Don't give me that best girl line. You're not too big or too old for me to set straight, you know."

"You know you love me, Sylvia. You wouldn't hurt a hair on my head."

He released her, and the two of them gazed at one another with smiles that held two decades of memories. The evidence of aging in the Whelans' oldest child was subtle. He was still lean and handsome, the pale blue eyes quick and mischievous. He still wore the light brown hair shaggy and unkempt and Sylvia shook her head and smiled ruefully at his stubborn refusal to manage it. There were laugh and sun lines around the eyes.

"When was the last time I saw you?" he asked with a frown, standing back to gaze down at her.

Sylvia crossed her arms over her chest and raised her brows. "Lord, child . . . it's been about three or four years. I think it was at one of those book receptions for your father. You and Diana got there late . . ."

He was nodding. "And left early. I remember. I hardly had a chance to talk to you."

"You could have if you'd gotten there sooner or stayed later."

"Yeah, well . . ." he said a little restlessly, running a hand through his long hair. "You know what it's like at those things. My father gets stroked and told how smart, intelligent and wonderful he is . . . and he believes it. He's difficult under the best of circumstances. But at those literary parties he's impossible . . ."

"Graham . . ."

"I know, I know," he said in surrender, putting up his hands against her admonishment. "I should have handled things better, and I don't have to push his buttons all the time. He doesn't have to push mine, either."

Sylvia sighed. It was a very old argument, and didn't seem any closer to resolution now that the Whelans were older and the kids grown and out of the house, than the first day she arrived at their apartment on Central Park West as their new housekeeper.

"When are you going to grow up and do something about your hair?" she questioned affectionately.

He grinned at her. "I'm like Samson. If I cut it I might lose all my strength."

She chortled in disbelief. "If you cut it you might get treated with some respect," Sylvia said, turning to head toward the kitchen area.

Graham followed her. He shrugged good-naturedly. "Why can't I have it just being who I am?"

"Sylvia? Is that UPS or FedEx? I'm expecting a set of . . ."

Paul looked only mildly surprised when he entered from his office and saw his son in the kitchen with Sylvia. "Did I forget you called to say you were coming over?"

"I didn't know I had to make an appointment to visit home."

Paul Whelan blinked at his son but gave no greeting and made no attempts to apologize. "How're you doing? Looking for your mother?"

Sylvia's attention went back and forth between them. The two men were about the same height and build. The father perhaps more comfortable in his body and still vain enough to watch his weight and looks. Graham's lifelong rebelliousness had not served him well, she thought. He still tended to look like a teenager who wanted to do his own thing.

The two men shook hands, which always struck Sylvia as odd. Like they were just acquaintances. But at least the first words out of Paul Whelan's mouth were not "Goddamn it, Graham. Will you get a decent haircut and stop acting like you're still sixteen."

"I figured she wasn't here. She would have come right away to say hi."

"Well, let's not stand here like you're making a delivery. Come on in . . ." Paul said, indicating the way to the living room with its panoramic view of Central Park.

The lobby phone rang just then.

"That must be your package now. I'll get it," Sylvia said, heading for the door.

"That's all right. I'll get it . . ." Paul said, leaving them.

Graham gave Sylvia a knowing look as if to say nothing had changed. He walked into the kitchen. He opened the refrigerator, reaching inside to help himself to a can of soda. "What do they have you doing now?" Graham asked, popping the tab on the can and drinking. He followed her as she went beyond the kitchen to a small den.

"Well, I'm inputting the revisions and changes on your father's newest manuscript."

"How's everyone?" Graham asked casually.

Sylvia sat at the desk and concentrated on saving her document and backing it up on the floppy. She took off her reading glasses and put them on the desk. Graham was now looking through some of the book titles that lined the shelf on the wall next to the window. His back was to her.

She knew he wasn't referring to his own family. "Oh . . . Mitchell is fine. You know he never was one to tell you what he was up to."

"Still trying to find himself?" Graham asked.

"No. He seems pretty settled. Has a really good job and a nice apartment . . ."

"Significant other?"

Sylvia turned to face her desk and found things that needed to be straightened. "He hasn't said and I don't ask. Mitchell keeps his business private."

"What you don't know won't hurt you, eh?" Graham said quietly. "Not like Reilly."

"Reilly was a different child, God rest his soul," Sylvia responded. "Your mother and I went out to visit him last week."

Graham continued his slow tour around the office, looking at photographs and framed awards. Handling the premiums and promotional products used over the years to market his father's very popular and successful novels. He stopped when a glossy program caught his attention. Graham picked it up to examine it and a small white business card fell out from the middle. Both he and Sylvia bent to retrieve it at the same time.

"I got it," he said, reading the information thoughtfully.

"I think your mother left that there. What is it?"

"Gayla's business card."

Sylvia reached out her hand. "I'll take it. I don't want it to get lost."

They exchanged looks, but after a moment Graham handed the card and program back to Sylvia. She slipped them under her computer keyboard.

"I heard that Dak was back in the city."

Sylvia gave him a stern look. "David Alan Kinney," she corrected. "Yes. He's an artist now, you know."

Graham nodded. "Mom told me. It's amazing the influence she had on us. Different from Dad."

"David is doing well. He's teaching and lives upstate. He bought a small house and is fixing it up."

"Is this the same David that was always trying to push me into a fight? Is this the same guy who hated the country place and complained about bugs and nothing to do?"

"Yes, it is," Sylvia said with a note of pride in her voice.

"I'm impressed."

"You should be. David is a very good example of how a person can turn their life around and move on."

Graham grinned and raised his brows at her. "Is that a message to me?"

"I'm not going to say anything on that. But sooner or later you have to stop blaming your parents for everything that goes wrong in your life. That's what being an adult means, Graham. You take responsibility for your own life."

"Yes, Mother," he said wickedly. Sylvia sighed as if he was hopeless. "Did he get married? Is he . . . involved with someone?"

"There was someone for a while but it didn't work out."

"You didn't mention Gay. How is she?"

Sylvia didn't turn around to face him. "Gayla's doing fine . . . Did you want to speak to your father about something? He should . . ."

"Does she ever ask about me?"

Sylvia sighed. "No, she doesn't. But you haven't seen each other in so many years." She looked squarely at him. "It's not like you two lived the same kind of lives, Graham. You and Gayla had nothing in common."

"We had you."

"That's different. I worked for your family. You are not my child."

He chuckled softly and became quiet. "I think about her, Sylvia. Gay was the one person who thought I could walk on water."

Sylvia became uncomfortable again and began needlessly moving and shifting things, making busy-work. "I know she . . . was very fond of you, too," she said softly. "But you were both just kids. She used to refer to all of you as her second family." Sylvia turned to regard Graham. "But I never wanted Gay to do that. Your family was *not* just like mine, and it didn't do my kids any good to pretend otherwise. Do you understand what I'm trying to say?"

"I hear you. But I don't agree," Graham said.

There were two transit file boxes stacked under the desk. Sylvia watched as Graham pulled them out and sat on the top one facing her. She recalled how when he was an adolescent he used to sit on the floor facing her like this. Filled with questions, voicing complaints, offering opinions. Endlessly curious, but indecisive.

"How come she just dropped from sight?"

Sylvia shook her head. "She was in school. She went on with her life, Graham. You got married. In a way you dropped out, too."

"It seemed the thing to do at the time," he said flippantly.

"Well, that's a fine thing to say. You didn't know Diana but a few months but you married her quick enough. To tell the truth your mother and I thought the child was pregnant or something. But Holly wasn't born for another two years."

Graham smiled wickedly again. "Fooled you." He quickly sobered. "So, what did Gayla think about me getting married?"

"Fine time to be asking, as if it could make a difference now. She never said anything about it. But I thought you needed more time."

"To grow up?"

She smirked. "You said it, I didn't."

Graham sighed, stared down at the floor. "Sometimes I wonder what would have happened if—"

"Sylvia, I need you to make a call for me. This isn't what I was waiting for."

Paul Whelan's voice from the hallway interrupted whatever his son was about to say. Sylvia knew the chance was lost when Graham suddenly stood up, pushing his temporary seat back beneath her desk.

"It's only eleven o'clock," she gently reminded Paul Whelan as he came into the office. "I'll check what time UPS and FedEx stop making deliveries for the day." She picked up her phone and punched in numbers.

"Thank you, Sylvia. Graham . . . How's Diana and Holly?"

"Good."

"Does Holly still want to play pro tennis?"

"Not this week. She's changed her mind and decided she might try out for the U.S. Olympic swim team. She's setting a few regional records in the backstroke for her age group, and springboard diving."

"Is this a day off, or are you working?"

"Appointment. I'm in town for a meeting at the Central Park Conservancy. They're taking bids for the redesign of the children's zoo."

" 'Bout time. That place has been an eyesore for too many years," Paul said absently. He accepted several letters from Sylvia that she wanted him to sign. "Well, like I said, you missed your mother. She may not be back until late this afternoon. Anything I can do?"

Graham and Sylvia exchanged glances at Paul Whelan's remote tone. Formal and polite. Graham hesitated and began pacing the small room. His movement raised Sylvia's antenna. She'd always been sensitive to the habits, motives and sensibilities of the Whelan children; maternal instincts and woman's intuition told her at once that something was wrong.

"I was hoping that I could say this to both of you . . ."

"Excuse me. I'll finish these calls from your office, Mr. P. . . ."

"Sylvia, you can stay. This is not a family secret or anything. Anyway, you're part of the family as far as I'm concerned."

"Well, what is it?" Paul prompted brusquely. "Did you get canned? Is Diana pregnant or something?"

Graham grimaced at his father's choices. "Always looking for bad news. Well, I won't disappoint you. Diana and I are getting a divorce."

CHAPTER SEVEN

Gayla felt the kiss on her neck. The lips moved to her nape in sensual exploration. She was relaxed enough to feel the tingling down her spine and the start of arousal in her groin. She contracted the muscles down there and moaned softly as the lips continued to her shoulder. At the same time a hand slipped under her arm and closed around her breast, massaging it and bringing the nipple to attention.

Gayla sighed deeply and rolled in the direction of the source of the caresses. She was kissed again, this time on the mouth and she lazily responded. She was halfway between encouraging the lovemaking . . . and wanting to go back to sleep. Experienced fingertips teased her breasts. She gently arched her back.

"Ummmmm."

"Remind me to buy Allison anything she wants when I see her again."

"What for?" Gayla muttered, still not awake.

"For deciding to stay with her grandmother for the weekend instead of coming home after her tennis tournament last night," Bill Coleman said.

"What about me? What do I get for letting her?" Gayla asked with playful indignation.

He laughed and slid his hand to her stomach, rubbing in a circle. "Let's start with this," Bill murmured, his fingers again exploring sensitive territory and eliciting a languid response.

The foreplay grew earnest as Gayla turned into his arms and Bill positioned her so he could half lie over her body. Gayla stretched out her legs and felt a wad of fabric at her feet, obstructing progress.

"Wait . . . what is this . . . ?" She reached at an angle to grab the item and pull it free. She held up a peach-colored nightshirt.

Bill took it from her and carelessly flung it on the floor. "I don't know why you bother," he murmured, nibbling her skin and squeezing her. "It's pretty . . . but it gets in the way."

"Next time I'll just wear a T-shirt, for all the notice you take," Gayla said, letting him have his way.

She didn't discourage him, but decided she would have preferred to get more sleep. Gayla was convinced, by the way Bill fairly pounced on her whenever there was a chance to be alone, that he wasn't seeing another woman. While they hadn't made any commitment to each other, she would have been put out to know he was playing her off with someone else. On the other hand, being the sole focus of his needs and attention made Gayla feel pressured. Obligated. She enjoyed his companionship. It was comfortable and certainly safe. It was gratifying . . . and satisfying. He was a good lover, nothing original or exciting, but it got the job done. She enjoyed his intelligence and that he always knew how to behave. And yet sometimes she had these fantasies. Sometimes she wished . . .

The telephone rang.

"Don't answer . . ." Bill said, his hand between her legs.

She was wet. Ready. He'd found the right spot with his middle finger. Gayla sighed deeply, undulating her body. The phone rang a second time, and she reluctantly pulled away.

"I have to get that. It might be Allison."

Bill flopped back on the bed in frustration. "Tell her her timing is awesome. And I take back my offer."

Gayla chuckled as she struggled into a half-sitting position and picked up the cordless unit. "Hello?"

"Have you seen the papers yet?"

"Good morning, Mitch. No, I haven't."

Bill groaned anew as Gayla identified her brother. He threw back the covers and got out of the bed, heading for the bathroom. Gayla settled back against the pillows. Her desire was quickly fading and, like Bill apparently, she knew that when she got off the phone they would not try to recapture the mood. The lovemaking had begun spontaneously, but the moment was gone.

"You didn't call me on a Saturday morning to ask about the news unless there is something in it I *really* need to know this minute, right?"

"Page fifteen in the lifestyles and culture section."

"Mitchell, I'm in bed . . ."

"Alone?"

"I haven't seen the papers. What is it?"

"I quote . . . 'The popular uptown gallery on the edge of Harlem has long been known for its support of black artists, and its commitment to reaching out to the community of middle- and lower-income residents. But they have gone a step further by bringing the 'hood into the gallery. The current show features a controversial but exciting and highly visual installation by an unknown artist who grew up in Harlem . . .' "

Mitchell had her attention, and when Bill returned to the bed Gayla barely noticed. Nor did she register, let alone respond, to his attempt to pick up where they'd left off by stroking her bare back.

"Bill," Gayla warned quietly to make him stop, but immediately regretted her indiscretion when her brother reacted with a throaty drawl. Not offended, Bill merely backed off and clicked on the TV to CNN with the volume turned low.

"Tell him I said hi. And if you don't want him, I do," Mitchell said calmly.

"Go on. What else does it say?"

" '. . . who grew up in Harlem. The program lists him as David Alan Kinney. But some Harlem residents might remember him as Dak. A former member of a now-defunct street gang known for petty crimes that included vandalism, Dak Kinney survived his early history to become an artist. He has called on his past experience to make bold and poignant observations on the black community and society in general.' "

"Oh, no . . ." Gayla murmured.

"Wait, there's more."

"I think I've heard enough."

"What's wrong?" Bill questioned.

"It's nothing important," Gayla said to Bill before speaking into the phone again. "Who was the writer on the article?"

"Rob Hanson. I've met him. I don't remember seeing him at the opening."

"He might not have been there. The show's been running for almost two weeks. He could have come at any time."

"Well, what do you think?"

"You think the same thing I do. Mom's not going to like it."

"What about Dak?"

"You mean David."

"That don't change the past, Gay."

"No . . ." She glanced furtively at Bill who seemed engrossed in the current world news segment on the TV. "But all of us have things we've done that couldn't pass close scrutiny."

"Ain't it the truth," Mitchell agreed dryly.

"Do me a favor. Don't tell Mom. Maybe she won't see it."

Mitchell sniffed derisively. "I can't believe I'm calling you about this."

"Well, it's not as if we don't know him."

"You know how I felt about him. I didn't like

David. I was afraid of him. But it was different when I saw him at Mom's."

"Really? What happened?"

"Nothing. He was pretty cool. He didn't act like he knew I was a faggot."

"That's not cute or funny, Mitchell. If someone actually called you that you'd be most upset."

"Well, I'm not sure he's really changed."

"Maybe he has. I wonder how David will feel when he reads that piece?" Gayla speculated softly.

"He probably won't even care. He could just blow it off. But if anybody tries to trash-talk him he'll probably just kick their ass."

Gayla winced at her brother's scenario. She didn't believe it for a minute.

"I want Bill to marry my mother."

Sylvia Patton, used to her granddaughter's ability to shoot from the "lips" and think about it afterward, merely regarded Allison across the table.

"Oh, really? And how does your mother feel about that?"

"I think she loves him. I always catch them sucking face . . ."

"Allison, please . . ." Sylvia admonished her for the vulgar expression.

"Sorry. But it's true. Don't you think they love each other if they're always hugging and kissing and whispering behind my back?"

"I think it means they *like* each other," Sylvia suggested. She carefully slid two more pancakes onto

Allison's plate. She put the frying pan into the sink, running water into it.

"I think Bill would make a good husband for my mother. She needs someone who is as smart as she is and who is a professional."

Sylvia shook her head and couldn't help laughing. "Did you count his teeth as well?"

"What?"

She poured herself more coffee, and moved the syrup dispenser closer to Allison as she took her seat again. With amusement and affection she watched her granddaughter. Sylvia reveled in her wholly unself-conscious beauty, in her bright inquisitiveness and outrageous observations. Her uncombed hair was a thick riot of twisted locks which only added a kind of wild-child charm to her countenance. But every day of this child's life Sylvia lived with the dread of discovery.

Sylvia still fretted over the knowledge that Graham had seen Gayla's business card. Of course, it was true he could have found out at any time where Gayla worked if he'd wanted to. She gnawed her lip, wondering if it wouldn't be a good idea for Bill and Gay to marry. It would certainly settle a lot of things. But she had to conclude that it would *not* necessarily solve any problems.

"Why all this sudden interest in your mother getting married?" Sylvia casually unfolded the morning paper, left outside her apartment door. She sipped her coffee and glanced quickly at the front-page headlines before flipping slowly through the inside pages.

"Well," Allison began with a thoughtful frown. "I don't want her to be alone. You know, Nana, when I grow up and go away to college she won't have anyone."

"She'll have me and Mitchell. She'll have her work and friends. She may marry Bill. She may marry someone else. Maybe she doesn't want to get married at all. But I can assure you, Ali, that she won't shrivel up and die."

Allison turned angry eyes to her grandmother. "She can't marry anyone else."

"And why not, if I may ask?"

Not having thought of a good reason beforehand, Allison frowned at her plate, absently pushing around her breakfast. "I don't want anyone else for a father. I mean, a stepfather."

Sylvia stopped her scanning of the paper to regard Allison. "Do you really want a stepfather? I didn't realize . . . Do you miss not having a father?"

"Well . . ." She looked at her grandmother, her gaze both confused and defiant. "I don't really mind so much for myself. But . . . I don't want Mommy to marry just anybody. Anyway, I know she didn't have a father, either. Don't you think that a stepfather is just as good?"

Sylvia stared at Allison, surprised at her consideration. "Honey, I don't think you have to worry. Your mother is very smart, and she knows how to take care of herself and you. If she was serious about Bill and he about her, I know they'd talk to you about it before doing anything.''

"I know, but . . . maybe I could tell them it's okay and then they can hurry up and do it.''

Sylvia smiled warmly at her. "Allison, why don't you let your mother and Bill work out whatever their relationship is, okay? You have enough other things *you* need to take care of.''

Allison groaned dramatically and scrunched her face up. "Aaauugghh . . . I don't want to go to piano lessons today. Can't I skip it this weekend?''

"Allison, we go through this every time you stay with me for the weekend. Now, I know you don't carry on like this with your mother. She won't stand for it and neither will I.'' Allison pouted, but remained silent. "The class is only an hour, and I've already told you we'd go and find those boots you wanted. But I don't like feeling like I have to bribe you to go.''

Allison turned beguilingly wide eyes to her grandmother. "It's not a bribe, Nana. Don't you remember I was supposed to get them for Christmas and they sold out?''

Sylvia sighed. "I stand corrected. But you're still going for your class.''

"My mother can't play the piano. Why do I have to? I like tennis better.''

Sylvia gave her a severe look to put the impertinence in check. "I couldn't afford to give Gay and Mitchell music lessons when they were your age. You don't know how lucky you are.'' She glanced at her watch. "You have about twenty minutes before we have to leave. Are you finished with that?" Allison nodded, sliding out of her chair and taking her breakfast things to the sink.

"Can we go to a movie later? Please?"

"It depends on how much you get on my nerves between now and five o'clock," Sylvia drawled playfully. When the phone rang, she put down her coffee and stood up, dropping open the newspaper. "I'll get it. Honey, rinse out my things, too . . ."

"Okay."

Allison hummed to herself as she did the simple chore. Her grandmother's voice was a comforting sound from the other room. Allison turned to the kitchen table, stacking the mug and plate her grandmother had used. But she was distracted by a photo in the newspaper, and put everything down to examine the image more closely. Allison was still reading the article when Sylvia returned two minutes later.

"That was my next-door neighbor. She wants to borrow my Bundt baking pan. Remind me to . . . Allison? Honey, what's the matter?" Sylvia came to stand over her granddaughter, searching for the cause of Allison's stony expression. "What are you reading?"

Allison jabbed the page. "He's a criminal. See, it says here that David Alan Kinney was a thief. Read it for yourself . . ."

Sylvia was trying to do just that over Allison's shoulder. "Calm down, Allison. Let me see . . ."

"I knew there was a reason why I didn't like him. He's a criminal!"

"He is not a criminal. Stop saying that."

"He is. It says so."

"It says he had been in some trouble when he was very young. That has all changed."

"Nana!" Allison said, scandalized that her grandmother would defend him. "But you don't know him."

"Yes, I do," Sylvia said. At her granddaughter's look of disbelief she reached out and rubbed her arm, as if trying to comfort her and break the news gently. "David had his problems when he was a teenager, but he's no criminal. I raised that boy for three years . . ."

"You raised him?"

"He had no one else. His mother was dead, and his father . . . well . . . you don't need to hear the whole thing, Allison. I took him in to watch over him."

"You mean . . . Mommy knew him a long time ago, too?"

"Yes, of course."

Allison's expression went through swift transformations but ended on a look of indignation. "She didn't say anything."

"Well, honey, maybe there wasn't any reason to. This was way before you were even born. After all those years Gayla was probably surprised to see him again." Sylvia frowned into her granddaughter's face. "Why do you feel you should have been told, Allison?"

Allison flounced away from her grandmother. " 'Cause I don't like him, that's why."

David stood at the window staring out into the street.

He felt trapped. For two days all he'd done was pace and ignore the telephone. His only connection to the outside world had been Kel. Which was both ironic and annoying as hell, because Kel was not the kind of lifeline David would have chosen. Even when they were young bloods he preferred speaking for himself. Kel would be the first to tell him *I got your back, man*, but David knew he had to watch his own back as well.

David heard the soft landing of King Tut on the window ledge next to where he stood. The animal butted its head into him, rubbing his neck and the length of his arched back against his arm. Tut meowed and looked up at David, demanding affection. David had to smile. The cat was smarter than he was. Tut wasn't going to give him the chance or time to feel sorry for himself. *Get over it*, King Tut seemed to be saying . . . *and scratch my back.*

Chuckling softly, David lifted the animal. Kel's reaction to Tut aside, David knew his old running crew would fall out if they could see him. He could imagine them laughing and goofing on him. But most of those guys were dead now. He balanced the cat in his arm, reluctant to admit to himself, let alone anyone else, what the animal's trust and love meant to him. Except for Kel, who'd been ragging him.

"Man, you better get yourself a woman and leave that cat alone. Ain't no pet in the world is going to take the place of *real* pussy."

When the phone rang, David didn't even bother to turn around. He waited for the current caller to either hang up or record a message. David had called Sylvia himself that morning to let her know he was okay, because he knew that she more than anyone else would understand exactly what that newspaper article had done to him. He was tired. He didn't want to fight or deny the past. He also didn't want to keep proving himself.

"Hi. If I've reached David Kinney this is Stu Warren from WQBR in Brooklyn. I saw your show yesterday and would really like to have you on our program to talk about your work and background. Give me a call at . . ."

The apartment intercom sounded, and David ignored that as well. It buzzed intermittently for another minute and then stopped. He had reluctantly given Kel a set of keys to the apartment because it was easier than having to be around waiting for his return every day. Besides, David didn't want to encourage Kel's habit of jimmying the locks.

The doorbell rang.

Fed up with the interruptions, and the feeling of being stalked, David went to the door. He hadn't expected the intruder to be anyone he knew. And he certainly wasn't prepared for the caller to be Gayla.

She blinked at David, not realizing until that moment he would not want to talk to anyone. It was an invasion of his space . . . and he probably didn't have much of it to call his own. Without a word David stepped back and gave her room to enter the apartment. Whatever response she had anticipated was not there, and her stiffness seeped right out of her.

Gayla walked past him with a scented coolness that hit him like a breath of fresh air. She proceeded without further invitation down the corridor into the center of the large front room. She took a quick assessing look around and turned to face him.

"I caught the door as one of your neighbors was leaving, since you didn't respond to the intercom."

"How'd you know I'd be here?"

"My mother. Why aren't you answering your phone? People have been trying to reach you for two days."

David was struck first of all with the lack of accusation in her tone. There was a time when Gayla would have come at him with claws drawn, her voice hostile and righteous.

David shrugged, slipping his hands into his jean pockets. "I was trying to work. The calls interrupt."

Gayla stared at him, her expression thoughtful and intense. "Was it that article? It made you angry, didn't it?"

His jaw began to tighten spasmodically. "Why do you say that?"

Her gaze never waivered. "David . . . I know that you're trying to get a life. The past haunting you like this can't help very much. You don't want to be reminded."

David frowned. What a surprise. Without answering he walked a bit past Gayla, picked up a chair and placed it so that she could sit down. He got another for himself. "So, why are you reminding me?"

Gayla sighed. "I'm not, but . . . when I saw the piece I suddenly realized that . . . all those folks out there who don't know anything about you are going to have opinions or judge you based on what was in the article."

David sat perfectly still. "So? How much do *you* know about me?"

Gayla slowly shook her head. "Almost nothing. I guess I'm as guilty as the rest of them. I've been doing the same thing for years. Not being fair."

"Maybe you had reasons."

"Maybe you did, too. Maybe . . . there was a lot of things you couldn't help. Mom always tried to tell me that. I didn't want to listen. And Mitch . . ."

"He always thought I was going to out him. Or worse." David shifted, bending forward to brace his forearms on his thighs, and frowned at his clasped hands. "I bet you didn't come here to make a confession or to say you're sorry."

"No," Gayla whispered honestly. "I just wanted to say that . . . I had nothing to do with the information that reporter used. I don't know where he got it. I swear."

David glanced at her with raised brows. "I believe you," he said.

She averted her eyes. "It's just that the author left you no secrets."

He shook his head. "My past isn't a secret. I have nothing to hide. He was just doing his job. I just don't like that the facts of my life might be used to pass judgment on me. Or to try and make me look bad."

"Well . . . there's been some good that came of it."

"Really? Like what?"

Slowly Gayla smiled at him. David was a bit startled because it was so genuine and brightened her eyes.

"You sold two more pieces. Attendance is way up for this current show, probably because of the reports on your art. People come in asking for you, hoping to get a glimpse of you, like you live at the gallery or something."

David couldn't return her smile, and he wished he could.

For her part Gayla was hoping that her news would soften the body blows he'd taken in the press. She hadn't expected David to jump for joy. But it would have been nice to see him smile again.

She sighed. "Come on. You can't tell me you're not happy about that. You are getting a lot of attention!"

He stood up and walked to the window. "That's the problem. *I'm* getting all the attention. Not my work. What is it people are really interested in, Gay? The mystery and bad parts of my life? Or my talent?

Why are you so excited? That the gallery is having a successful show, or that you'll make money, too?"

Gayla stood up and joined David at the window. "That's not fair," she said indignantly. "You forget, I didn't make the choice to put you in the show. I didn't know you were so . . ." She stopped. David turned to her with alert eyes, prompting her to go on. "I didn't know you were so . . . so good. So creative. There. I've said it."

Now he did slowly grin. "Hurt that much, eh?"

Gayla had to laugh and with that she began to relax. "So this is what crow tastes like. Ugh!"

They stood grinning at one another. The sense of ease and familiarity with each other was not lost on either of them.

Tut's meow came as an eerie intrusion. Gayla looked in surprise as the gray cat walked right up to her and continued to meow.

"Oooh . . ." She bent and picked up the animal who accepted her cuddling and stroking. "What a beautiful cat. Is she yours?" Gayla asked in disbelief.

"He. Actually, I belong to him. I do whatever Tut tells me to."

"Tut?"

"As in King."

Gayla laughed out loud. She caressed the cat under the chin and was treated to complete acceptance by the swish of his tail back and forth. She grinned, watching the cat crane his neck as he rubbed against her and ignored David for the moment. Gayla chuckled.

"What's so funny?" David asked. He reached out to add to the animal's ecstasy by tickling the top of his head.

"I don't know. I never would have thought of you as being an animal lover."

"Just another thing about me you didn't know," he said without rancor.

"How long have you had him?"

"I found him about four years ago. He was hurt. Looked like he'd lost a fight with a bigger animal. Probably a raccoon. I patched him up, and he stayed."

"Why King Tut?"

David shrugged sheepishly. "It's not very original. I was reading a book on Egyptian art that week." He watched Gayla stroking the cat and nodded. "You've got good hands. Tut approves."

The comment embarrassed her because of the incredible imagery it evoked. And because her response was so unexpected Gayla gently passed the cat to David.

"I have to go."

David watched her but didn't respond.

Gayla took a deep breath. "There is one other thing."

"More bad news?"

"And good news."

"Let me have the bad news first."

"There's a publication that would like to interview you."

"No."

"You haven't heard what magazine it is yet. You don't know the point of view they want to take." He was shaking his head. "They're willing to pay . . ."

"No."

She sighed in exasperation. "Look . . . this is free publicity. Let it work for you. I happen to know that this journal reaches a huge audience. You want to be taken seriously? You want people to look past your background and mistakes? Then talk to them. Be open. Give people a chance to hear your side."

David watched her carefully. He put Tut back on the floor, much to the animal's displeasure. "Since you've already told them I'd come, I guess we'd both look pretty bad if I said no."

She didn't deny it. "How did you know?"

"You didn't ask. You told me. And you're here in person to tell me. If you'd called, you would have risked me hanging up on you."

She was surprised. "Would you have done that?"

"Probably."

Gayla shook her head in bewilderment. "I don't understand you."

"Don't give up now," he said with more earnestness than he wanted her to hear. "You're getting the hang of this. What's the magazine? When's the interview?"

"Maybe tomorrow. I'll call them back. I told them I had to run the idea past you first."

He nodded reflectively. "Okay. I'll do it." He tilted his head and regarded her slyly. "So what would you have told them if I'd refused?"

Her smile was coy. "I didn't think you'd really say no."

"Sure of yourself, aren't you?"

She sobered and shook her head. "No, David. I wasn't. But I counted on your grabbing this chance to have your own say. Okay, you messed up when you were seventeen." She hesitated, looking uncertain. "I . . . I messed up when I was nineteen. It doesn't have to dog you your whole life. You've paid your dues. Besides . . . I think my mother is right."

"About what? What did she say?"

"I don't think I'll tell you," Gayla teased quietly. "You'll start to believe your own press." He grinned. It wasn't the smile she was looking for, but it was nice.

"So, what was this other good news you had?"

"The board of the gallery has agreed with my decision to extend the show. Probably for two more weeks, at least."

"Why?"

"Well . . ." She watched him, preparing for his reaction. "I want to take advantage of the attention. The number of people coming to see the show will look good on my grant proposal to NEA in the fall. Is that okay?"

He shrugged. "Sounds like a smart idea to me."

It was not lost on Gayla that this was the first real agreement on anything she and David had ever had.

When they heard a key in the door, they looked at each other. David's expression showed his apprehension. Gayla's was harder to read. Because until that moment she had not considered the possibility that David was involved with someone. That a lover might walk in on the two of them. Gayla felt oddly guilty at the thought and didn't understand why.

The door opened and a tall, stocky figure filled the doorway.

"Honey, I'm home!" the voice said in a falsetto before bursting into deep male laughter.

Tut stiffened and lowered his belly to the floor, skulking away across the room. David caught the movement out of the corner of his eye, appreciating the cat's instincts. The animal retreated to relative safety on top of the bookcase, his second favorite spot. The first was being held by him.

As Kel slowly entered the room, Gayla watched his approach with open curiosity. Kel looked from one to the other with a broad smile on his face. David could see the way Kel was scoping her out.

"Afternoon." He nodded to David. "Hi . . . I'm Kelvin Monroe," he said, holding out his hand to Gayla.

He was dressed casually, but in expensive designer labels. Clean. He also carried a navy blue canvas duffel packed with what David assumed were more of his personal things.

"Hi. Gayla Patton."

It was clear to David that Kel wasn't going to need him . . . or want him . . . to act as middleman in the introduction. David was amused, waiting to see how Kel would handle a woman who wasn't immediately fascinated with his obvious masculine appeal. He wanted to see how far Kel would go to play her . . . right before his eyes.

Kel frowned quizzically. "I believe I've seen you before. At the gallery uptown . . ." He gave a cursory glance at David. "Where Dak is showing some of his work."

David didn't react.

Gayla smiled apologetically. "Did I meet you? I'm sorry I don't remember."

Kel laughed with self-deprecating ease. He shook his head in apology. "No, we didn't actually meet. I saw you, and Dak told me you ran the gallery. You were just leaving with a beautiful young girl . . ."

"My daughter, Allison. Are you an artist, too?"

Kel laughed lightly. "I'm afraid not. He's the one with all the talent. We've been friends a long time. I just hang around and stand in his shadow."

Gayla smiled, nodding. She glanced at David, who so far had not said anything.

He took that as his cue to come forward. "Kel is staying with me for a few days . . ."

"Just a week or so . . ." Kel corrected.

"Well . . ." Gayla said awkwardly, avoiding Kel's intense, smiling stare as she began to move toward the door. "I have to leave. I just dropped by . . ."

"Business or pleasure?" Kel fished.

Gayla hesitated. His voice was so teasing and charming, she wasn't sure she should take offense. "About David's work."

David finally took over, afraid that Kel wouldn't

be able to keep up his facade of civility. "I'll walk Gayla to the door."

When they reached the door, neither knew what to say.

"Well . . ." David began, stopping short.

Gayla nodded. "Well . . ." she also said.

He opened the door for her. "You'll let me know about that interview."

"Yes. I'll call, but you'll have to pick up the phone," she said dryly.

"Fine. Bye."

Gayla raised her brows at his brief goodbye. With a half-smile she turned to the elevator.

When David closed the door again he had no time to reflect on her visit. No time to think about the barriers which had come down between them, although he had no idea yet what was going up in its place.

"Here. This is for you."

David stared at the bills Kel extended to him. "What's that for?" he asked quietly.

Kel pushed the money into his hand. "For taking me in, man. I can see I'm messin' up your social life." He grinned.

David was glad that Kel had not said something more crude about Gayla being there. But he frowned at the money. He folded what he calculated to be about a thousand dollars and shook his head as he held it out to him. "I don't want your money. I said I'd help you out."

"No, man. Take it. I told you I had something lined up. You know I'll take care of you, bro."

"I don't need this, Kel."

Kel laughed. "To my way of thinkin' that ain't hardly enough!" He jerked his head in the direction of the open room of the apartment. "You ain't exactly living large. Get yourself something nice. Get that Gayla something nice. 'Cause if you don't, I might go after her myself."

Kel walked away. David watched him, wanting to give him the benefit of the doubt. But he was left trying not to think about whether Kel's interest in Gayla was real or just boasting . . . or where the money came from.

"Oh, my God . . ." Gayla whispered when she saw the man standing in front of her building. Her recognition was instant.

He was dressed in khaki slacks and boots. A polo sweater under a lightweight purple ski jacket. The perennial jock, she thought. The dark blond hair looked like it had been recently cut, but in the attractive and carefree disorder of a Robert Redford. It made the man boyishly handsome, and a standout in the predominately black neighborhood.

For a fleeting moment Gayla thought of turning around and walking away. Perhaps returning in a half hour on the chance that he might have left by then. But she didn't have a half hour.

She would have known Graham Whelan anywhere, besides the disconcerting fact that he didn't seem to have changed since the last time she'd seen him. Gayla looked at her watch anxiously. This couldn't have happened at a worse time, but there was a part of her that knew it would have, sooner or later. The irony of the moment struck her as cruel. For a while after she'd first arrived at college she prayed every day that Graham would show up to take her away. After Allison was born she stopped caring. It terrified her to even consider what had brought him to stand in front of her building now, looking nervous and out of place.

Gayla had the advantage, and she used it. She walked toward her building waiting for Graham to notice her. But she pretended to be searching for keys.

"Gayla!"

She stopped and glanced up, as if distracted. Graham stood in front of her, grinning broadly. His blue eyes sparkled with pleasure. It was genuine, and threw her off guard.

He spread his arms. "It's me!"

With that announcement Gayla could see that he expected to greet her with a hug, as if it might rush them through the past to catch up with the present. She made no attempt to accept the offer, and her smile was distant.

"Graham. Isn't this a surprise."

He dropped his arms, but the grin held. He looked her over with a shake of his head. "You look great."

So do you, she thought. But it didn't make her feel

either sad or reminiscent or regretful. In just that instant of reunion Gayla realized she was free.

"I know it's been years," Graham said brightly, as
if it hadn't been nearly fifteen years.

"I haven't given it a lot of thought," Gayla said
calmly enough. "Life goes on, you know." She could
see his exuberance die to uncertainty. "How did you
get my address? What are you doing here?"

He was forced to retreat by her cool attitude. "Not
Sylvia. I didn't even ask."

Gayla waited.

"I found your business card at my parents'
apartment."

And waited . . .

"I thought . . . well, I wanted to see you, Gay.
That's all."

She stared at him. "That's all?"

The warmth deepened in his eyes, but Graham no
longer tried to couch the encounter in a familiarity
that belonged to the past. He put his hands into the
coat pockets. "I've been hearing from my mother and
Sylvia about how well you're doing at the gallery.
And I . . . I've been thinking about you."

Gayla tried to stay calm, aware of the time. Any
moment Allison's school bus could pull up to the
building. She shook her head. "I don't know why
you would."

He now seemed at a loss for what to say next.
"You were an important part of my life. I've never
forgotten. I guess I thought we could . . ."

"Not relive old times or pick up where we left off.

You're wasting your time if that's why you came here, Graham. I'm not sixteen anymore," she said more impatiently than she meant to. She no longer had hard feelings toward Graham Whelan. She just wanted him to go away.

"Okay, I guess you're not glad to see me," he murmured ruefully. "Can we talk?"

"About what? Old times?"

"Why not? I want to hear about the gallery. And Dak."

"David."

"Twenty minutes. Okay?"

She wanted to say no, but had a feeling that that would not be the end of it. She remembered how persistent Graham could be. She didn't want to have to do this again. She was running out of time, and resisted the urge to look behind her for the approach of Allison's school bus.

"I only have a few minutes."

"Is there somewhere we can go for coffee?"

She merely nodded in response and walked past Graham. He fell into step next to her. They turned the corner and headed two blocks west to Broadway. Gayla led the way to a small unpretentious café called Rosa's. It was overheated inside, with the smell of pork and garlic, coffee and sweet breads wafting in the air. At one table sat two elderly men smoking and chattering in Spanish. Gayla took a table near the front and Graham sat opposite her, leaning his elbows on the faded plastic tablecloth.

"Interesting place," he commented.

Gayla had never been in Rosa's, but Allison had said the shop had great *sapopillas.* A woman hurried toward them to take their order for coffee and left. Gayla and Graham did not attempt any conversation until the order had been served. And then the steaming cups sat between them untouched. The years had taught Gayla great patience, and she had no intention of giving him an opening.

But Graham was staring out the window to the street, seemingly fascinated by the activity. It occurred to Gayla that Graham had probably never been this far uptown before without being on the highway passing through. It suddenly confirmed for her how little he'd ever known about her.

"So," he began, bringing his gaze back to her. He took time to study her closely. "I want to say how beautiful you are, but you might think I'm handing you a line."

Gayla shook her head. "I wouldn't. But what makes you think I'd care?"

His smile wavered and he flushed. Graham tore open two packs of sugar and poured them into his coffee. He slowly stirred. "You used to care very much. I remember when . . ."

Gayla pushed back her chair so suddenly that it scraped across the linoleum floor. She jostled the table trying to stand up and her coffee sloshed onto the surface. Graham was caught by surprise. He reached out and grabbed her arm.

"Gay, I'm sorry. I'm sorry. I didn't mean it the

way it sounded . . ." She tried to pull free and he released her. "Please, don't go."

She glared at him.

"Please . . ."

Slowly, she sat down again. She watched warily as Graham gulped his coffee, combed his fingers through his hair and took a deep breath. "This isn't going well . . ." he said.

"You shouldn't have come. What did you think would happen?"

He looked bewildered. "I . . . don't know."

"How's your wife?" Gayla asked quietly.

He became alert. "Why are you asking?"

"Does she know you're here with the daughter of the family housekeeper?" He stared bleakly at her. "There is nothing between us, Graham. We met by circumstance, not because you would otherwise have sought me out and been interested in me. We are from different backgrounds. Downtown boy and uptown girl. We're as different as . . ."

"For God's sake, Gayla, don't say it. That had nothing to do with how I felt about you."

"Black and white. Why not call it for what it was? At least it would be honest. I'm not interested in rehashing the past. And I'm *not* interested in picking up where we left off."

All the cockiness drained out of him. "What I want . . . is a friend." He stared into his coffee, hunched over and reflective, like a drunk trying to figure out how his life turned upside down. "Diana . . . my wife and I are getting a divorce.

That's definite." He chuckled dryly. "Actually, it was probably inevitable. It just took all these years to admit it."

Gayla looked at his bowed head. "What about your daughter?"

"Holly? We haven't told her yet."

Holly . . . "How old is she?"

"Not quite twelve. Tall for her age. Shy. She looks like me."

Gayla sighed inwardly. She no longer felt the intense anger grip her. Or the wave of resentment and disappointment. She could only feel those things if she still cared, and she no longer cared about them for herself.

Holly.

Gayla shook her head. "No. I can't help you with your . . . marital problems. I don't have the experience."

"The marriage is over. I'm trying to save myself." He leaned across the table. "My mother said you have a daughter, too. Allison."

Gayla was afraid to acknowledge it, as if his knowing kept them connected. She didn't want to be that close to the Whelans again. She remained silent.

"You never married."

"I chose not to."

"I used to wonder . . ."

She swallowed. "About what?"

"What it would have been like if we'd gotten married."

Gayla pushed her cup away and once again prepared to get up. She reached into her pocket and pulled out two dollar bills. She put them on the table. "We never would have."

"How do you know?"

She stood up. He didn't try to stop her this time. "You would have had to see me as your equal. You would have had to tell your parents that you loved me. You would have had to ask me. You never did. This is my treat . . . I have to go." Gayla headed for the door. She didn't say goodbye.

"Gay, wait. I really would like to be friends. We used to be. We were almost like family."

His words stabbed at her, opening old wounds and leaking secrets.

"I don't need any more friends, Graham. And I have my own family." Gayla opened the door and turned once more to him. "I'm sorry it didn't work with you and Diana."

Gayla closed the door, leaving him sitting at the table alone.

Chapter Eight

〰〰

Gayla opened her eyes just long enough to check the time on her watch. Another hour. She absently rubbed her elbows and flexed her fingers and feet. She felt cold. Gayla sighed and slowly shifted her body to a more comfortable position, gnawing her lips when the ache in her arms turned momentarily sharp. The unread magazine, newspaper and folder of papers on her lap slid off sideways to the floor. She made a futile attempt to grab them but missed. It was a full ten seconds before Gayla made any move to pick up her things.

David, seated next to Gayla, noticed her clumsiness and bent to retrieve the scattered items. He silently handed them back to her.

She found it an effort and had to use both hands. "Thanks," Gayla said in a thin, flat voice.

She wasn't surprised when she got no response. David sat back in his seat and closed his eyes again.

The last hour and a half since boarding the Metroliner out of New York's Penn Station headed to Washington, D.C., had been passed in absolute silence between them. It was beginning to get on her nerves. Gayla realized, however, that perhaps she had unnecessarily provoked David by again making a decision for him.

Fumbling, Gayla managed to put away the reading material in her leather tote. Except for the manila folder. She turned to study David's profile. His long legs were stretched out and crossed at the ankles. His hands were clasped on his lap where he held a book that also had not been opened. She watched the way his head swayed gently with the train motion. He looked like he was sleeping, but Gayla knew he was not. He wasn't really relaxed. His brows were drawn together and his mouth was closed tightly. She could see the muscle in his jaw working.

He was still angry.

Gayla shifted yet again, more toward him. "Look, I know you don't feel like talking to me. I know you'd rather not be here, but you are. I really need to go over some things with you. Please . . ." she said reasonably.

He remained still for so long after she'd finished that she suddenly wondered what she was going to do if David really refused to talk to her. But he shrugged his shoulders.

"So go ahead and talk. You're going to do whatever you want without my say-so, anyhow."

"What are you mad about? I told you about the interview . . ."

His mouth curled cynically. "Except for the fact

that it was going to take place in Washington on national TV . . ."

"The TV thing didn't really happen until yesterday. I told you as soon as I knew."

David glared at her. "That's the problem. You told me; you didn't ask if I wanted to do this. But I'm just an ex-con. Why worry how I feel about anything, right?"

Gayla could almost feel the coiled tension in him. She'd hit a nerve. Her own were beginning to feel bruised and tender. But she couldn't blame David for that. "You're overreacting."

"Where do you get off making decisions for me like that, Gayla?"

"You could have just said no," she reminded him calmly.

He looked incredulous and shook his head, frowning at her. "Are you trying to test me? Do you want to see at what point do I break and go off?"

She could feel the start of pressure in her chest. Like a cough waiting to happen. The buildup was distracting and Gayla tried to calculate how much time she had before it would take over and the demands of her body superceded anything else.

Gayla didn't respond right away, but watched his face and eyes. Somewhere during the diatribe Gayla felt herself weakening. Somewhere the truth of his accusations hit home, and she didn't have the energy to deny any of it. But she couldn't go down in flames, either.

"If you calm down for a minute, you'll see this is a great opportunity to get publicity for your work . . ."

"Fuck the work, Gayla! Forget about publicity. What about *me*?"

The question stopped her cold. She considered David for a moment, and his anger was raw and naked and suddenly painful to witness. Gayla averted her gaze, unable to answer David, because she didn't have a simple response . . . or even a very good one. She'd made a mistake . . . and he might never forgive her.

Gayla sighed, hugging herself close and feeling the attack steadily invading her body. There was no need to be concerned yet, although the timing was bad. Damage control with David was needed right now, because she realized that perhaps he was right. But for the moment, her most important concern was getting through the next twenty-four hours before she had a crisis.

The ache seemed to be spreading fast and furious to all her joints. But any meditation she might have used to help her focus was continually interrupted by the image of Graham Whelan standing in front of her building. It bothered her that he'd reappeared after so long. But in truth, Gayla was more upset by what was going on right now between herself and David.

She eased herself into another position. "Look, I agreed to this telecast because I thought it would be great exposure . . ." He ignored her. "I'm used to making this kind of arrangement for people. It's part of my job at the gallery for promotion and marketing. TV appearances are hard to get, but this is a little different. You'll be taped in a studio in D.C., and the program goes out to satellite station hookups at colleges around the country. So the audience will be mostly students and teachers. The moderator is a local news reporter. I think there are two other people on the program with you . . ." Gayla opened her folder and quickly located the information. "One is a photographer and the other is a musician, so you won't be alone. Now, the theme of the interview is . . ."

"What do they know about me?"

Gayla closed the folder and looked at him. "Only what I've told them."

He turned to gaze earnestly down at her, waiting.

"I told them . . . you were one of the most exciting artists we've had in a long time. I said that you didn't have much formal art training, but that you have an excellent eye for observation." He looked as if he was waiting for more. "And I gave them the usual bio stuff, that you were born and raised in New York, started out at Bronx Science High School, but didn't finish . . . I remembered that. Mom always said it was criminal that you didn't finish. No pun intended." He wasn't amused. "I said that you went to college upstate for a few years and, until recently, were living in Dutchess County. And you taught art for a while. I didn't say where."

A shock of awareness flashed in David's eyes at Gayla's revelation. "How did you know all that?"

"Mom, mostly. And I did some checking. It wasn't like prying or anything. The information is pretty much public, and we needed it for our records and for insurance purposes."

David frowned quizzically. "Why didn't you ask me about it?"

"Because I didn't know what you wanted to tell me. I don't have many of the details, only the recorded facts." She hesitated, blinking at him. "I wasn't sure you were willing to trust me with things about yourself that were . . . personal."

"All you had to do was ask," he said simply.

"I'm sorry. I really am," Gayla whispered quietly.

It was as much a surprise to hear herself saying it as it was to David.

He narrowed his gaze on her. "Are you sure?"

She raised her brows. "Yes, I am. Are you going to ask me to prove it?"

"I might." He leaned forward to pull a small nylon duffel from beneath the seat in front of him. He unzipped it and dropped his book inside.

"Look, why did you agree to take part in the exhibit? Why did you come back to New York if you didn't want any recognition?"

He shrugged. "I got tired of running. I can't change the past, but I don't want it to be what I'm most known for, either."

"You're being too hard on yourself."

He arched a brow. "Now you tell me."

"You know, you could have outright refused to make this trip. Why didn't you?"

"Because despite the fact that you weren't open with me, I knew you thought this was a good thing to do. We both would have looked bad if I'd backed out. Besides . . ." He hesitated for a second. "I saw this as a way of getting over a major stumbling block."

"What? Suspicion of my motives?"

"No," David said with a shake of his head. He looked squarely at her. "Fear."

Gayla willed herself to keep moving. She knew her movements seemed slow and awkward. The dull ache in her wrists and elbows had relocated to her lower back. And she felt very cold. That's how she knew she was running out of time to handle the onset of the crisis herself.

She glanced surreptitiously at David, who was reading signs and maneuvering them through the Union Station crowd toward the exit and the taxi stand. Common sense told her she should say something. Stubborn self-will and denial kept her silent. Gayla estimated it had been close to five years since she'd last felt this kind of pain. Not unheard of but still counted as unusual. And because she had ignored the signals, taken her prolonged remission for granted, she was about to pay the price. She'd even forgotten the over-the-counter painkillers that would have helped.

A sharp pain shot through her arm when she was accidentally jostled, and she uttered a strangled sound. It was unavoidable and made her falter in her steps. David gazed at her alertly, but Gayla pretended nothing had happened. If they could just get to the hotel she knew exactly what to do. But Gayla had not counted on the congestion of cars picking up or dropping off travelers outside the station. Nor had she counted on the line already formed to wait for cabs. She began to focus her breathing. She concentrated on getting in a lot of air, and then evenly exhaling, searching for a meditative state that would help her navigate the escalating stages of the attack.

The line moved. Slowly. When Gayla and David finally climbed into an available cab, she no longer had a choice.

"Which hotel?" David asked her, as the driver looked over his shoulder for instructions.

"Not the hotel," she said softly. "Please take . . . take us to the . . . Capitol City Medical Center."

David's head turned abruptly. Gayla was grateful to see the instant understanding that there was a problem. He turned back to the driver.

"You got that?"

"Yes, sir."

The cab pulled away from the curb, and Gayla slumped against the seat with her eyes closed.

"Why didn't you say something sooner?" David asked. He relieved her of her overnight case. She tried to hold onto the shoulder tote, but he took that as well.

She didn't resist. "If we had arrived an hour sooner, I could have handled this myself."

"Where do you hurt?"

Gayla fleetingly opened her eyes to look at his face. He was concerned, but calm. "My . . . back. My hands . . . and I'm cold. I need to get warm . . ."

The words were barely formed when David shrugged out of his navy blue sports coat. He tried to get it around Gayla's shoulders with a minimum of movement.

"Put your hands in the pockets," he ordered. He leaned forward to speak to the driver. "How close are we?"

"About ten blocks," the man responded nervously, looking through his rearview mirror at the woman in the backseat breathing heavily. "She gonna have a baby? Listen, mister, I don't know nothin' about birthin' no babies."

"I don't either," David said. "So you better get us to the hospital, fast."

David sat back and put his arm along the back of the seat behind Gayla's neck. He sat close, but only to make his body a firm support against the swaying of the vehicle rather than to hold her. He knew that touching her could be uncomfortable.

In another two minutes they were pulling into the curved driveway of the emergency room. The driver quickly got out and came around to open the back door. Gayla was able to slide out of the taxi and to stand on her own, but she winced with every motion. David dug into his pocket and hastily stuffed a bill into the driver's hand, who nodded a thank-you and beat a retreat.

David watched Gayla moving with a kind of stiff

dignity and determination. He didn't try to help because she didn't seem to need any. And she wouldn't want it. David knew that for a fact because now he could see there was a lot about them that was the same. A do-or-die mentality of not giving up and never admitting defeat.

But he also knew something must be seriously wrong.

At the emergency room desk she waited to get the attention of two receptionists who were already handling the room filled with dazed visitors in varying states of distress. One woman finally looked up at Gayla.

"Yes?"

"I . . . I'm SS hemoglobin," she said in a strained voice. With shaky coordination she took her shoulder tote back from David and reached inside. Gayla pulled out a card carrier and flipped it open to show the attendant some information. "I'm on the edge of a crisis . . ."

The woman scanned it quickly and nodded. "I have to take her in, right now," she said to her co-workers. "Call the technician on duty and tell them I need blood drawn for a chemistry workup, and CBC." Turning back to Gayla, she beckoned her to come around the desk. She gave David, who stood alertly watching, a questioning glance. "You wait here. We have to get an IV started . . ."

Gayla managed to give him a reassuring glance as she disappeared around a partition. He had to assume, for the time being, that she was going to be okay.

He remembered a time long ago when he'd found Gayla in tears of pain, wails of agony. He had tried to ignore her, but curiosity for what was happening to her won out and drew him to her.

He'd heard the sounds coming from a small supply shed behind the house in Vermont. At first David had thought it was an animal who'd found its way inside. But it was someone crying. Sent to put away a wheelbarrow, he'd left it outside the shed while he went in to investigate, quietly opening the door and stepping inside. David thought better of calling out, and cautiously approached and peered behind a riding mower. Gayla was curled up in a fetal position, on a canvas tarpaulin used to cover the machine in winter.

David looked around, wondering if someone else had been with her. Had she been attacked? Was she hurt?

"What's the matter with you?" he asked.

Her body jumped, startled by the sudden voice. Other than that, she didn't move. "Go away. Mind your own business."

"You sick or something?"

"I said, go away! Leave me alone."

Her voice ended on a moan.

David came closer and squatted down next to her. He looked at her but didn't see any cuts, bruises or blood. But Gayla was obviously in a lot of pain.

"I'm going to tell your mother . . ." he said, starting to stand.

Gayla gasped and turned to glare at him. Her face was wet and puffy from crying. "No, don't," she pleaded. "Just . . . leave me alone."

"What if you're dying or something?" he said.

"Stupid. I . . . I'm not dying," Gayla muttered between sobs.

David stood up to leave.

"Dak . . ." she called out frantically. "Don't tell my mother. I . . . don't want to go to the hospital. She'll . . . make me . . ." She squeezed her eyes closed, stubbornly refusing to give in.

David stared down on her. He had been prepared to walk away and leave her there. But he didn't. "You just going to stay there and cry?"

"I'll go back to my room. Everyone . . . will think I'm just taking a nap."

She tried to stretch her legs out to sit up, and would have toppled over if David hadn't held out a hand to her. Gayla took it, holding tightly, grunting as he used his arm strength to help pull her into a standing position. She was trembling.

"I'm cold," she whispered. She hunched her shoulders and wrapped her skinny arms around her chest, swaying in front of him.

"We better get out of here before Mr. Whelan comes in."

"I . . . I don't want my mother to see me," she whined.

"She won't," David promised. He walked back to

the shed door and glanced out. "Come on." He beckoned, keeping watch as Gayla slowly joined him. He reached behind for her hand as he walked out.

David had to pull her along, listening to the tears and grunts of pain. But he didn't stop, heading for the back door into the house, hoping Sylvia wasn't in the kitchen, and that everyone else was out somewhere on the property. They made it into the living room, to the den that was Gayla's room. They could hear voices of Mrs. Whelan, Sarah and Reilly, but they didn't see anyone. At the den, David released Gayla's hand and stood back as she stumbled past him into the room, closing the door.

The next morning they'd had to take Gayla to the hospital anyway in Randolph Center. She was there almost a week.

And she never said anything to him again about that incident.

Whatever was happening to her when she was fourteen seemed powerful enough to kill. Was it happening again?

Glancing around, David spotted a seat where he could wait for the duration. He knew it might be a while before anyone came back to give him news. He had experience with emergency wards. A memory began sneaking up on him then. He didn't want to think about it; he'd trained himself not to go there. David sat back and closed his eyes. The sounds around him were impersonal and disturbing and he wanted to shut them out.

The dark side of his memories clutched at his

chest, stimulated by the distinct medicinal smells of antiseptics and disinfectants and the echoes of emergency personnel shouting orders as they had tried to save his mother's life . . .

"Mr. Patton . . . Mr. Patton . . ."

He felt a gentle tap on his shoulder and came instantly alert. He found himself looking at a woman dressed in a white uniform. "Gayla?"

"She's fine. She's getting her things together now. You can leave when she's ready."

David stood up with the bags. He questioned her carefully. "You're letting her go. It wasn't all that bad, eh?"

The nurse began walking away and he followed. "No, this was a mild attack. But she was pretty uncomfortable by the time she got here. Mostly we see folks when they're just about ready to climb the walls," she joked. "Your wife is lucky because her case was never severe to begin with."

He didn't bother correcting the nurse. Anyway it was irrelevant just then. But he knew that had the subject come up with Gayla, she would have set the record straight in a heartbeat. David checked the time. Nearly four hours had passed. It was a little after eleven in the evening.

He caught up to the nurse as she stopped at a desk and began making notations in a record book. "She was in a lot of pain when we got here," he commented in an attempt to prompt more information.

"Well, we had to medicate her at first, but she has a pretty high pain threshold. Her blood count was not bad. She only needed one bag of saline." The nurse gave him a sage but comforting look. "You can take it from here. Get her home and warmed up. She didn't say what kind of work she does, but stress doesn't help."

With that she walked away to other duties.

David headed down a short hallway where he could see a triage area of little treatment rooms, separated by only a curtain. He spotted Gayla right away. She had just finished donning her coat and stepping into her shoes. She absently pushed and patted her hair, trying to give it fullness after it had been flattened in the back from lying on a pillow. Her movements were coordinated but slow. To David she appeared tired.

Gayla looked up, sensing that she was being watched. She saw David and wondered what was going through his mind. His expression didn't give much away. Gayla put her tote on her shoulder and walked slowly to meet him. She gave him a brief smile.

"Sorry 'bout that," she said flippantly.

David didn't return the smile. "They said you can leave." She nodded. "Do you have everything?" She nodded again.

For a second they just stood there, each waiting for the other to do something. David finally held out his free hand. Gayla hesitated only briefly before accepting the offer. Not of help or comfort or reassurance, but as a connection back to the familiar. The strength of his hand grounded her, bringing her back from the sense of being too light, and floating on air. His hand was warm, and she held it tightly.

They didn't acknowledge their separate reactions.

They found a cab waiting outside the hospital. Not much was said of any consequence during the short ride to the hotel, and their conversation picked up as if there had never been a need to stop at an emergency facility. But even the air was different around them, filled with knowledge of the experience they had just shared.

The small, elegant hotel was not a known tourist accommodation, but the kind of hotel frequented by business travelers. Courtesy of the hosting publication, they had dining privileges in the hotel restaurant, but they didn't really feel like eating. After they checked in, David escorted Gayla to her room to make sure she got safely inside. Still no mention was made of the hospital side trip or what had made it necessary. Gayla steadfastly refused to meet David's gaze, as if nothing unusual had happened . . . or as if hoping it would just go away. David then went to his own room, two floors up.

He had very little to unpack, and when he was finished he felt too restless to either watch TV or go to bed. He was thinking about Gayla, and what was wrong with her. Even that summer she was fourteen and spent a week in the Randolph Medical Center, he'd never found out the name for what had happened to her. He didn't know now.

After a while David left his room and headed back to Gayla's. It was almost midnight. He wasn't sure what he was going to say to her once he got there. He couldn't even anticipate how she was going to respond. He was acting on instinct, taking a chance.

David hesitated for a moment outside her door. He could hear nothing from inside. He started to turn away; what if she was already asleep? But what if she wasn't? Finally, he knocked for admission. The voice came back muffled and weak.

"Yes?"

"It's David."

There was a long moment before the door was unlocked and quietly opened a crack. She was dressed in a long knit nightgown. Gayla didn't look at him directly, nor did she say anything. She left the door open and turned back into the room. David entered and by the time he closed the door Gayla had climbed back into bed with the covers pulled up around her shoulders. He stood looking down at her without feeling the least bit uncomfortable about being alone with her in a hotel room. Obviously she didn't feel it either, or she wouldn't have let him in.

"I'm okay," she said, reading his thoughts.

He pursed his mouth. "Can I use your phone?"

Gayla frowned. "Go ahead."

He called room service. "This is room four-eighteen. Can you please send up a pot of hot . . ." He glanced at her in question.

"Tea."

"Make that one tea and one coffee. Thanks." He hung up and casually sat down in the chair diagonally across from the bed.

"I don't feel like . . ."

"The nurse said to take you home and get you warm. Why?"

"Why?"

David nodded. "Is there some reason why you can't tell me what happened? That cab driver was pretty happy you didn't have a baby in his backseat. Are you pregnant?"

A surprised laugh was forced out of Gayla, but she quickly sobered. "No, I'm not." She closed her eyes. "I . . . don't talk about it."

"You want me to ask Sylvia? What do you think she'll say when I tell her we spent half an evening in the emergency room of a D.C. hospital?"

"This is none of your business," Gayla informed him softly but firmly. David merely sat back in his chair and waited. "I'm not going to talk about it with you."

"I'm not doing the program tomorrow," he quickly countered.

She snorted. "You think you can blackmail me?"

"I'm calling your bluff. Or if you prefer . . . you show me yours and I'll show you mine."

"I'm not going to play this game . . ."

"I just spent half an evening in a D.C. hospital and I want to know why. You know I can find out. But I want you to tell me."

"Why do you need to know?"

"Is it a secret? Maybe I could have helped you sooner. Maybe what happened could have been prevented. You expect me to trust everything you do or tell me without a lot of questions. But you're not willing to give as much in return. Is that how it works with Bill Coleman?" David asked bluntly. "You're in charge?"

She closed her eyes but otherwise didn't move. "That's none of your business, either. You're in no position to harass me about this."

"What have I got to lose?"

Gayla shifted positions under the covers until she was flat on her back and staring at the ceiling. Finally she sighed.

"It's not such a big deal. It doesn't happen a lot. That's why I don't say anything. Especially not to my family. I think the last time I had an attack was about five years ago. Something like that. I was supposed to take Allison to her first ballet performance. I couldn't disappoint her . . ."

"Did Sylvia take her?"

Gayla shook her head at David. "No. Mitchell filled in. I think I told him the only reason he was willing was because of the chance to see some good-looking guys in tights." David looked askance. "Mitchell has more of a sense of humor than you think."

He shrugged. "I've never been given a chance to see that. What's SS hemoglobin?" he asked.

"It's a level of blood cell count that indicates one of three kinds of . . . of sickle cell anemia."

He nodded slowly. "I've heard of it."

"Black folks are prone to getting it. My parents

were carriers but never had it outright. I have it. Mitchell doesn't.''

"Allison?''

"She has the trait.''

"Does she know?''

"Yes, but I don't think she likes to think about it. I don't want her to. She's not going to ever get sick because of sickle cell. And I don't want her to feel . . .'' Gayla stopped.

"She could lose you?'' She nodded. David sat forward in the chair, bracing his elbows on his knees. "Could she?''

"It's . . . very unlikely. I'm considered to be at tolerable risk level. So now you know my deep, dark secret. Are you satisfied?''

He pursed his mouth. "No.'' He saw surprise register on her face. "Stop feeling sorry for yourself. You can still do just about anything you want to. Already you're ahead of the game.''

"You have a lot of nerve. Where do you get off thinking you can tell me how to act or feel?''

David stood up and slipped his hands into his trouser pockets. He thoughtfully considered Gayla from across the room. "You have a family who's there for you. You have a beautiful daughter. From where I stand, you're not doing so badly. You could be sicker. You could be alone. That's not nerve you hear . . . it's envy.

"There's not a day goes by that I don't wish I had done things differently when I was seventeen years old. I also wish my mother was alive. But the good news is I'm free, black and lived to be more than twenty-one. The way I look at it, I have a lot to be grateful for. So do you."

"I didn't know they teach Philosophy 101 in prison," she said. Gayla could tell by the telltale flexing in his jaw that she'd hit home.

"Prison taught me a lot more than that. There's no substitute for freedom, self-respect or family. I have two out of three. I'm working on what I'm missing."

Gayla was surprised and moved by David's honesty. But she remained silent.

There was a polite knock on her door with the announcement of room service. David slowly walked to answer.

"So, you have Sickle cell. It's nothing to be ashamed of. You don't have it because you're being punished. I would have respected your secret if you'd trusted me. You have a long way to go, too." David opened the room door.

"You ordered tea and coffee?" the delivery man asked.

David turned back to look fleetingly at Gayla as he indicated that the tray should be placed on the desk. "For the lady," David responded as he stepped out of Gayla's room, closing the door as he left.

Then he stood outside her room debating if he should go back in. He couldn't see the point. David headed for the elevator, but instead of returning to his room, he took it down to the lobby and headed for the hotel bar. There were about a half-dozen men, mostly in conversation or watching the TV which was on Conan O'Brien.

David ordered a beer, although he didn't really want one. He would have preferred a cup of coffee. He would have appreciated Gayla's company. He wanted her respect even more, but they were still sometimes engaged in attack and retreat. It was dispiriting. He drank only half the beer and returned to his room.

He could hear the phone ringing as he put the passkey in the door. He caught it on the third ring.

"Hello?"

"Where were you?"

"Why do you want to . . . Gayla, is it another attack?"

She didn't respond right away. When she did her voice was quiet. "I'm fine, David. I . . . I just wanted to let you know . . . you forgot your coffee."

"I didn't forget it. I left it because . . ." David started to explain and then stopped, considering. "Should I come and get it?"

"It's still hot. I don't want it to go to waste."

David thought about it. "You know it's way after midnight."

"I know, but I'm wide awake . . . and free of pain. Let's play hooky."

He grinned. "I'm on my way."

"Aaaaaaggghh . . . aaaaawwwwwohmyGod. . . . shit . . . oooh, shit . . ." Kel moaned as he surged forward and tried to bury himself deeper into the womb of the woman who lay beneath him. She had her hands splayed over his taut, pumping buttocks, pulling him into her, aiding the release. She expertly raised her pelvis, rotating against him, eliciting another long groan as the last of his physical explosion ebbed away.

"Mmmmmmmm, yeah," she mewled as if in ecstasy, and then softly hissed through her teeth while Kel tried to grind the last of his pleasure into her. "Mmmmmmmmm, baby . . . that was so good."

He collapsed against her, his heavy body crushing her into the mattress. "Damn!" he got out weakly.

She began to gently rub the top of his shoulders, sliding her hand across his neck. Her manicured fingernails teased the skin behind his ears which, immediately after Kel's climax, was now highly sensitive.

Kel grunted and rolled over to lie next to her. He seemed on the verge of sleep until he suddenly sat up on the side of the bed. She twisted toward him and continued to stroke his back.

"You sure know how to use your thing," she drawled. She planted a gentle kiss between his shoulder blades. She slowly maneuvered a hand around his waist, seeking the now limp, damp organ and working it like it was a joystick.

"Okay . . . that's enough," Kel said dismissively, his voice back to normal. He slapped the woman playfully on her thigh.

"Aaaaoow!" She exaggerated the impact. "Hey . . . I'm not into that spanking stuff."

He picked up the cellular phone from the floor

next to the bed and used his thumb to begin punching in a number. "Get me something to drink, will you?" he ordered the woman.

She lazily sat up, but took inventory first before following his instructions. Smoothing her hair. Using a hand towel to wipe the milky residue from her inner thighs. Checking her nails for cracks or chips. And then sliding off the bed and heading barefoot and bare-ass to the kitchen.

She turned to Kel at the doorway. "I have to use the bathroom."

"So, use the bathroom," he said indifferently, listening to the ringing on the other end of the cellular.

"But the cat's in there."

"Open the fucking door and let it out," Kel instructed impatiently. She sighed and turned away. "Get me my drink first . . . Yeah, it's me. What's up?" he said into the small hand unit. "I know I'm late. I had something important to take care of and it couldn't wait." Her chortle could be heard from the other room. "We on or what? . . . Did you check out where that door goes? Good . . . Okay, but what about Boo Boo? You sure he knows what he's doing? . . . I don't give a flying fuck whose brother he is, man. I don't want to end up holding my dick in my hand, you got that? . . . Naw, forget Dak. He's out. The brother's not down with that no more. But I'm tellin' you, he's cool . . ."

Kel didn't bother looking up when the cute young thing returned to the bedroom. She stepped over the clothing on the floor and leaned forward to place the can of beer on the top of the TV in front of Kel.

"We got lots of time. I checked it out. It's gonna be a snap."

He reached out to roughly stroke the young woman's rear, trying to get his hand in the tight space between her legs. She resisted, trying to twist away. Kel caught her wrist and jerked her around. The short battle excited them both, igniting the fuse which hadn't burned out yet.

"You just make sure you got my back," Kel said into the phone as she teased him with the calculated movements of her naked body. She freed her hand and, well aware that Kel's eye was on her and his interest was rising again, sashayed out of the room with a provocative wiggle of her high, rounded butt.

"Huh, huh . . ." Kel uttered in appreciation. "Yeah, I'm listening . . . okay . . . I'll be there."

He popped the tab on the beer can and swallowed nearly the entire contents by the time the woman had returned from the bathroom. She climbed on the bed, kneeling and sitting back on her heels. The position thrust her ample breasts forward.

"What did you say the man who lives here does?"

Kel reached for her as he sat back on the bed, leaning against the wall. "He's an artist."

"Oh, yeah? He one of them guys that likes to draw naked women? You *know* that's just a line so he can get some . . ."

Kel began rubbing her arms, cupping her breasts and squeezing them together. He boldly spread his legs with his member at full attention. He urged her closer and she crawled toward him. "The brother's not like that. I think he's the real deal 'cause people buy his shit. Mmmmm, baby . . . come on over here, I have to make this quick. I have work to do . . ."

She sucked her teeth at the need for urgency, while she positioned herself between his legs. He held the sides of her head, directing her.

"You said you was going to take me to eat . . ." she whined.

"Yeah, baby. I will . . ." He moaned as she took hold of him and her mouth closed over the bulbous head of his penis. Her tongue flicked lightly across the sensitive opening at the top. "This is like . . . the appetizer."

She understood exactly what to do to slake his hunger.

CHAPTER NINE

—————∞∞∞—————

Gayla stood in conversation with the public affairs coordinator of *Black Dialogue*. She nodded on cue, making a herculean effort to stay focused on the non-stop conversation of the gregarious young woman. Every now and then Gayla sipped from her tea or flipped through her program notes. She maintained contact with the senior staffer, charmed in spite of herself but exhausted by so much energy at seven-thirty in the morning. She mostly listened, employing "Oh, really" or "I know what you mean" whenever a response was called for. And Gayla knew that later she wouldn't remember a thing.

She smiled and chuckled often, letting the sound carry across the green room as a signal that she was fine, and nothing was amiss this morning. She was aware each time David cast a brief glance in her direction before returning to his own conversation with a co-participant.

"I couldn't believe this man. We all thought he was going to be cool and say all these funny things, and then he didn't say more than five words during the entire broadcast. Someone called in a question and all he said was, 'I can't answer that.' We nearly died. It was so embarrassing. We *scrambled* to fill in."

"I know what you mean," Gayla murmured sympathetically.

In her peripheral vision she made note of the other guest on the show. An attractive light-skinned woman with 'locked hair and an elegant manner. She was dressed with contemporary simplicity in a long skirt and an oversized, brightly printed top that was Afrocentric in style and colors. She was, in fact, a fabric and clothing designer replacing the photographer originally scheduled. The designer's work incorporated not only the influence of African culture, but also elements of Chinese and Indian fashion. She was regal but friendly . . . and she had David's undivided attention.

"Okay, we're ready to head out to the studio and get all of you seated on the stage and hooked up to microphones. Come this way, please . . ."

Gayla stood back to let the three program guests follow the producer from the room. David walked by, still in conversation with the designer, and Gayla found herself taking up the rear. They were led down a series of nondescript corridors to a door marked STUDIO 4. It was a huge open warehouse-like space with one side set up to be a cozy sitting room complete with plants, comfortable chairs and a coffee table. Opposite was a theater arrangement of chairs occupied by an audience of about fifty.

The program moderator was a popular D.C. news

anchor who was telegenic and articulate. He introduced himself to all the guests and took his place on the stage. Gayla watched the final preparation as David was seated and he was instructed by one of the stage sound technicians how to thread the mike wire so it would be as unobtrusive as possible. He appeared at ease, casually attired in dark brown slacks and a rust-colored long-sleeved polo shirt under a camel-hair sports jacket. His neatly groomed close cut beard emphasized the lean and sculpted line of his cheek and jaw. From a distance, he seemed to have the poise and presence of someone famous. The interested attention of the designer notwithstanding, Gayla suddenly saw David as someone who appeared worldly, professional, urbane. It occurred to her as she continued watching that her mother's faith in David Alan Kinney had been justified after all. Unlike Graham who had disappointed so many people in so many ways. The comparison was confusing.

The audience was diverse in every respect. Running the gamut in age and gender. Mostly black; there were several whites and one Asian photographer. A few appeared to be reporters, with notebooks and recorders ready.

David suddenly looked up and caught Gayla's eye. She hoped she hadn't appeared to be staring at him when in fact that was exactly what she was doing. She quickly improvised a pantomime of straightening the collar of his shirt where the small black audio device had been attached. She watched him pick up on her signal, but in no other way did he acknowledge her.

"Okay, we have two minutes to the opening sequence, and then we lead right into the introduction with Brad Michael Davis. Please remember, everyone, *not* to look directly into the camera. Just pretend they're not there. Direct your comments and answers to Brad Michael, or to each other. One minute . . ."

The lights began to dim in the studio, except for the stage area. The director went to silent hand signals, taking his cue from his headphone communications with the sound booth above the studio. He raised a hand for attention and used his fingers to count down the final seconds.

They were on the air . . .

After the first ten minutes Gayla began to relax. She'd given David an outline for the discussion along with questions the moderator would ask. He had done his homework. And even if he hadn't, he clearly was more than capable of thinking on his feet. He was knowledgeable about art and the sensibilities of an artist. He talked about fooling around with drawing when he was a kid, and how he never thought it would develop into a career. He mentioned those who influenced him early on, including her mother . . . and the photographer Emily Whelan. He explained how he used his work to talk to the viewer about black history, pain, disappointment, loss, love and hope.

He mentioned in passing that he now taught art as well.

"My work is rough," David readily admitted at one point. "I didn't study when I was a kid, and didn't take this seriously until I started using it as a way to ask questions and look for answers. I really didn't know what I was doing until someone said, hey . . . that's interesting art. Oh. Is that what I'm doing? I didn't know." The studio audience laughed.

And so did Gayla.

He played off the other participants, and a healthy debate and disagreement kept the conversation going. The designer talked about using fabric as a canvas to create images, using the top she wore as an example of wearable art.

"I could use about a half a yard of your top for something I'm working on now," David commented at one point.

Again the audience laughed.

There were two breaks for FCC-required station identification during which everyone got to relax for a few minutes, drink liquids, get coaching from the moderator. Gayla kept her attention focused on David. He never once looked in her direction and it occurred to her rather ironically that he was doing well on his own. But Gayla, like the audience, was being exposed to a side of David Alan Kinney she didn't know existed. He was charismatic, but in a quiet, self-deprecating way. He came off as perhaps a tiny bit nervous but he never fumbled for a response to questions directed to him, and he wasn't afraid to admit when the discussion turned to something he had no knowledge of. He simply listened attentively to what the other guests had to say.

David unexpectedly looked at her. Caught, Gayla flinched as if he'd just read her mind. She quickly recovered, however. She smiled and gave him a thumbs-up sign.

In the second hour of the taping the format changed and the moderator asked for comments and questions from the audience. From distant campuses across the country, phone calls were made to the studio. Gayla checked the time. Ten more minutes and it would be over. The moderator signaled a young white woman in the studio audience with her hand raised to stand and ask her question.

She was dressed in a coordinated business attire that was smart and contemporary, professional but attractive. She was young enough to pull off wearing a skirt well above the knees, displaying beautiful legs.

"I have two questions for Mr. Kinney. I happened to be in New York a few weeks ago and caught your show. It was great . . ."

David was paying attention but he silently waited out her comments.

"My question is, since you've already said that your life was an influence on your art, was watching your mother being murdered by your stepfather one of them?"

For long seconds every person in the studio was frozen in place. Gayla's stomach somersaulted in shock. She looked first to David, who only appeared to be calmly thinking about the question. She looked to the young PR coordinator, who appeared disoriented and unable to react. The producer looked to the director, who looked to the moderator, who sat with a theatrical smile that seemed inappropriate, foolish and locked in place. He was used to a script and a TelePrompTer for his cues, and momentary confusion and panic stiffened his features. He pointlessly shuffled his lap notes.

"Well, I don't think . . ."

"Of course it was an influence," David spoke up.

Everyone held their breath, their eyes on him. Gayla tried unsuccessfully to get his attention and signal him not to answer. But David was looking at the slender woman with a kind of bright narrow focus that effectively closed out everything else, as if he was locked in one on one with her.

"I was only nine at the time. For years I thought it was my fault that she died. That memory of helplessness and guilt is in a lot of my work. I thought I should have done something to stop him. Anything."

"That's all we have time—"

"My second question . . ." she cut in, impervious to the stir she'd created and boldly pushing on. "Did being in prison for almost three years play in your decision to pursue art? Like group theory or something? Was making license plates how you got started? By the way, I really like your street moniker, Dak. It's got a nice sound."

There was an audible gasp in the audience, and several people hissed at the woman. She paid no attention. The director signaled for a break, but once David started to speak again, everyone stopped, wanting to hear what he had to say.

"Being locked down only showed me how stupid I was to get myself in there in the first place. I learned the hard way to appreciate freedom. I realized that with some work and some luck I could do something better with my life than go out like a chump. That would have dishonored the memory of my mother. I was lucky to meet up with some good people who believed in me and wanted to help me start over.

"And just to set you straight, we didn't make license plates at my facility. We worked with the highway department paving and repairing roads . . ."

The moderator forcefully stepped in, his smile almost maniacal as the camera centered on him. "I'm sorry, that's all we have time for. Thank you for your questions."

There was a final wrap-summary, announcements and a commercial plug for the sponsoring magazine. A repeat mention of the current books, projects or exhibits that the guest speakers were currently involved in, with the encouragement to the audience to buy, read or see for themselves. The studio lights went up, and Gayla could hear the collective release of held breaths.

The attractive woman, oblivious to the tension she'd created, marched right up to the stage, extending her hand to David and introducing herself with a smile. Gayla finally moved. She was prepared to run interference if she had to . . . but she didn't have to. She stopped when David accepted the woman's greeting. Despite the fact that she'd just peeled back the scab on two painful episodes in his life, David merely appeared curious and alert.

The woman talked with animation and poise and David tilted his head toward her to hear what she was saying.

Gayla stood indecisively, watching the exchange. David didn't bother to seek her out and she felt superfluous and even foolish wondering what was being discussed, and what was going to happen next.

"I'm so sorry . . ."

Gayla forced her attention to the distraught young PR coordinator. "What?"

"We had no idea she was going to do that."

"Who is she?"

"Her name is Maron Connelly. She writes a column for the *Washington Post*. Not that she needs to work. Her father is a bigwig in D.C. He's high up in the Justice Department."

"Why would she be interested in this kind of event?"

The coordinator chuckled. "For the shock value, probably. She's good at doing stories about people on the edge of society. And you're not going to believe this. She's the only white writer who's a member of the National Association of Black Journalists. They couldn't keep her out . . ."

"I know . . . it would have been discrimination," Gayla murmured absently. "Very smart."

Gayla felt excluded as David and Maron Connelly stood talking. Clearly David was neither upset nor offended by the personal and intrusive questions asked of him on the air. If anything, Gayla sensed that David was fascinated by the reporter's in-your-face approach.

"I sure hope she's not trying to create a scene and get him angry."

Gayla watched them. Deep in conversation, neither David nor the woman seemed to be aware of the activity around them as the station crew dealt with equipment and the audience was escorted out. Gayla slowly shook her head. "I don't think that's the problem at all."

"Are you cold again?"

It was a second or so before Gayla realized David was talking to her. She turned her head and frowned.

"Excuse me?"

He didn't repeat the question, but stood up to retrieve his sports jacket and passed it to her from the overhead baggage rack.

"Thanks," she murmured, accepting the garment and draping it around her shoulders.

David sat down again and stared blankly at the seat back in front of him, deep in thought. Gayla stole a quick glance at David's profile. He didn't seem inclined to talk. But then, she recalled, he never did. That didn't mean he didn't want to.

"Where did you teach art? Mom never said."

David shrugged lightly. "I guess I could have asked."

"You could have."

"It's not that I wasn't interested," she quickly put in. "I know that you did, but . . ."

He glanced at her when she hesitated.

"I never thought to ask."

"I started out at a vocational facility for boys. It was a pilot program that was supposed to be a woodworking shop. But it wasn't really about making napkin holders or picture frames. I think we were supposed to learn how to stay focused. How to start something and finish it. How to think, even."

"How did you get into it?"

"A friend of mine saw a newspaper ad and sent it to me. And he gave me a good recommendation. After that I did a few short-term things before getting a job at a junior college. By then I was doing my own work and being encouraged to show it."

"What happened to the junior college? Did you . . ."

"No, I didn't lose my job. I took the semester off. I had some business I needed to take care of. I was commissioned to build a small one-room studio. That led to other work. Then at the last minute I was asked to exhibit at your gallery. So, here I am back in New York."

"But only for a while. You have a job to go back to."

"I don't know. It depends."

"On what?"

He gazed at her for a moment. "On whether I get a better offer to stay."

David checked the time on his watch, and drained the last of his coffee. He'd finished his breakfast—just toast and juice—fifteen minutes ago. But Kel was still plowing through a cholesterol mountain of eggs with sausage, pancakes with syrup, and grits with a little pool of melted butter. No question he could put it away . . . like he might not eat again for a long time. If he didn't get himself killed beforehand, he'd probably die of a heart attack. That's how Kel was about everything, David knew. All or nothing. Now or never. A big man hungry for everything.

David frowned, staring down at the toast crumbs on his plate. "You going to work today?"

Kel shoveled a fork full of eggs into his mouth and chewed before answering. "Work?"

"You told me you'd found a job. That you'd be getting your own place and settling down for a while."

"Yeah, yeah . . ." Kel nodded. He glanced up at David as he washed his food down with a deep gulp of his coffee. "Trying to get rid of me, man?" he teased.

"Trying to get back to my routine." David hesitated, and then sat forward to lean over the table, to talk to Kel in a low voice so that no one else would hear. "Listen, Kel. I can't remember when we didn't know each other, man. We went through some rough times together . . ."

"But we sure had some fun," Kel interrupted with a soft cackle.

"Yeah, we did. But things are different now. I . . . I have a new life. Different from what I did before."

Kel nodded, poking around in his plate with the fork before using it to hack off a wedge of the stack of pancakes. "I know, man. It's a damned shame."

David narrowed his gaze on him. "What?"

Kel chewed and swallowed the bulge in his mouth. "I don't know if you frontin' or what. But it's like you trying to be somebody else."

"I am," David admitted without hesitation.

Kel leaned in closer, using his fork to poke at the air for emphasis. "Dak, you're a fucking ex-con. That ain't ever going to change. And no one's ever going to let you forget. Why you want to change up now? Things used to be so good. We had everything. We can still have everything . . ."

"I don't want everything, that's what you don't get. I just . . ." David struggled to make it simple for Kel to understand. "I just want a life where I work, I make money, I pay my own way, I don't owe anybody anything, I have a decent place to live . . ."

"Fuck that shit," Kel uttered scathingly. "You don't get brownie points for being good. We got fucked over when we were kids. By our families, cops, the system, the white man. I ain't for that no more. I'm getting all I can get right now."

David saw two things in Kel's eyes, in the mouth twisted with his words and ideas. First there was the bad-ass kid who was quick and could always be counted on to come up with ways to have fun . . . and get into things. And then there was the Kel he'd last seen who'd come close to getting killed, but had been caught and sent to jail instead. For the second time. That was the Kel sitting opposite him now.

"I thought you had a job?" David asked quietly.

"I do."

"Doing what?"

"I know this guy who owns a small trucking outfit. Does short-distance hauls. I'm one of the drivers."

David stared at him. "That can't pay very much."

Kel shook his head, forked more eggs into his mouth. "It doesn't," he admitted. "But it keeps clothes on my back, food in my mouth, and I can give you a couple of dollars for letting me stay at your place. Like I said, it's only for the time being. I'm working on a few deals. I'm going to be away for a few days. Leaving tonight. Give you some privacy. In case you want to bring someone home for the night. Don't forget to bag it up." He laughed in amusement.

David went back to looking at the crumbs. He pushed the plate aside. "I don't need any more trouble, Kel."

"You're not going to get any."

"What I don't know won't hurt me, right?"

Kel shrugged with an innocent lift of his brows. "I don't see why it should."

CHAPTER TEN

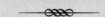

Gayla listened to the voices and laughter, the low-playing live music that came from the gallery one level above. She glanced around the incredible transformation of the Guggenheim foyer, where flowers and candles and bistro tables created a fantasy of light, colors and smells. Tonight the space was more than a museum entrance. More than a warehouse of art. It was a theater for a happening, a showcase for the wealthy and well-connected.

What she liked about coming to a museum was the excitement it stimulated in her for returning to her own work. Gayla was also envious of the fact that David . . . just did it. No excuses about not having time, or not being good enough. Just putting his heart into it, and being honest. David used his own life, good and bad, to fuel his imagination. She had been afraid to. But there had been a reoccuring idea lately, a theme to be executed through the print-making processes of intaglio and silkscreen. Gayla really wanted to do it.

She felt Bill's hand on the small of her back as he

put away the coat check ticket and steered them toward the registration desk. Several Junior League women greeted them and gave them a seating scheme for dinner. They were immediately handed glasses of champagne from waiters standing like sentinels at the end of the table.

"We don't have to stay too long," Bill whispered as they began the ascent up the wide circular walkway, spiraling to all the exhibit floors.

"I take it some of this is about business. We can stay as long as you like."

"Sure you don't mind? I know how you feel about these charity events that only seem to benefit rich causes."

Gayla shook her head as they walked. "That's not it. But a fund-raising event to benefit the library of a private school seems redundant," she said wryly. "I would have been more impressed if it was for a children's shelter. Or a hospice for the terminally ill."

Bill smiled down at her. "Deserving programs. But not sexy. You know how this works. You run a not-for-profit center, and you're always looking for sponsors and money for exhibits and promotion. View this as an opportunity to meet some of the rich and famous. Shmooze the hell out of them . . ." Gayla chuckled. "And get them interested in your favorite charity. If these rich folks want to give up money, let them give it up to you. A gallery in Harlem for start-up emerging artists; for your after-school art program for junior and senior high school kids. For maintaining your archives of African-American, Caribbean and Latino artists. You know how to work a room. And you'll get dinner."

Gayla smiled. "Maybe I should let you do the talking. That's why you're on our board."

Bill lightly placed his arm around her waist and his fingers squeezed gently. "I sure hope that's not the only reason. I have a real interest in the gallery. But I expect to get something in return."

Gayla was instantly alert, heat rushing to her face with the acknowledgment of the affair they'd been having for more than a year. She hadn't considered that Bill had gotten involved with the gallery primarily as a smoke screen to get to her.

She stared at his profile as he smiled and greeted people he knew, and introduced her. Many were engaging and interesting and important to know. A lot of lawyers and their wives. Several CEOs and their wives. A selection of artists and writers and dancers . . . with their various significant others.

"Gayla, hi."

Gayla came out of her reverie to smile in surprise at the bespectaled, redheaded woman thrusting a hand out to her. "Hi, Nancy."

"It's great to see you. It's been such a long time."

"I know. But don't take it personally."

Nancy laughed. "Of course not. There's work, kids, meetings, kids, the unexpected and . . . you get the idea. Take your pick. Hi, Bill." She reached forward to get an air kiss on her cheek.

"Where's Sid?" Bill asked the petite woman.

Nancy made an airy gesture over her shoulder.

"Back there. We got separated about two group encounters ago. He got waylaid by Judge Hanlon. I swear, you men do not know how to chill out. For you these things are just a chance to continue office work. Gay, I've been meaning to call you about something."

"Oh, really? About a job with more money and real benefits, I hope," Gayla joked.

"As a matter of fact that's exactly what it's about. We have an opening that needs to be filled by the summer, and I thought I'd speak to you about it. I was telling the director of the Department of Cultural Affairs about you and he'd like to meet you."

"Really? Why?"

"The department has just created a new position for a liaison to the many arts programs around the city. They're looking for someone who can work with the city and various funding sources, and the communities. You'd be perfect."

"But I was just joking. I already have a job, Nancy. I like what I'm doing."

"That's what I told the director. But other people have mentioned your name as well. Your track record is exactly why he thinks you could do well with the department."

"I'll be honest with you, Nancy. I'm not interested in being the token minority to make the department look good."

"I understand. But there are a good number of programs in minority communities, and the director wants to place someone who has a sense of community needs."

"Who can relate."

"Exactly."

A reasonable and smart goal, Gayla had to admit.

"And I told him you are a fine artist . . ."

"Nancy . . . I appreciate the thought, but I think you should continue your search."

"Well, don't say no so fast. You haven't heard what they're bringing to the table. There's nothing lost in listening to what they have to say, is there?"

"No, I guess not," Gayla said, rubbing her temple. She didn't have a headache so much as feeling the pressure of things getting out of her control. One surprise too many.

Bill's intense growing interest.

David's metamorphosis.

Hers.

"I'll give them your number. Why don't you call me after you've spoken to the director?"

A gong began to gently vibrate through the great rotunda-like center of the museum. Bill took hold of Gayla's arm. "They're announcing dinner."

"Listen, we'll talk," Nancy said. "I better go find my husband . . ." And she was gone.

Slowly the milling groups of people started clustering in one large mass as everyone headed to the dinner, set up in the gallery on the top level of the museum. The movement was slow and Gayla absently glanced around at the other guests. Through the crowd she spotted a black man in formal wear . . .

with a phase beard and a sculpted, masculine face. Gayla stumbled.

"Watch your step," Bill cautioned, grabbing her hand to steady her. "Are you okay?"

Gayla wanted to turn around again but nodded at Bill with a smile. "I'm sorry. I literally tripped over my own feet."

They fell back into step, and at the earliest opportunity Gayla hazarded another look behind her. She scanned the faces quickly but did not see the man again, the one she thought was David Kinney.

The guests flowed into the dining area looking for their tables, greeting tablemates and finally sitting down. Bill again introduced her to several guests at their table, but Gayla was too distracted to remember a single name. She covertly tried to look around at all the guests without appearing to do so. But she didn't see that familiar face.

After the introductions at her table and the pouring of the dinner wine came the inevitable inquiries about what everyone did. One of the women was the owner of a midtown gallery. She had heard about, but not yet seen, the new show at Jump Street Gallery. She was already interested in representing David Alan Kinney.

Gayla's reaction was not exactly one of excitement. She felt a reticence that was unexpected and odd. She wanted to say that *she* was David Kinney's representative for his work . . . but that wasn't exactly true. Gayla also recognized, after a moment in which the sensation swept quickly through her body, that the very idea made her feel apprehensive. Threat-ened. But all she could do was to take the woman's card and promise to have David contact her for an appointment to show his portfolio.

She tried to stay in the moment. She smiled and asked questions and responded, but she wasn't hav-ing a good time. It bothered her that so much of her thoughts, her associations, even her socializing lately, always seemed to include the name of David Alan Kinney.

Gayla was relieved when the dinner plates were removed and coffee poured. The evening was almost over. She whispered to Bill and excused herself from the table.

She slowly maneuvered back in search of the la-dies' room. Gayla smiled vacantly as she passed sev-eral tables. Her gaze roamed briefly, and found that face again. And he had seen her and was studying her openly. It *was* David. Gayla couldn't control her startled look. Consumed with curiosity about his presence, she hesitated for a fraction of a second, intending to be gracious and say hello. But then she saw that he was not alone. And in fact gave all the appearance of being the escort of the younger of two women seated on either side of him. Gayla saw and recognized her, too.

She was almost level with their table, but at the very last moment decided against saying anything, merely smiling pleasantly as she walked past his table. But Gayla already knew that in not saying something, she had given herself away.

*   *   *

David silently let Gayla pass his table. He'd been hoping, after first seeing her during the reception part of the evening, that he might get through the night without coming face to face with her. The idea made him very uncomfortable. He felt very much, in Kel's words, like he was frontin'.

She was wearing a navy blue dress with a simple, collarless scoop neckline. Adorning it was a white gold chain that had what appeared to be diamonds spaced every inch and a half along the length. The dress fell to just above the knees. Tasteful. Fashionable. The bodice of the dress sparkled with tiny rhinestones. Her hair was combed off her forehead and framed her brown face smoothly. She was easy to spot in a sea of blondes and pale bare arms and faces and necks. But David realized that the single immediate thought that went through his mind when he'd first spotted Gayla, before he recognized her, was that she was a striking, attractive woman. Not the truculent girl he remembered, or the sassy and fearless teenager. But a grown woman of style, grace and maturity.

"It's pretty boring, isn't it?"

David turned his attention to Maron Connelly. He couldn't help smiling at her, because she was right. "I'll survive. I'm not used to being out and about in society."

"Now you're being sarcastic. You have more confidence and you're more interesting than any three men in here put together."

"Oh, really? What makes me so interesting? Besides the obvious."

She laughed, leaning toward him, ignoring the covert glances of speculation from the other guests at the table. "You find all of this so pointless."

"So, why did you invite me?"

"I told you. I wasn't even going to bother coming up from D.C. at all for this unless you agreed to be my date. It was really a last-minute decision, but there were other reasons. Number one, my father is on the board of the museum, and I'm an alumnus of the school the benefit is for. Number two . . . I wanted to see you again."

"Number three, you wanted to shock everyone by showing up with a black man."

She laughed again. "Silly. That's not going to shock anyone. What's been shocking everyone is that no one has ever heard of you. Where are you from? Who's your family and what school did you go to? What do you do? I've love to see the reaction on people's faces to your answers. But it's really none of their business, is it?"

David chuckled, though he didn't share her breezy confidence. She had privilege written all over her. From her bearing and confident manner, to the haute couture dress that fitted her thin but shapely body to perfection. From her social ease and amusing banter, to the indifference she obviously felt for anyone's opinion of her.

David liked her.

Maron was completely honest, and exactly what she appeared to be.

"You made it your business," he reminded her.

"Well . . . I did start out with very noble intentions. I wanted to write the real story of David Alan Kinney. I really think you should sign your artwork as Dak. It's a very strong name. Very titillating."

"I'm glad I can entertain you."

"Bullshit," Maron whispered with a sweet smile, for his ears only. "You never would have said yes to my invitation if you thought I was trying to get over on you." Her smile broadened. "Go on and say it. You've never known anyone like me."

David pursed his mouth. "Actually, I have. Someone I used to know a long time ago."

"Well, that's okay, then. So, what did you think of my father?"

"Seems like a straight-up guy," David said at once.

"He meant it, you know, when he said he'd like to see more of your work."

"Did he? Or did you twist his arm?"

"I did urge him to see the show and he did. And he was impressed. I can be persuasive, but my father is no fool. And I can't manipulate him at all. Well . . . not anymore. I showed him the piece I wrote on you. I told him about your background. The only thing he's interested in is what you plan to do with your life now. He believes in second chances. He's had a few himself. I'll have him tell you about them sometime."

David shifted in his chair. "Maron, look . . ."

She wouldn't back off, not afraid of the other guests noticing her attention to him. Not put off by his own unease.

"I know a lot of people who get two and three chances in life, David, who really don't deserve it. But they know people. Have money. It's so refreshing to meet a man who came back from the dead with pride and a purpose for his life." Her voice became soft as she gazed intently at him. "You're really good-looking on top of that."

He frowned in surprise at her observation. He could see the clear invitation in her hazel eyes. He was not indifferent. But David felt the need to be cautious, to go slow. And he couldn't shake the sensation that he was being watched. Not by the people around them. He didn't care about them or what they thought. But something else was tugging at his consciousness that he couldn't get a firm grasp of.

"I bet you say that to all the men," he teased, for want of anything else to say.

"Let's leave," was Maron's response.

He carefully studied her. "And do what?"

"Go for drinks or coffee. See what develops. Let's play it by ear."

"What would your father think?"

She gave him a quizzical look. "You're kidding, aren't you? I'm a grown woman. If you want I can prove it to you." She leaned closer to him. "Or are you afraid of me because I'm white?"

"I take it you don't see that as an issue?"

"Not at all. I was raised in an environment of enlightenment," Maron said airily.

She stood up and held out her hand to him. That got everyone's attention. "Come on. People are starting to leave now anyway."

David took her hand, just because he didn't want her to continue to stand there with it held out to him. That sent the wrong message. But he released it as soon as he was standing. He momentarily stepped back for Maron to precede him from the room. There were quick and polite good nights exchanged as they left.

It bothered him greatly that he was concerned with running into Gayla on the way out. But they didn't, and David felt a profound relief when he and Maron climbed into a waiting cab and pulled away from the museum.

"I'm sorry you didn't have a good time," Bill said as he and Gayla stepped off the elevator on her floor and headed for her apartment.

She had her keys already in hand, and they jangled as she prepared to unlock the door. She felt very distant and distracted. Tense. She forced her attention back to Bill.

"It's not that I didn't have a good time. But . . . sometimes these evenings seem so tiring and so pointless."

Bill stood gazing at her with a crooked smile. "PMS?" he questioned.

Gayla looked stunned, and then she started to

laugh. "I did sound like I was whining. I'm sorry. I had a good time. I always do with you."

"Do you mean it?"

"Of course. Why would I lie about something like that?" she murmured, putting the key in the door to unlock it. "Anyway, I got to see Nancy. I like her. She's very good about getting us money from Cultural Affairs for the summer jazz series in the gallery garden. And she's managed to persuade several companies to purchase artwork for their corporate collections."

"See. I did you a favor by bringing you . . ."

Gayla chuckled. "Thanks." She unlocked the door and opened it. She could discern the light on in the living room, and the very low volume of the TV.

"George McCaffrey was there," Bill said as they entered and closed the door.

"Yes, I saw him and his new wife. The third, I'm told."

"Fourth. I caught a glimpse of Sandra Forrest as she was leaving with her son. And surprise . . . David Kinney."

Gayla blinked as she glanced over her shoulder at him. "You did?"

"I wonder how he got invited. A little out of his league, don't you think?"

She blinked again. "What do you mean?"

Bill leaned against the wall next to the door, watching as Gayla removed her coat and hung it in the hall closet.

"I mean, come on . . . the guy's an ex-con. I don't

mind giving him a chance to show his stuff. His work is not bad. Undisciplined, but it grabs your attention. From jailbird to peacock is a bit of a stretch. David Kinney is not the kind of man I'd invite to dinner, or to necessarily meet my family."

Gayla stared at Bill. "I'm surprised to hear you say that, Bill."

All conversation stopped when the baby-sitter appeared. A nineteen-year-old who lived on the floor below, she gave her report of the evening, was paid and said good night. Bill picked right up with their discussion.

"Would you invite Kinney to your house? How do you think Allison would feel? Anyway, you don't have anything in common with the man except the connection to the gallery."

"There's another one," Gayla found herself saying.

"Excuse me?" Bill said, confused.

Gayla licked her lips and lowered her gaze. She walked into the living room and turned off the TV. Bill followed. "I've known David Kinney since I was about seven years old, although I haven't seen him in the last fifteen years or so."

Bill was shocked by the revelation. "You never said a thing, Gay. Why? How did that . . ."

"My mother took David in after his mother . . . died. He had been in foster care for about four years and . . . was having some problems adjusting. When my mother found out he was getting into trouble, she stepped in to try and help."

Bill shook his head. "Apparently it didn't help much."

"Well, not at first. When he got sent upstate, my mother said it was for something that wasn't his fault. He was innocent."

"Gayla, that's what they all say."

Gayla sat on the arm of the sofa. She felt a strange tightening of the muscles between her shoulder blades . . . at her temples and the corner of her mouth. "I'm just telling you what happened then. And I . . . I don't think David's the same person."

Bill looked skeptical. "You believe that?"

"You've met and talked with him. What do you think?"

"I don't know. I don't much care. I'm a lawyer, Gay. I'm not a criminal lawyer but I have lots of friends who are. Eighty percent of released cons end up back in the can. Those are the facts."

"Which means the other twenty percent don't," she said, a bit testy. "He's . . . almost like family. To my mother, at least. Like a distant cousin we haven't seen in years. My mother felt sorry for him."

"As long as you see him as a charity case, I guess it's okay. Just watch yourself around him."

She nodded, but the tightening had moved to her forehead. "Was he by himself?" she asked.

"Kinney? No. He was with a young white woman." Bill smirked. "I don't even want to go there," he said when he saw the stare on Gayla's face.

"Hi . . ." a voice said softly from behind an opening door.

Gayla stood up quickly. "Allison? Honey, I'm sorry we woke you up." She put her arms lightly around her daughter's nightshirt-clad shoulders and kissed her cheek.

"That's okay," Allison murmured in a childlike, sleepy tone. She rubbed her eyes and yawned and gave Bill a brief hug. "Hi, Bill."

"Hey. You were supposed to be asleep."

"I know. But I heard you come in."

"Allison, go on back to bed. Bill is leaving in a minute. I just want to say good night . . ."

Allison nodded and took slow steps back toward her bedroom. Then she glanced at Bill. "Well?"

Gayla frowned, looking between Allison and Bill. "Well, what?"

Bill waved the child on. "Good night, Ali. I'll take you and your mother out to dinner on the weekend, and you'll hear all about it then. Okay?"

"Don't forget," Allison said before obediently returning to her room and closing the door.

Gayla frowned at Bill. "What was that all about? What are you two hatching behind my back? I'm telling you right now, Bill, I will not let you buy Allison a Coach knapsack. She's too careless with her things and . . ."

Bill shook his head. "It's not about the Coach bag. Maybe for her next birthday. Then I'm allowed to get her what I want." He slowly approached Gayla and drew her lightly into his arms.

Gayla had the immediate sensation that he was not holding her so much as containing her. As if she might fly off the handle at him.

"What is it?"

Bill smiled down at her and kissed her forehead. Her lips lightly and chastely. "Something I've wanted to do for a long time. Actually, Allison wants me to buy this for you, too."

"What?" Gayla asked, holding her breath, afraid to hear the answer.

He bent to kiss her in earnest. "An engagement ring."

It was almost four-thirty. David had to get up to leave, but had no idea how to get out of the bed without awakening Maron. Her arm was draped across his chest. David lay still for a moment, letting the rhythm of her breathing match his. He was afraid to admit that he liked it. Going to bed with Maron Connelly was about more than the satisfaction of them both getting off.

They had stopped somewhere for coffee, a quiet little café around the corner from her high-rise New York apartment building, shared with a girlfriend who was a producer for one of the network stations and who traveled a lot. The apartment was classy, expensive, and overlooked the East River from the eighteenth floor.

David absently stroked Maron's back, only to have her moan and wiggle closer to him. Her silky hair tickled his neck and throat. Only a sheet covered them from the hips down. He glanced down at their naked and exposed bodies. The first cognizant thought was that he was in bed with a white woman. Opportunity and lust aside, Maron Connelly would not have been his first choice to have a fling with. David knew that she understood that and wasn't offended. But it was painfully ironic to David that Kel was right when he'd told him what he needed was a woman. True, he needed the release of sexual tension, but he really wanted something more.

His thoughts shifted to that look on Gayla Patton's face at the benefit dinner a few hours before. David wondered what she had been thinking when she'd recognized him. And . . . why hadn't they acknowledged each other? Had Gayla seen and known who he was with?

Carefully, David tried to ease Maron off his chest and onto the bedding. She twisted against him.

"Maron, I have to go."

She protested. "You're kidding," she croaked, trying to snuggle up to him, her long pale limbs contrasting against the brown of his skin. "For God's sake, it's the middle of the night. You're not going to tell me there's someone waiting at home, are you? I'm going to be pissed off if you do."

He let her have her way as she crawled back into position, her small breasts flattened against him. Her groin sensuously rubbing on his. David gritted his teeth and tried to fight the inexorable rising of his flesh.

"There is. My cat."

It was a moment before Maron responded by lifting her head. Her features were completely veiled in sleep, and she squinted open her eyes to blink at him. "Your cat," she said flatly, as if it was something unknown to her. "Your cat." She sputtered and started laughing, collapsing on David in girlish giggles. "That is so . . . so sweet," Maron laughed merrily.

He felt foolish. "He needs to be fed. I didn't expect to be out all night."

"Well, I did." She looked at him again, sweeping her hair from her face and gazing at David with drowsy amusement. "I can't believe you're thinking of leaving while you're in bed with a naked woman who's willing and ready. I can't decide if your concern for your pet is absurd or endearing." She slid off his body and lay next to David with her head cradled on his shoulder. "Or maybe it's me? Look . . . I was raised in a very liberal household. No holds barred. No propaganda. My dad taught me that people are people are people." She tilted her head to gaze seductively at him with her hazel eyes, stroking a finger around his stiff male nipple. "A man is a man is a man . . ."

Why look a gift horse in the mouth? David asked himself. Why deny that he hadn't exactly tossed her out of bed . . . even though it was her bed. Or that kissing and caressing her had certainly done it for him. Eyes closed, it made no difference, did it. A woman was a woman was a woman.

Maron kissed his jaw, working her way to his mouth. "What's your cat's name?"

David sighed, stroking her arm. His penis was already hard and sandwiched between their bodies. Even *that* was stimulating. Idly his fingers moved to her breasts and stomach. "Tut. King Tut.".

She chuckled in appreciation. "Cute. You have a sense of humor, too. Listen . . ." She licked around the shell of his ear. Her cool hand slid down his chest. "Your cat will wait another hour or so to get food. It has nine lives. You don't."

David couldn't help laughing softly. He was having fun.

But he frowned as guilt rolled in, and memory blanketed him. This was reckless. He was being foolish. And then Maron touched him, wrapping her hand gently around his already stiffened penis and working it with an expertise that made David hold his breath. He felt like fireworks were going off in his body. Man . . . he needed it, *bad*.

"Wasn't it good for you?" Maron teased in a little-girl voice.

David let the long-held groan out and let her have her way. Letting her stroke him until he could feel the building force of the explosion. Then he rotated his body to lie on hers, her arms welcoming and holding him, her kiss demanding and bold and sweet. Maron held him off briefly in a silent reminder to protect them both. David obliged with a rubber. She opened her legs, and he had no trouble thrusting into the warm and wet sheathing of her body.

The lift of her pelvis urged him into the cadence of intercourse. He didn't need a second prompting. He didn't want to stop.

It had been a *very* long time.

But it was just like riding a bicycle.

Chapter Eleven

He stared at the building entrance, afraid to even blink. He didn't want to risk missing anything.

There were more people leaving now, for school or work, than when he'd arrived an hour earlier. That had been at 6:30 A.M. In the meantime, dawn had become an overcast spring morning. Easter was just a week away. It was warmer than he'd expected, but Graham sat in the driver's seat of the Trooper 4X4 with the windows up. The tinted glass hid him.

Graham had long ago accepted that he'd blown his chances with Gayla forever. Seeing her the other day had confirmed that. He had been sincere when he'd told her he wanted her for a friend. But it was probably too late for that as well.

He checked the time. Almost seven-thirty. He had only a vague idea of what he was doing outside of Gayla's apartment building. It came to him on his drive back to Connecticut the last time he'd seen her. It had been gaining momentum ever since, until Graham could think of nothing else. He'd awaken in the middle of the night, going over the conversation with

Gayla, and her attitude toward him. Suddenly trying to recapture that summer before she'd left for school and he'd gotten married.

And she had a baby.

It had stunned him to realize how quickly Gayla had become involved with someone else. She had said she loved him. She had declared she'd never love anyone else. But *he* had been the one to betray her. So then why didn't it make sense to him?

Graham rubbed his eyes, wishing he'd thought to buy several cups of coffee. Maybe it was just as well, he thought caustically. He was so pumped up the caffeine might kill him. He hadn't been able to get back to sleep after awakening at a little after one in the morning. By four-thirty he'd gotten out of bed to sit in the darkened living room, gnawing over an idea that, the more he considered it, didn't seem so far-fetched. By five he was on the road heading for New York, and Harlem.

Graham was so tense that when the door to the building suddenly opened and Gayla stepped out, he accidentally pressed his car horn. But she paid no attention and didn't look at the green Trooper parked several doors down from where she stood. He again felt real regret at how things had turned out between them.

Gayla was dressed in jeans and sweater, and had an armload of clothing for the dry cleaners. And she was alone. But she just stood in front of her building glancing down the street to her left, as if waiting for something or someone. Graham reached for the door handle and prepared to get out. But Gayla looked behind her as the door opened again and a tall adolescent girl came out. Gayla turned to her in conversation.

Allison . . .

Gayla reached out to brush something from the girl's shoulder, who listened and nodded in response. Graham saw that she was dressed like most teens her age, but Gayla's influence was evident. He squinted at a pendant she wore around her neck. Silver, although he couldn't tell the shape at this distance. Graham found himself leaning forward, pressing against the glass to see better, but no longer daring to get out of the car.

Allison . . .

She was tall and thin. All long legs, neck and arms. She was as tall as her mother. But the daughter was lighter in skin tone, her features fine and delicate. She had an abundance of hair that, around her temples and ears, was almost blonde. Graham's view was suddenly obstructed when a yellow school bus churned to a stop between himself and the mother and daughter on the sidewalk. It only took fifteen seconds, but when the bus pulled away only Gayla stood there, watching as the bus drove away. Then she turned in the opposite direction to run her errand.

Graham felt his stomach muscles contract and twist. He suddenly felt too hot, as if he could suffocate. His mouth went dry, and he was unable to move. His body felt like a leaden weight. He closed his eyes on a grimace and passed a shaky hand over his forehead.

"Sweet Jesus . . ." he groaned.

"Have you told Allison?"

Gayla finished basting the ham and repositioned the foil over it. For a moment she didn't know what her mother was talking about. There seemed to be so much that she'd kept from her daughter. There was not sharing with her David's relationship to the family. Not telling her about Graham. Either one had the potential to make Allison angry. Or to hurt her deeply.

"No."

Sylvia finished layering the last of the sweet potatoes in a baking dish, and sprinkled brown sugar generously over the top. "Why not?"

"Because I haven't gotten around to it. Between school and after-school things and my work schedule . . ."

Gayla didn't finish the sentence, and Sylvia waited her out. "Those are excuses. They don't have to do with anything, Gayla. How long does it take to tell your daughter that the man you've been seeing, that she seems to be crazy about, wants to marry you and be a stepfather to her?"

Gayla closed the oven door with more force than she intended. "I don't think you can just blurt that kind of thing out. I should sit down with Allison when she's not bopping all over the place and I'm not in the middle of so many things."

"Then it will never happen."

The two women turned and faced each other in Sylvia's tiny kitchen.

"There's a lot to consider. There's—"

"No, there isn't," Sylvia cut in. She assumed the position of motherly authority, one hand on her hip and the other waving in the air and pointing at her daughter for emphasis. "It's very simple. Either you love the man or you don't. Either you believe that he can make a good home for you and Ali, that you can be happy together . . . or you don't." Sylvia turned to fuss at something else on her cluttered countertop. "What you really mean is that you don't want to marry Bill Coleman."

"That's not what I said."

"You might as well. You sure don't sound happy that he asked you."

"Do you think I should marry him? Do you think he's the one for me?" Gayla asked her mother.

"Well . . ." Sylvia began. Her back was turned to Gayla, and she took a long time to respond. "Bill is a wonderful man."

"I know that. But that's not what I asked you."

"Nana, where did you put your albums?"

Allison appeared in the doorway, her hair loose and framing her face. She had on the current fashion of sweater and jeans that were not just oversized, but which looked like they belonged to someone else.

"They're in a box someplace. Look in my room."

"What albums is she talking about?" Gayla asked when Allison left them.

"The ones of you and Mitch when you were small."

Gayla grunted. "Goodness. I haven't seen those pictures in years. They should give Allison a good laugh."

"She's seen them before, but she never gets tired of looking at them. I was going to pack them away with some other stuff. What else is there to do?" Sylvia asked, looking around the kitchen where Sunday dinner was being prepared.

"How about some iced tea?"

"That's a good idea. And there's still time for a small casserole of macaroni and cheese."

The doorbell rang.

"That's probably Mitch. He said he would try and come over . . ." Sylvia said.

Gayla went to answer the door, passing through the living room, where Allison was kneeling on the floor absorbed in the photo album which was spread out before her on the coffee table. Beside it was a small dish of peanuts and a can of soda.

When Gayla unlocked the door and opened it, she found herself facing David Kinney. The surprise was, she wasn't surprised to see him. There was instead an odd sense of the familiar. Like an unexpected family member suddenly showing up and their presence is just taken for granted.

David, on the other hand, instantly wondered if somehow Gayla knew that he'd spent the night with Maron Connelly. Yet she smiled uncertainly.

"Hi," Gayla said.

"Hi. You're not going to ask what I'm doing here?" he couldn't help saying.

Gayla stood back for him to enter. "My mother invited you for dinner, I suppose."

"Actually she invited me last Sunday, but I couldn't make it." David kept his voice smooth, his expression bland, as if that would keep Gayla from detecting what he had been doing. And with whom.

"Who is it?" Allison asked, appearing behind her mother and peering over her shoulder.

"Hello, Allison."

Allison wrinkled her nose. "What are you doing here?"

David stepped through the door. "Visiting your grandmother. Is that okay?"

Gayla looked at her daughter, waiting for her to answer. She seemed nonplused by David's asking permission. But so was Gayla.

Allison looked down at her stocking feet, wiggling her toes against the wooden floor of the foyer. With her head lowered she shrugged. "I guess so."

"Thank you. I appreciate that," David said.

Gayla glanced at him sharply but realized that he wasn't being sarcastic. As she closed the door and Allison went back to the living room, she noticed that David was holding a bundle of purple irises partially behind his back.

"How pretty."

David brought them forward. "They're for Sylvia."

"That's very thoughtful. She'll love them. She's in

the kitchen," Gayla informed him, and David followed her.

Sylvia looked up when the two of them came into the kitchen. "David! I'm so glad to see you . . ." She held out her cheek for him to kiss her.

"I'm a week late."

"You know very well you're welcome to come to my house anytime you want. This will always be your second home."

Gayla went back to her chores, although she was listening. Her mother and David Kinney had a very comfortable relationship. She felt proud that what her mother had been able to give to him he obviously held with great respect and love in his heart.

"These are for you. Better get them into water," David said, giving the wrapped bouquet to Sylvia.

"Oh, David. You didn't have to do this." Sylvia accepted the flowers, and kissed him in thanks.

"Here, Mom . . ." Gayla passed her mother a cut-glass vase from the top shelf of one of the cabinets.

"I'm going to put these right in the center of the dining table."

"Anything I can do to help?"

"Not really . . ."

"Yes," Gayla countered. David looked askance at her. "You can set the table . . . and maybe keep Allison company."

He nodded. "Okay."

Once Gayla had pointed out where to find flatware, napkins and the good china, David left the two women. In the living room he found what was needed in a hutch and sideboard. Allison ignored his presence.

"Allison, I could use your help. Just for a minute, if you don't mind."

"What for?" she asked suspiciously, glaring at him from her seat on the floor.

"I need to move the table away from the wall, and I'm not sure where everything goes on the table. I don't want to mess up."

Allison considered the request for a moment. Unable to find a reason to refuse and not raised to be completely thoughtless, she grudgingly stood up and came to the table. Together they repositioned it, and she helped spread the tablecloth. That was all he'd intended. But without further bidding Allison helped with the rest of the place settings. Once David caught her staring at him. She quickly finished her part and returned to her album.

When David himself was finished, he came and sat on the sofa. The TV was on to a tennis match, and he watched for a minute.

"You like tennis, I see."

"Mmmm hmmm," she murmured.

"Do you play?"

She slowly turned another page in the glossy album, her concentration focused on the fading images. "I was state champion for my age group last year," Allison said offhandedly.

David was impressed. "Outstanding. Then you're really good."

"I'm going to the regionals next month with my school team," Allison boasted.

David smiled to himself. She had a healthy ego. Lots of confidence. "Are you interested in going pro?"

She gave him a hesitant glance, her head tilted on the side. "I'm not sure."

"It's a tough life. But it could make you rich and famous. Your mother will have to come to you for an allowance. She better not make you mad."

Allison fought it, but she broke into giggles.

"When I was growing up tennis was not the game of choice."

"Basketball or baseball," Allison said assuredly. "That's what the boys I know all play."

"No, that wasn't it for me. Swimming was my thing." She looked at him, processing the information and trying to fit it with the opinion she'd already formed about him. "Do you swim?" he asked.

Allison averted her gaze. "Yeah, but I'm not that good. Besides, I don't like getting my hair wet."

David nodded, glancing at her slightly crinkly-textured hair with its light brown and blonde highlights. It was not a Patton characteristic. He sat forward, pointing to the album in front of her.

"What are you looking at?"

"Nana's album."

"Oh, yeah? Anybody in there I know?"

Allison shrugged. "It's family, mostly, but I don't know all the people."

David slid across the sofa until he was seated adjacent to Allison. He took the liberty of turning the opened album a little in his direction. "Let me see . . ."

For several pages David just scanned the images. It was, as Allison said, mostly her family. Pictures of Sylvia with Gayla and Mitch as very small children. Mitch, a shy little boy with a finger in his mouth and staying close to his mother. Gayla, bright and forward, with a gap-toothed grin as she posed for the camera.

"Your mom looks funny without her two front teeth," David commented.

Again Allison giggled. She leaned over the page, her eyes following the movement of David's finger as he pointed at the faces. "The clothes are so wack."

He hid his smile at her slang. "Your children are going to say the same thing about you twenty years from now."

Allison shook her head. "I'm not going to have kids. I don't want to get married."

"How old are you?" David asked her.

"Thirteen."

"You'll change your mind."

"No, I won't," Allison said firmly. Then she frowned and looked at him. "How do you know?"

"Because you'll grow up to become smart, beautiful and talented, and you'll meet a guy who'll think he can't live without you and who'll make your heart flip around in your chest. You'll think he's handsome, smart and talented and want to have his children. That's who love works."

Allison made a face filled with doubt and embarrassment. "I don't think so."

"Wanna bet?"

She shook her head, but bent over the album in retreat. "Have you ever been married?"

"No."

She looked slyly at him from beneath her long lashes. "Do you have any kids?"

He shook his head. "No. I didn't have much to offer a wife for a long time. But it doesn't mean I don't want a family." David considered his next thought, pausing as he weighed the risks of voicing it. "I envy your mom."

"How come?"

"Because she has a family, a satisfying career . . . and a beautiful, smart daughter. That's the whole deal. You're very lucky, Allison."

She didn't seem to know what to say to that, so she opted to remain silent and return her attention to the photographs. Together they looked through the rest of the album. They came to a page near the back of the collection. The picture wasn't well focused or composed, but it showed Sylvia with a tall, skinny black teenager who stared unsmiling and indifferent into the camera. David pointed.

"Do you know who that is?" he asked. Allison leaned closer to see but only shook her head. "That's me."

"For real?" She quickly looked back and forth between the page and David. "It doesn't look like you."

"No." David agreed. "I didn't have a beard, for one thing."

Her laugh this time was distracted. "Let me see . . ." She turned the album fully to her and spent long moments closely examining the details.

David half-expected Allison to make an impertinent adolescent response. The kind meant to keep him at a safe distance. The kind she'd been giving him ever since they met. He watched the thoughtful expression on her face, fascinated and awed that Gayla had produced this child.

"Nana said that she raised you," Allison began quietly.

"In a way, she did. Did she tell you she took me in to live with your mother and Uncle Mitch?" Allison nodded. "Did she tell you why?"

"She said because your mother had died. Is that true?"

"Yes."

"Was your mother sick?"

David heard an agonizing strangled scream in his head. He didn't flinch helplessly from it as he had for years after what happened. "No. She was killed."

Allison's eyes grew round. "Really?" she breathed. "Did . . . did you see it happen?"

"Yes, I did." He spared her and himself the details. "Sylvia was a friend of my mother's. She's been good to me. She kept me from doing some pretty stupid things when I was young."

Allison frowned at the photo again and then at

David. "Well, how come I never heard of you before? How come you never came to see Nana until now?"

David sighed. He realized that he had the opportunity to say any number of things to Allison to put her at ease. He could put the best possible spin on his history because no one knew it better than he did. But he remembered being thirteen when no one took him seriously, and he couldn't talk about the pain and fear he lived with, and he felt alone and angry. He would have loved to have been where Allison was right now. Secure in her world and surrounded by love. But when all was said and done he still had to deal with the truth. It was the only defense he had.

"I've been living someplace else for about ten years. Before that . . . I was in jail."

Gayla looked out of the kitchen and into the living room. She was rather surprised to see her daughter sitting on the floor next to David, riveted to whatever he was saying. He was earnest, gesturing with his hands for emphasis. As if what he had to say was important and he wanted her to understand.

"It sure is quiet in there," Sylvia said. "What are they doing?"

"Talking," Gayla responded, turning to her mother. "I wonder what they're talking about."

Sylvia smiled peacefully, unconcerned and trustful. "I don't think it matters."

David turned off the engine but continued to sit in the dark car and stare out into the night. He needed a private space to himself for a few minutes, and didn't immediately get out to go to his building. It was only eight o'clock in the evening, and Kel was probably still in the apartment before heading out for his usual late-night prowl. He had to admit that Kel seemed to work at not getting in the way, not being around all the time. But the smaller confined space of the car also allowed David time and quiet for recalling the evening at Sylvia Patton's. More important to him, however, was the end of the evening.

He had driven Gayla and Allison home afterward, but David didn't think Gayla's good night and thank-you to him had much to do with the offer of a ride. Perhaps it was her sincerity. And the smile of understanding when, even after the shared moments at Sylvia's, Allison had still gotten out of the car without so much as a good night.

"I'm sorry," Gayla apologized. "I don't know what's wrong with Allison. She's never this rude."

"She's not being rude," David said. "She's just expressing her feelings the only way she knows how."

"For what? David . . ." Gayla said in exasperation. "My daughter doesn't seem to like you, and I can't understand why."

He considered Gayla carefully, enjoying her bewilderment; she was so different from the adolescent who·had been so quick on the draw. "It's not that she doesn't like me. It's that she's unsure of me."

"I don't know what that means," Gayla said in confusion.

"It means that she doesn't want anything to

change. She's very comfortable with her life the way it is."

"Well, what does that have to do with you?"

"Maybe Allison thinks I could change things."

"That's silly. I don't see how."

"Right. So don't worry about it. She'll come around."

Gayla had watched through the windshield as Allison had reached their building, letting herself in but not starting upstairs on the elevator. Instead, she sat in a lobby chair until her mother joined her.

Gayla turned to David. "I hope she didn't pick that up from me."

"What?"

"Walking away and not dealing fairly with things that . . . bother me. Not listening."

He raised his brows in innocent inquiry. "You do that?"

Gayla laughed. "Come on. I was a little bitch when I was her age. I was mean to you."

David shook his head. "Things were different then."

"It didn't bother you?"

He looked at her. "Yeah, it bothered me."

Gayla blinked, trying to interpret the look in his eyes. She shifted her gaze to the sight of Allison inside the building. "I'm glad you came to dinner."

David kept his expression pleasant. "Thanks."

"I mean it. Anyway, I've been meaning to call you." Gayla looked thoughtful, and a little bit nervous.

"Did I sell another piece?"

She smiled absently and shook her head. "Not this week. I . . . wanted to apologize for the way I acted when we were in D.C. You were really nice and patient about what happened. I wasn't very grateful. And . . ." She sighed as if what she had to say next was hard. "I'm sorry that I never tried to understand how bad things were for you years ago."

David shifted in his seat toward her. "You know . . . you and I can go on all night apologizing and confessing and beating our chests. I guess the list is kind of long about what we did or said to each other. But it's probably not nearly as bad as what we did to ourselves. Listen, Gay . . . I made some really bad decisions when I was young. I'm really glad I didn't destroy myself before I wised up and saw that I was my own worst enemy. I can't blame anyone for what happened to me."

Gayla looked at her hands clasped in her lap. "I know. I guess I made bad decisions, too. Didn't I?"

"If you're talking about Allison, you know I can't speak on that," he said quietly. "Looks like you did fine. Everything worked out, didn't it? You have her."

"Thank you," Gayla said, putting her hand unconsciously on his arm.

"Why are you thanking me?" he asked.

Gayla shrugged in an almost shy gesture. "For being patient and open with Allison. Like I said, I don't think she's been very friendly."

"Man," he murmured. "Sorry. Thank you. All in one night. I wonder what's coming next?"

"Who knows?" Gayla whispered before finally getting out of the car and hurrying to her waiting daughter . . .

Who knows?

David's imagination was running away from him. The very question laid the groundwork for any number of possibilities to come to mind. Including several he could resurrect from years earlier. Fantasies. The what-if kind.

David finally got out of the car and locked it. He was pensive, but he also felt an unfamiliar surge of hope. About himself, and for his future. Having let the clouds of the past burn away, he could now turn to creating real dreams and perhaps making them a reality.

Chapter Twelve

———∞∞∞———

David slowly approached the restaurant and stood so that he couldn't be seen. He watched Gayla through the window where she was seated at a small table just on the other side. He had seen her many times since he'd returned to New York, but never like this, from a distance, unguarded and open.

Gayla had always been different from the girls and women he'd known. From the start he had not understood her. He'd thought she was stuck-up and put herself above him. He had to grow up and see her again to realize that unlike himself, Gayla had been given enough love to be secure in herself. What he had seen as conceit was really self-esteem.

David suddenly recalled the afternoon at the Whelan summer house . . . the last time he or Gayla and Mitchell would ever visit there . . . and he'd found her crying in the gardening shed just off the kitchen in the back of the house. Actually, David remembered that he'd followed her there. It was not like the time, three years earlier, when she'd had the attack that, as it turned out, was related to sickle cell.

This was about something else, and he had his own guesses as to what.

He could hear her sobbing as he approached the shed. The wrenching sound brought a flashback of seeing his mother on the floor at his feet, already dead from her wounds and knowing he would never be able to speak to her again. He stood pacing outside the door, agitated. Then he knocked on the door and slowly opened it.

Gayla jumped and turned around to face him, her face wet and distorted. But instead of telling him to go away and mind his own business, she stared at him before dissolving into tears again.

"Hey . . . someone's going to hear you," he warned uncomfortably.

"I . . . don't care."

"What are you crying for? 'Cause they're going to sell the house? 'Cause Mr. Whelen is on Reilly's case again? They do that all the time. 'Cause Graham is getting married?"

"Shut up . . ." she moaned.

"You're going away in September anyhow. I know you like it up here but . . ."

"Will you please shut up!" she screamed.

And then her face changed with a wide-eyed look of stunned surprise. She gasped and suddenly coughed as she bent over. David grabbed the nearest thing at hand, a clay flowerpot, and shoved it under her face. She began to vomit, the violent contractions cutting off her tears until the purging ended. Weakened, she covered her mouth and leaned against the shed wall. He touched her shoulder, awkwardly trying to comfort her by rubbing it. Then he found himself urging Gayla away from the wall, and she transferred her weight against his side, her head tilted onto his chest.

It had been an extraordinary moment for him. He'd forgotten that he was comforting Gayla and began to draw a kind of comfort from her—a healing—for himself. It didn't last very long. She was still crying. Quietly now. She gazed up at him, her eyes watery, pleading and confused. David couldn't remember how long they stayed together like that. Longer than was wise. Then Gayla stood up, gently pushing him away. She walked out of the shed with one arm across her stomach and the other hand wiping her face as she slowly headed away from the house, aimlessly down the footpath leading into the woods. He let her go.

David realized now the experience had been the beginning of a rebirth. Not that it mattered in the next few years of his life. But it had given him one of several reasons to change.

He entered the restaurant, and Gayla glanced up at his approach. She smiled as she watched him pull out his chair and sit opposite her.

"Sorry I'm late." He placed a large black book on the floor next to his knapsack.

She pointed, curious. "Is that your sketchbook?"

"Yeah. I was up at Fort Tryon Park and the Cloisters this morning."

Gayla regarded him closely, her smile warm and her eyes bright.

David chuckled. "I know what you're thinking. You've come a long way, baby."

"You're right. But don't say it like it's funny."

He inclined his head in thanks. "What about you? Surprised?"

She drank from her water glass, looking at him over the rim. "I don't think so. I think you always had it in you, as my mother would say. Can I see what you've done?" she asked, holding out her hand.

David reached for the black book and passed it to her over the table. Gayla balanced the book against the edge of the table and her lap. She appraised each page, occasionally stopping longer over one drawing or another. Occasionally raising her brows, or pursing her lips. Once smiling in pleasure.

"What do you think?"

She closed the book and handed it back. "I think they're good."

"I wonder if Allison would say so."

Gayla chuckled. "Allison only knows if she thinks a picture is pretty. She doesn't necessarily know or understand what makes it good." She shook her head in reflection. "It's amazing, you know? I wanted desperately to become an artist. Emily Whelan was a great influence. I had all those classes at the museum and studied at a special high school . . ."

"While I ran wild in the streets . . ."

"And became the real thing."

He frowned, skeptical. "I don't know . . ."

"David . . ." She reached across the table to touch his arm. "You're very good. Just say thank you."

He turned his hand over to grab hers. "Thank you."

They sat like that, looking at one another.

"Did you ever believe that we would one day sit across from each other without lobbing hand grenades and cursing each other out?"

His grin was lopsided. "No. But I did hope."

It took a second for the admission to sink in. Gayla's smile didn't waver, but her gaze was uncertain. She quickly tried to interpret David's meaning. Whatever conclusion she came to made her withdraw shyly, and she pulled her hand free of his.

"I was surprised when you suggested lunch," he said smoothly, stepping right over the momentary awkwardness.

Gayla sighed in relief. "Yes, well . . . I have something for you. Lunch is my treat. It's kind of a congratulations." She picked up her purse and pulled an envelope from inside. She held it out to David.

He accepted it and silently opened it. It was a check from the gallery in the amount of nearly ten thousand dollars. He kept reading his name, the amount. Counting the zeros. "I sold that much?"

Gayla nodded, pleased with his modest response. "You sure did. We've only had one other artist who ever did as well, but she was known in the art community already. What are you going to do with it?"

"Pay off some bills," David said wryly, folding the envelope and sticking it inside his knapsack.

"Well, here's to more of where that came from."
Gayla lifted her water glass to toast him. Their
glasses gently clinked, and they laughed at the simplicity of the celebration.

"I guess this should be champagne. And I should
be taking you to lunch for taking a chance on me.
Order the filet mignon."

Gayla shook her head. "I don't eat meat. I'm a
vegetarian."

He nodded, not even questioning her. "Strict diet.
For your sickle cell."

She was touched that he had remembered. Even
Bill had to be reminded for several months what her
restrictions were.

"Then one day I have to take you for the best,
most expensive plate of asparagus we can find."

Gayla laughed. They gave their orders to the
waiter. "You know, the show closes out in another
two weeks. What are you going to do then?"

David shrugged. "I have no idea."

"What are your options?"

"Not many. I could go back upstate. I have a small
house there . . ."

"Really . . ."

"It's not much, but it's mine. I thought about staying here, but I don't know what kind of work I
could get."

"What about going back to what you were doing
before? Teaching, right?"

"I had a one-year renewable contract to teach at a

youth-detention facility. But it didn't pay very much. I wasn't sure I'd go back."

"I heard about a position at an organization here in the city. They're looking for someone to act as a kind of community liaison to arts programs."

David shook his head. "I wouldn't be good at that. You want someone outgoing who can talk a lot and be persuasive."

"You teach. It's the same thing."

"Yeah . . . but I can get a student to listen to me. Grown-ups are more difficult. You always have to prove something."

"You know . . . it's true. Well, maybe you can get a teaching job here."

"Maybe."

"I can give you a great recommendation."

He stared at her thoughtfully. "You'd be willing to do that?"

"Of course."

"Of course," he repeated with a touch of irony. As if another kind of history hadn't existed between them that had taken years to overcome. He shifted uncomfortably in his chair. "I . . . want to thank you, Gay. There has been a lot of stuff between us. I didn't think it was ever going to change. I appreciate that you've been . . . fair."

She pursed her mouth. "It takes a long time to grow up," she said quietly. "And I've learned that I don't know as much as I think I do." She hesitated, blinking with a kind of vulnerability. "I really want to thank you, too. For proving me so wrong."

* * *

David half-expected Kel to be in the apartment when he arrived, but it was empty. David had to admit that Kel, for the most part, tried very hard to keep to himself. Not that they didn't have nights of sitting and talking, and sometimes going out for drinks. But Kel was always running into people he knew, or was constantly cruising the women. At least twice David had come home alone while Kel had taken some attractive female up on her offer for the evening. It had become clear to David that he and Kel had little in common anymore. The past that they'd once shared was not enough.

He was surprised when King Tut did not immediately greet him. David gave a whistling signal for the cat and he received a soft meow from behind the sofa. Tut appeared from the space, dragging a length of cloth with him. He struggled and shook his hind paw, trying to loosen the item from his claws.

"What have you got there?" David murmured to the cat. He lifted the animal to the sofa, and carefully unhooked him from what turned out to be a shirt. "Now you know you're messing with the wrong thing. Kel will fry your fur if he catches you," David warned the cat.

He looked around the sides of the sofa for a box or bag belonging to Kel that the shirt might have come from. But all of Kel's things were neatly stored against a wall, with nothing showing an opening that the animal might have gotten into. David was about to just fold the shirt and leave it on the sofa bed for

Kel to find later, when he noticed another object just visible beneath the sofa. David tried to pull it free, but resistance told him it was caught or attached to something else. He craned his neck to peek behind the sofa, and finally grabbed the bottom of the frame and lifted the end of the sofa away from the wall.

For a moment he frowned at the two boxes, not remembering having stored anything behind the unit. But there was also a black canvas bag which David knew wasn't his. The trailing cloth was coming out of the top of the partially unzipped bag. David stared at it, knowing he had two choices. He could just leave everything as it was and return the one shirt to Kel with an explanation of Tut's caprice, or he could listen to the sudden alarm that went off with the recognition that these things had been deliberately hidden from sight. He made the decision instantly and squatted down to open the bag completely.

David lifted out the rest of a shirt and beneath that a towel. But packed in the cavity of the bag was piled jewelry, credit cards and a considerable amount of cash. He gently shook the bag to shift aside some of the contents, and spotted the handle of an automatic pistol. David stared at the gun for a long moment. He knew better than to touch it, and felt dread and anger because of what it meant.

He reached to open the two closed boxes, and did change his mind. He could guess what was stashed in them, but he was going to make Kel tell him instead. For a moment David thought of putting everything back and pretending that he'd never seen anything. But he knew that was no longer an option. He was going to be forced to do something he'd been avoiding.

David had just finished closing the bag when he heard the key being inserted in the front door. He stood up and walked to the hallway, watching as the door was opened and Kel walked in.

"Hey, bro," Kel called out in his usual carefree manner. "I didn't think you'd be back so early."

"I'm surprised to see you, too," David said, as Kel walked toward him.

"I'm going back out. I gotta change."

"Have a date?" David asked when Kel was almost in front of him.

Kel laughed. "Yeah . . . if that's what you want to call it. I met this sister . . ."

He stopped right in front of David, but got distracted by the displacement of the sofa, and the presence of the two boxes and the bag behind it. David watched Kel's face closely as it first registered shock, and then cool unaffected acceptance. Kel shook his head in disbelief. He looked at David as if offended.

"Yo, man. You been going through my things?"

"Not exactly. The cat got into one of the bags and got tangled in a shirt or something. I was going to put it back and I came across those."

David handed the one shirt to Kel, who reluctantly took it. He marched over to the sofa and bent down to look at the boxes. For all intents and purposes nothing looked disturbed. David had even left the canvas bag half-zippered, in case that had been planned by Kel as a checking measure for anyone's interference. Kel glanced sharply at David, trying to read his expression. Unable to, Kel relaxed with an irreverent grin.

"Thanks, man. I'm glad you got to your cat before I did. I might have drowned his ass in the toilet."

Although Kel chuckled at his own threat David knew it was not an idle one. He kept his gaze on Kel. He turned to face his friend, knowing that there was no help for it but that they were going to square off.

David took two slow steps closer to him. He had to get into Kel's space, right into his face so there was no mistake about his meaning. "I don't want to know what you're up to, Kel. I don't want to know where your money is coming from. But I want you to tell me you're not putting my ass on the line along with yours."

Kel fingered the shirt in his hand as he stared at David. He lifted his shoulders. "You know me better than that, man. Homey don't play that game. Not with my boys, know what I'm saying?"

"I hear you, man. I don't know if I can trust you."

Kel's jaw tightened. He lost his relaxed stance and stood tall. He'd never been afraid of anyone in his life, and that included his friends. "If I tell you everything is cool you can take that to the bank. I'm better than Allstate," he boasted.

David's objective was not to try and stare Kel down to see who would blink first. It was to look into the heart of his childhood friend and see if the person he'd always known was still there.

"Are you strapped?" he asked bluntly.

Kel lifted his hands in surrender and shook his head. "Hey. You want to check me out?"

David had his answer.

He kept his attention on Kel and jerked his head in the direction of the sofa. "What's in the boxes?"

"You didn't look?"

"Do I have to?"

Kel slowly grinned, his expression a conning leer as he sized up the situation. In order to keep pace with him and protect himself, David knew he had to take on that old role of thinking like a hood. He knew how to play. His life could depend on it.

"I told you, man. I hooked up with some brothers and we're doing business."

"Out of a truck. Hauling," David said with obvious skepticism.

"Yeah, that's right," Kel maintained, his smile challenging David to say otherwise.

But already David could see Kel taking the offensive position. After just five minutes they stood facing each other as potential enemies. Kel stood with his legs akimbo, his jacket open and his arms relaxed at his side. His hands were opened, the fingers flexing a little. Slowly David put up his hand in front of Kel and looked at him squarely.

"I'm not going to let you fuck up my life, Kel. I'm not going down."

"So what are you saying? I played you? You not

going to take my word?" Kel suddenly jabbed his finger at David. His face twisted into a malevolent scowl. "I saved your fuckin' ass, Dak! You'd be dead meat if it wasn't for me."

"I appreciate that." David nodded smoothly. "But that was a long time ago." Again he pointed at the sofa. "I need to know what you've been hiding in my home." His voice was hard with purpose and fearlessness.

Kel just stared at him, leaving the next move up to David. The silence stretched. It was finally broken by the soft tentative meow from the cat, as if he could sense the tension between the two men. It was no longer possible for David to back down.

"Shut the fuck up!" Kel yelled at the cat.

David knew the animal was on top of the bookcase. The only place it felt safe when Kel was in the apartment, because it wasn't easily reached. David was the first to break eye contact. He turned to the boxes, reaching for the opening on the first one.

"Back off, man. I'm tellin' you," Kel thundered.

"So it all comes down to this, Kel? You and me over a bunch of stolen goods?"

Kel grabbed for David's arms from behind. But David gripped the box flaps and pulled them open. The box was packed with plastic-wrap bundles of a white powdery substance, small vials and Baggies with other drugs.

"Get off my stuff!"

Like a kid who was protecting his toys, David thought. The image jarred him because Kel had always been someone who was selfish, egocentric, remorseless and a bully. He tried to pull away from Kel and they struggled. The contents of the box spilled onto the sofa and floor. Kel tried to swing him to the floor as well, but David held his balance as they bumped into furniture and knocked things over. The bookcase rocked back and forth precariously. With a wild scream of fright, King Tut leaped away. He landed on Kel's arm, his front claws digging through the jacket and tearing into the skin. The cat's hind legs dangled as he swung back and forth, unable to get his claws free.

Kel growled, cursing violently at the animal as he grabbed it ruthlessly by the neck and pulled it away with a jerk. Without hesitation he flung the terrified animal aside. Again Tut bellowed and hit the floor with a thump. He quickly righted himself and scurried away into the kitchen to crouch next to the refrigerator, meowing plaintively.

David stumbled to his knees. He twisted around, grabbing Kel around the thighs. Throwing his body weight forward, David toppled them both to the floor. Kel was hampered by his long coat and for a moment David had the advantage. Kel pounded on his back with his clasped hands but David retaliated by thrusting his arms upward to break the hold. With his fist he slammed Kel in the side of the head. Kel got in a blind punch to David's face, catching him on his left cheek.

And then Kel tried to get his hand inside the loose coat, and David had to switch his tactics to stop him.

But Kel had had lots of practice in the art of dirty fighting. He hadn't survived this long without being able to protect himself when he had to. The gun came free in Kel's hand and David grabbed his wrist to keep the gun pointed away from his head. He brought up a knee and pushed it forcefully into Kel's groin to hold him still. But Kel was heavier and had more power behind him. He forced his way up and rolled David onto his back on the floor. David held tight to the gun hand, however, forcing the muzzle into the air.

They grunted and struggled for breath.

Someone began banging on the door. "What the hell is going on in there? Quiet down, will ya? Before I call the cops!"

Kel had David pressed flat on the floor. They glared at each other. It was a fight for life, but David wasn't going to let it be a fight to the finish. For sure he'd lose everything then, no matter what the outcome.

"You . . . you have . . . a choice," David gasped. "You can . . . use this on on me or . . . you can . . . take your shit and . . . get the hell out. No pursuit. No . . . cops." Abruptly he gave up struggling with Kel. He let go of Kel's arm and raised his own above his head. He stared Kel down.

Kel, still wildly enraged, cocked the gun and stuck the muzzle against David's throat. He labored for breath too, baring his teeth. "Mother fucka!" he grunted.

David lay still. "Your call, Kel."

Kel's hand was rigid, his finger on the trigger. In

another moment he lifted the gun and eased off the ready. He stumbled up from the floor, staring down at David. He put his gun away and, without saying a word to David, began throwing his things together.

David got up, wiping his face. His nose was bloody. He watched closely as Kel packed his belongings, tying or taping the boxes and stacking them against the wall in the foyer. He didn't ask him where he was going, or if he had another place to stay. Weighing on his mind was the clear memory of Kel protecting him from a trio of rival gang members. They hadn't set a trap for him, but had simply lain in wait until he walked unknowingly in harm's way. They'd wanted revenge for the police raid on their crib which had collared five of their members and resulted in a shoot-out with a sixth because an informant had passed information.

David knew it wasn't him, but that wasn't going to save him as the three jumped him on a stairwell and pounded him. Caught by surprise, David's one thought was to avoid getting shot or stabbed. But the three seemed to want to beat him until he was helpless and defeated first. Maim him and leave their mark. Then they would have killed him. It never came to that. Suddenly Kel was there out of nowhere, throwing his body into the middle of the attack with backup from their crew.

How do you repay someone for saving your life? David only knew that Sylvia Patton had never asked him to. Kel wouldn't let him forget.

Kel stopped long enough to stand and face David.

His brow was wet from the exertion of the fight and hustling to get his things together . . . all his worldly possessions as far as David could tell.

"You're not coming from where I'm at anymore. You've gone . . . downtown," Kel muttered.

"And where are you, Kel? What's your agenda for the rest of your life? When do you just settle down, raise your kids, work at something that's real?"

Kel grinned. He wiped his brow with his forearm and placed his hands on his hips. "You call what you got real? You're living in a dump that's not yours with no furniture, nothing. You have some fucking cat for company. Now you're some goddamn so-called artist and you're too good for me. I saw you with that broad at the gallery. She the one you told me about who was stuck up and messing around with some white boy in the family her mother worked for? Didn't I hear at the time that her brother was a faggot in the making? Man . . . she got you pussy-whipped. You trying to prove you're good enough for her. She the one you said treated you like shit when you lived with her family. You're an ex-con. She not going to go down for you."

David didn't outwardly react other than to take a step closer to Kel. "Leave her out of it. You got a problem with what's happening right now, put it on me. I could have turned your ass away the first night I found you here. I owe you, Kel, but I'm not willing to give up my freedom again to prove I'm for real."

Kel grinned malevolently. "Can I use your phone?"

David nodded silently. He retreated to the other

side of the room. His mind went briefly to the cat, but couldn't take the time to hunt him out and see if he'd been hurt. Five minutes later Kel was finished with his call.

"I'll give you a hand getting those boxes downstairs . . ."

"I'm cool. I can do it."

David grabbed Kel's arm and got his attention. "Look. We've both said what we have to say and we've said enough, okay? I'll get these two boxes . . ."

With that David bent to lift the first of the boxes, moving to the door.

He and Kel didn't have much to say as they stood inside the entrance of the building waiting for Kel's ride. A van pulled up shortly, and Kel's things were quickly loaded and secured. The driver never got out and was never introduced to David. In a minute Kel and David were facing each other.

This was it. The end. There were not going to be any goodbyes.

"Now we're even. Right?" David asked clearly.

Kel's smile was cryptic. "We're even." He got into the van and it sped away.

David knew he'd made the only decision he could. There was more at stake than their friendship. In any case he had things on his mind Kel couldn't begin to relate to. Wanting to find a permanent place to live. Wanting to make a living. Wanting a family . . . kids. David had only the sketchiest idea how any of it was going to happen. The check from the gallery notwithstanding, he had no viable means of income. A letter from the center upstate where he'd taught the year before had arrived indicating they weren't going to renew his contract.

David returned to his apartment to look around. Kel was right. He was not in great shape.

Then he saw the envelope on the sofa. David picked it up and looked inside, already knowing what he'd find. He didn't have to count it to know it was not an insignificant amount of money. He stared at it, trying to determine if it was supposed to be a thank-you, a handout, a payoff. Or a setup.

Tut began to meow weakly from the kitchen, still frightened. David whispered soothingly and coaxed the skittish animal out into the open. He lifted Tut into his arms, comforting the stiff, scared cat.

"It's okay, old man. You left your mark." He sat on the sofa and the cat crouched next to his thigh, licking its fur.

David thoughtfully fingered the fat envelope and thought about the letter from the center. The check given him by Gayla was still in his bag. He thought about his mother and Sylvia; about all the people who had done what was best for him—including Emily Whelan, Maron . . . and Gayla—and those who had not. He listened to the silence of his apartment as he considered his future and what it might be. He casually tossed the envelope on the sofa, causing the cat to start.

David picked up the phone and dialed a number, beginning the final break from the past.

Chapter Thirteen

—∞∞∞—

Gayla heard the soft knocking on her open door, and glanced up from the report she was word processing on her desktop. A black man stood in her doorway, grinning at her for all the world as if they knew one another. She tried to place him, wondering if he was someone she'd met at the exhibit. He was dressed casually but expensively in obvious designer labels which struck her as being . . . adolescent.

"Good morning," he said brightly, with a charming smile.

Automatically Gayla returned the greeting, but waited for him to clarify the mystery of his identity.

He shook his head in understanding as he entered her office. "You don't remember me, do you? Dak's buddy. We met a couple of weeks ago at his place. Kel Monroe." He held out his hand across her desk.

"Oh, yes." Gayla's smile became genuine, and she shook his hand. "I'm sorry. I'm a bit distracted . . ."

"No apology necessary," Kel said, taking a seat.

Gayla was a little surprised by his forwardness. "Is . . . David with you?"

"No, no . . . I'm on my own. As a matter of fact, I don't see much of him these days. I think he's got, you know, a little side action going on," he said slyly and laughed.

Gayla continued to smile, but she found herself immediately thinking that David must have a girl-friend. She couldn't interpret her reaction just then to that possibility, but . . . Maron Connelly came briefly to mind.

"As a matter of fact I thought he might be here with you."

"Did you?" she murmured.

"Well . . . you two knowing each other almost all your lives and all . . . living in the same house."

Gayla's smile lost some of its warmth and was replaced by a growing sense of caution. "He . . . told you about that?"

Kel shifted comfortably in his chair, crossing an ankle over a knee. He was wearing two expensive gold rings. One had diamonds in it.

"Well, of course I knew that for about three years or so, after he got out of detention for trying to kill his stepfather, that a woman took him in. A friend of the family. That would be your mother, right? When he introduced us that time, I remembered. Said the girl was into art and hated his guts."

Gayla studied him. "Why are you telling me this?"

"No reason. Just making conversation. Dak cares a lot about your family."

"Thank you," she said, feeling like it was forced out of her.

"The brother owes me, you know. Big-time."

"Excuse me?" she asked, confused.

"He never told you? When they sent him upstate that time, after he left your family and went out on his own. He was in the wrong place at the wrong time when some stuff went down. He got pulled in with everyone else. Accessory after the fact. Accomplice. Aiding and abetting . . . all of that."

"What was your part in it?"

He grinned. "Let's just say I had information to set the record straight."

Her smile became thin. "You saved him, is that it?"

"So to speak. More than that I once saved his as— his life." Kel nodded. "He'd do the same for me."

"*If* you were innocent," Gayla felt the need to qualify.

"Of course."

"Well . . . this is all very interesting, but David hasn't told me anything about . . . his troubles. He seems to have gotten his act together."

"Looks like it." Kel shifted his gaze to the office in general. "Not the same old Dak, though. He's headed for the big time. Making legit money now."

She was careful, feeling the tightening of the muscles across the back of her neck like a warning. She was alert to Kel Monroe's innuendos, but couldn't figure out where he was headed. Gayla decided not to ask. "There's a lot of interest in him right now," was all she said.

Abruptly he became serious, watching her so intently that Gayla thought he could see right inside her.

"Does that include you?"

She blinked, incredulous. "What did you say?"

He shrugged. "I don't mean to be nosy or anything, but . . . living in the same house. Spending all that time together. You know . . . things happen."

She took her time answering, finally taking the offensive by merely smiling. "You *are* being nosy. I don't have anything to say about what happened in the past."

"What about now?" he persisted smoothly.

"What about . . . you saying goodbye and letting me get back to work? Which, I might point out, you don't seem to do much of. How do you support yourself? Or are you . . . independently wealthy?"

Kel howled with laughter. He slapped his thigh and shook his head. "Man! You got me. That was cold."

"You haven't answered the question," she reminded him.

"I got a few things going on. I'm a man of resources." He grinned.

"Look, this has been interesting, but I . . ."

He held up his hands and stood up. "I'm gone. Don't want to interrupt what you're doing."

"Why did you come here?" Gayla asked bluntly.

He pursed his mouth. "No reason. I was just in the neighborhood." He headed to the door. "Sightseeing. Scouting a bit. By the way . . . how's that beautiful daughter of yours?"

Unconsciously she rubbed her hands together. They were cold. "She's fine, thank you."

"Good, good. You take care now . . ." With that he was gone.

Gayla stared at the empty doorway. She wasn't sure if she should feel apprehensive or not. There was the question, of course, of Kel Monroe's motives for coming to see her like this, out of the blue. And how had he managed to get to her office without being detected? Teddy would have called her if he'd known someone wanted to see her. But all of that faded in comparison to his sudden interest in her life . . . and in Allison.

"You didn't enjoy the movie very much, did you?"

Gayla tried to smile reassuringly at Bill, but the truth was, she wasn't able to get into it. "I'm sorry. I was very distracted. And I was really looking forward to seeing that film, too."

Bill put his arm around her shoulder and drew her gently closer to his side as they walked away from the theater. "When you snap out of your funk, I'll take you again."

"Don't bother. I'll wait until it comes out on video."

He chuckled. "Then that's even better. We can watch it together from bed with popcorn and beer."

Gayla gazed off across the street, taking in the bright lights, noise, and both vehicular and pedestrian traffic on a Friday night. Lots of couples with plans for the evening, the coming summer . . . the rest of their lives. But for her, even watching a video some months from now seemed like too much of a commitment. Where would it lead? What if this was not what she wanted? What if . . .

"What is it about the idea that you don't like? The popcorn and beer? The in-bed part? Or all of the above with me?"

"I didn't think your suggestion required an answer," she said with a nervous laugh. "The video won't be out for a year. A lot can happen in a year. Let's not try to plan so far ahead."

She could feel Bill watching her. That intent stare he had when he was busy interpreting, reviewing and getting ready to respond to something she'd said. The lawyer in him probing for hidden meanings.

"I think you're taking my suggestion too seriously. Want to tell me what's on your mind? Is everything okay with Allison?"

Gayla shook her head impatiently. She didn't want to play twenty questions with Bill. He was already asking questions she didn't want to answer.

"Why don't we stop to get a drink or something before we head home?"

Home . . .

They maneuvered through the hordes of people milling about the Cineplex theater near Lincoln Center and made their way to a small café tucked off Columbus Avenue. The pre-theater diners had already gone and the restaurant was only half-filled with customers.

After being seated and given menus, Bill and Gayla were mostly silent until giving their orders for cappuccinos and one dessert to be shared.

"Did Allison get that information I sent her on those Thurgood Marshall cases? She said she had a special end-of-term report to do."

"Yes, thank you."

Bill reached across the table and took hold of her hand. He held it, stroking her fingers. "You know you don't have to thank me. That's what I'm supposed to do."

She frowned, shifting her hand slightly to end the stroking. "What do you mean?"

His smile was indulgent. "Taking care of business. Taking care of my woman and family. Like a husband should."

Gayla had so many thoughts and images rushing through her head at that moment that she felt almost dizzy and out of breath.

She thought of the difference between Bill and the men she'd ever fantasized into the role of husband and father. There was no question that he was better suited, more capable, willing and able. But she also factored into her consideration David Kinney, then and now. Horrified, Gayla realized that her thoughts had drifted to David. What if he was involved with a woman as Kel Monroe had hinted? So what?

She was embarrassed when Bill had to gently shake her hand to bring her attention back to the moment.

"I can see that idea didn't exactly bring stars to your eyes."

She laughed nervously and shrugged. "I . . . guess I was trying to see you in the role."

Their order arrived, and Bill held off on responding until after the waitress had left.

"Trying?" he questioned flatly.

She started to sip from the hot liquid, but changed her mind and put the cup down again. Gayla was afraid to look him in the eye.

"I want to marry you, Gay. I want to make plans for our future. I want to help raise Allison. And I want kids of my own . . . with you."

Gayla lifted her chin and looked squarely at Bill. His expression twisted her insides. "I know," she whispered.

"Look, you're not concerned about Sickle Cell Anemia, are you? You made it through with Allison with no problem. I'm not a carrier so we're safe."

"That isn't an issue with me," Gayla told him.

Bill spread his hands wide. "Does that mean yes . . . or no? Do you want to marry me or not?"

"It means . . . I . . . I'm still thinking about it." He was watching her again and Gayla felt besieged by his lawyer's stare.

"I don't understand what there is to think about," he said quietly.

"Then . . . I guess I'm just not sure. I'm sorry, Bill. But it seems like such a . . . a major decision. And I'm so used to being alone and taking care of myself and Allison, and . . . not having any other expectations. Marriage is such an upheaval in my life, in the routine Allison and I have created."

"Marriage is a union where two people, you and me, agree and *want* to share all of those upheavals, whatever they are. I'd be there to protect and help you. To love you, Gay. And Allison."

"I know, I know," she uttered in agitation. She felt awful not being able to give him the clear answer he wanted. She felt scared of her reasons.

"What do you want to do?" he asked.

She sighed anxiously. "This is a big decision for both of us. I haven't spoken to Allison about it yet. I was getting used to the idea myself. Let me see how she feels about this. Give me a little more time."

Bill smiled in understanding, his hope renewed. "Of course. Take your time."

Hurry up, Gayla said to herself.

David stared at the skyline beyond the terrace door. It was a fabulous view. The city was bejeweled and looked magical at night. It was much more appealing than the stark reality that daylight brought to it. He remembered a well-known singer once saying, during a concert date at Carnegie Hall, that New York was like a sexy and glamorous woman . . . who'd been screwed too many times.

He turned back to the living room, and set his untouched wineglass on the glass and chrome coffee table. He could see himself in the highly reflective surface. A man waiting on a woman and feeling uncomfortable. A black man waiting on a white woman, and feeling worse.

What was he doing here? David asked himself as he looked impatiently at his watch. No. He knew why he was here. For the companionship. For the energy of a woman who was smart and genuine, talented and more than capable of matching his needs in bed. For the fact that she accepted him just the way he was. And neither of them had any expectations. Which was why David knew he had to leave.

He glanced at Maron as she paced behind her plush brushed-suede sofa, a portable phone pressed to her ear. She was talking to a prospective subject about setting up an interview. Maron was being strong but feminine in her persuasion. David recognized her modus operandi; it had gotten his attention in the first place. David got a kick out of watching her. She was raised in privilege and taught to be confident . . . and she didn't take for granted her sense of entitlement.

Maron returned his gaze and, without missing a beat in her conversation, blew him a kiss. She held up a finger indicating she needed one more minute and she'd be finished.

David looked at the time again. He went back to stare out the window. He never thought he'd want to return to the city that had nearly destroyed him, but now he was glad to be back. Even the hard stuff seemed to make sense. His probation officer had once told him, during one of those therapy-type sessions together, that things happen for a reason. And things happen when they're supposed to happen. He just had to pay attention and use all the signs to make his life what he wanted it to be. The choice was his. His life was his own. *Well, in that case,* David considered, *I know what I want.*

"Darling, I'm sorry," Maron crooned, slipping in front of David and giving him a light kiss. "Nothing waits on the news. I've been trying to get ahold of that woman for weeks. I have two hours tomorrow to listen to her side of why she had her own son arrested. With her lawyer present, of course."

David accepted her kiss and watched her as she moved away to get her own glass of wine. He'd never known a woman as openly affectionate as Maron. "You gotta do what you gotta do," he murmured wryly.

She sat down on the sofa, kicked off her expensive shoes and curled her legs to the side. She shook out her dark hair, and it settled in loose waves about her jaw and neck. She patted the space next to her. David didn't move. After a moment of regarding him, she stared down into the glass and sighed.

"You're not staying, are you?"

David flexed his jaw muscles. It would be so easy . . . "No."

"Are you angry about the constant interruptions? That I'm in Washington most of the time and . . ."

"No. I don't have a problem with any of that. You're a dynamite woman, Maron, and you have a career, a life."

"And you don't really feel a part of it, is that it?"

"You're not really a part of mine, either."

She rolled her eyes. "David, you know I'm not pretentious. I don't give a shit what your background is, or that you spent time in jail, or . . ."

David came to sit on the coffee table in front of her. He leaned forward and grabbed her hands to stop their waving, and then he rested his palms on the sides of her face. Her hands covered his, holding them in place. David was aware of the contrast of their skin sandwiched together. He thought at first it would bother him, but it really didn't. But that wasn't the point, either.

"I know, I know. Maron, it's not you. You are amazing, you know. Incredible."

She nodded. "It's true. Tell me more."

David wasn't sure what he expected from her, but he felt relief that Maron wasn't being difficult. "Your parents did a great job with you."

She blinked at him. He'd never thought of her as being vulnerable, but it was there in her eyes.

"What are you saying? That it can't work between us? Or . . . is it something else?"

Her expression made him sad. "Of course it can't work between us, Maron. You're not in love with me. And . . . I'm not in love with you. What happened between us was opportunity meeting head on with . . . need. There's a whole bunch of things going on in my life right now that I need to sort out. But I can't go on seeing you knowing . . . knowing that . . ."

"You might be in love with someone else," she surmised in a whisper.

That stopped him short. He didn't have the nerve to say it himself. David still couldn't tell if it was true. He dropped his hands.

"You know I wasn't just getting my rocks off, being with you, right?"

"Oh, David. I know that." She nodded. "I'm good at reading people." She managed a sly grin from beneath her long lashes. "I knew you were smart and honest. And I knew you'd be terrific in bed."

He cringed. "No stereotype intended."

She shook her head, reaching out to stroke his cheek. "None at all. Everything else about you was a bonus." Maron uncurled herself and bent forward to put her arms around his neck, to lay her cheek against his shoulder.

David held her close. "I'm sorry."

"I guess it's not a good idea to ask you to stay tonight anyway. Just because . . ."

"I don't think so. It . . . wouldn't feel right."

"Speak for yourself," she said dryly.

Graham felt like a fool. Worse, he felt like a common stalker.

Once again, he found himself waiting for an opportunity to see the thirteen-year-old girl. He no longer bothered to try and not make himself so noticeable. He was not so out of place on the streets of Harlem, since no one paid any particular attention to him. He didn't return to the apartment building where Allison and Gayla lived, and he didn't *dare* attempt a school rendezvous. Instead, he picked the one place where he wouldn't draw attention. The small art gallery where, two days a week, Allison met her mother after school.

The fact that he felt forced to do this didn't help Graham's conscience, either. But if Gayla or Sylvia found out how covert he was being they might never forgive him. On the other hand, they had long had a secret which was his as well.

Graham was determined to meet his daughter.

He'd only gotten a glimpse of her over the past week, and never from closer than about twenty feet. But each time he saw Allison just added to his acceptance of her, and his great joy. That more than made the risk worthwhile. Still, what he was doing was not without consequences. Graham had yet to figure out how to tell his estranged wife, and his own daughter, Holly, about Allison. He also knew that his parents didn't have a clue that Allison was their grandchild, too. But also . . . he had no idea how Allison would feel about him. What had Gayla told her all these years?

What if Allison wanted nothing to do with him?

Graham paced back and forth outside the gallery entrance. He was positioned so that he couldn't be seen by anyone on the inside, and so he could spot Allison first, as she approached. He squinted off down the street, looking for the tall young girl who tended to daydream as she walked . . . and then he saw her.

He gnawed a thumb cuticle and constantly raked his hand through his hair. He took deep breaths to settle the tumult in his stomach. He was suddenly gripped with a near-paralyzing fear. What was he to say to her?

Graham started walking toward her, closer until Allison realized that there was a man standing in front of her. She automatically shifted to walk around him.

"You . . . must be Allison." His voice was still filled with uncertainty. She focused on him, slowing her steps. Cautious, but not fearful. Graham smiled to put her at ease but didn't try to get any closer. "You're Gayla's daughter. I'm Graham Whelan. Your grandmother, Sylvia, used to work for my family. She works with my father, now." His heart was pounding.

"Oh, hi," Allison said cheerfully. She had not stopped, however, in her progress toward the gallery entrance. She reached out for the door handle.

"I . . . I stopped by to see the new show. Especially David Kinney's work. I know him, too." He awkwardly stuck out his hand to her.

Politely, Allison put her hand in his. He found it limp and soft, but he squeezed gently, holding it for a brief moment before releasing her.

"It's very nice to meet you, Allison," Graham said with heartfelt sincerity.

"Thank you," she responded shyly. She pulled on the door.

"Well . . . I guess you're on your way to see your mother so I won't keep you. Maybe . . . we'll see each other again." Graham raised a hand to wave goodbye, but she'd already turned away, swinging through the glass doors.

"Bye," Allison said airily as an afterthought.

Graham watched her disappear, unable to say another word.

Chapter Fourteen

$\approx \infty \approx$

Mitchell shifted in his seat and sighed. His gaze drifted from the arena and the choreography of the Disney characters from the animated film *Pocahontas* to his niece. Allison was watching attentively, although slouched in her seat. She was also mindlessly mutilating the straw from her last container of soda, chewing and twisting it with her teeth.

She's really into this, he thought ruefully, seeing any chances of their leaving early disappear. He checked his watch. They were an hour into the program and he knew it had to be over soon.

Suddenly Allison giggled. "That was a neat jump. Did you see that, Uncle Mitch?" She turned her head to regard him briefly before looking again at the action of the Ice Capade production.

"Sorry, I missed it," he said, trying not to sound bored.

The number finally ended and the audience applauded. Again, as he'd been doing all afternoon, Mitchell let his attention wander. Not that he was expecting to see anyone he knew. This was a children's show, and there were thousands of them in attendance with their parents or other relatives and guardians. He shook his head.

"It's a good thing I think you're cute and I like you," he said to Allison.

"What do you mean?" Allison asked, sitting up and fidgeting in her seat now that the latest routine was over and a musical overture set up the next and final segment of the show. She leaned over to sip from her uncle's half-finished soda.

"This is not how I planned to spend my weekend. You and your mother owe me, big-time."

"It's a good show," Allison declared, now nibbling on leftover popcorn and swinging her leg restlessly beneath her seat. She suddenly jumped up, putting her container on the floor. "I'll be right back . . ."

"Wait a minute. Where are you going now?"

"To the bathroom," she said.

"You just went not fifteen minutes ago. Can you wait? This is almost over."

"I know, but when I have to go I have to go."

Mitchell couldn't argue with that. He didn't even try. "Okay. Here's the deal. It's going to be a mob scene when this is over and there's going to be a stampede of little kids. So when you come back from the little girl's room, we get a head start out of here, okay?"

"Okay," Allison agreed readily. She stepped over Mitchell's feet and kissed him quickly on the cheek before sprinting up the stairs.

Having already visited the bathroom twice Allison

knew exactly where she was going. She was in and out in no time flat, but didn't immediately return to her seat. The music from the last number blared on and she began humming the theme which had been prominent in the film. Dawdling, she passed the concession stand again and, once more, looked at the display of Disney merchandise on sale in connection with the show. She'd pretty much outgrown the desire to have those kinds of things, but liked seeing what was for sale.

Allison lost interest halfway down the counter, and turned to head back to her seating gate.

"Hi, Allison."

Hearing her name, Allison stopped and turned around. Her eyes blinked at the few people standing near the counter, but she couldn't focus on anyone she knew.

"Remember me? We met last week at the gallery where your mother works. I'm Graham Whelan."

Allison blinked at the smiling man. He was walking toward her but stopped about four feet away. She nodded. "Oh, yeah. I remember you."

"Are you enjoying the show?"

"Yes," she answered simply.

"I'm here with my daughter and some of her friends. They seem to be having fun."

"You have a little girl?" Allison asked, interested. Graham grinned. "Holly. She's almost twelve."

"I'm thirteen," she said.

"Yes . . . I know," he murmured.

"Do you have other kids?"

Graham hesitated and swallowed, watching the questioning innocence in her eyes. "Yes," was all he could manage to respond. "Are you here with . . . your mother?" he asked smoothly.

"No, with my Uncle Mitch."

"Your Uncle Mitch," Graham repeated, surprised.

"I gotta get back. My uncle is waiting for me . . ."

"Yeah, me too," Graham said, although he didn't move. He put one hand in his pants pocket and waved with the other at her. "Well . . . you enjoy the rest of the show."

"See ya," Allison said, turning away and hurrying to her seat.

"Ready?" Mitchell asked as soon as she was back.

He passed Allison her jacket, and motioned for her to pick up their empty snack containers for disposal in the garbage. He was more than ready to leave, and started up the stairs to the exit.

"Do you have everything?" he asked over his shoulder.

"Yes."

"I might make a pit stop myself . . ."

"I saw Mr. Whelan again," Allison piped up.

Mitchell walked another few feet before he faltered, stopped and turned to frown at his niece. "What did you just say?"

"I said, I saw Mr. Whelan."

"Mr. . . . Whelan? Paul Whelan?" he asked quickly.

Allison shook her head. "No. It was another one." She started to walk ahead of her uncle, but he grabbed her arm.

"Wait a minute, Ali. Wait . . . Now, tell me this again. When did this happen?"

"Well, I saw him at the gallery when I was going to meet Mommy, after school."

Mitchell was totally confused. "And you told your mother?"

"No." Allison shrugged. "I forgot."

"But . . . that was . . . when?" he probed.

"I don't know. Last week sometime, I think."

"Oh," he whispered. Maybe it wasn't as bad as he thought. He started walking again, but already other people were beginning to file out, too. He reached for Allison's hand so they wouldn't get separated.

"But I saw him again," she added suddenly.

Again Mitchell stopped in his tracks. He turned on Allison. "When? When did you see Whelan? Are you sure his name wasn't Paul?"

"I'm sure." Allison blinked at him, somewhat confused by her uncle's questions and sensing something might be wrong. "I was standing at the concession stand and he was there, too . . ." Her uncle muttered on oath under his breath. "Uncle Mitch, are we leaving?"

"Yes, right now . . ." he said, picking up his pace to get out of the building. He kept glancing behind at Allison, asking her questions. "Did . . . did he say anything to you? Did he ask you any questions?"

"Mmmm hmmm," Allison said.

"What?"

"He asked me if I was enjoying the show . . ."

"No, Ali, I mean . . . Never mind . . ."

They were out of the stands. Mitchell looked all around, trying to spot the quickest exit from Madison Square Garden. He forgot completely the need to go to the bathroom.

"Uncle Mitch . . ." Allison whined after a moment. "You're going too fast!"

"Sorry. I just want to get us out of here . . ."

From the quickly thickening crowd an arm stretched to grab Mitchell's shoulder. He looked over his shoulder and into the face of Graham Whelan. He couldn't say anything. Graham didn't have to. They were stopped now, with people swarming around them trying to get to the escalators.

"Hi, Mitchell," Graham Whelan said above the crowd. His greeting didn't leave room to be ignored.

A look of stunned surprise spread over Mitchell's face.

"Uncle Mitch, that's the man I was telling you about," Allison said, pulling on his hand.

Neither man acknowledged Allison, but for the moment just kept focused on each other.

"We need to talk," Graham said agreeably.

"Not here." Mitchell shook his head. "You have to talk to Gayla. I can't . . ."

"Let's not make a scene," Graham suggested.

Mitchell turned to face him, moving to the side out of the way of the crowds. He more or less pushed Allison behind him out of sight. "Look, this is not the time or the place to handle this."

"I don't want to make trouble," Graham reasonably. "But you know I should have been told."

"It's none of my business. I don't have the right . . ."

"No, but I do," Graham interrupted.

Allison peeked out from behind her uncle's back, at the man with the blond hair and yellow jacket. "I told my Uncle Mitchell that I saw you."

"I know, sweetheart. Thank you." Graham smiled warmly at Allison.

Mitchell put out his hand, almost touching Graham's chest. "You'll have to talk to Gayla."

"I've tried that, Mitchell. I talked to her, Sylvia . . . I'm talking with you right now. I've tried giving everyone a chance to tell me what I should have been told years ago."

"What's wrong?" Allison asked neither man in particular. "How come we're standing here? Where's your little girl?" she finally asked Graham.

He was staring at her with that same fascination and tenderness he'd felt from the very first moment he'd set eyes on her.

"Please don't do this, man. Can't you wait until . . ."

"Holly is going to leave with her friends and one of the other fathers. I told her I'd catch up to them in a little while. But . . . you're my little girl, too, Allison."

He got it out so quickly and smoothly that Mitchell couldn't even prevent it. He wasn't even sure there was any point to trying. It wasn't as if Graham was wrong, or demented, or being difficult. Graham had the right.

Allison blinked at Graham, her small face a study in youthful bewilderment. She glanced at Mitchell, but he remained silent. She frowned at Graham and quickly shook her head.

"No, you're not."

"Do you know anything about your father?" he asked her.

"Graham, for God's sake . . ."

"I'm sorry, Mitchell. But do you have *any* idea what finding this out did to me? No one would tell me. I had to figure it out on my own. That's not right. You know that's not right."

"I don't have a father," Allison answered in a small voice. She crowded close to her uncle, her gaze questioning as she stared at Graham Whelan.

He smiled kindly at her. "Everybody has a father. Sometimes we don't get to meet them right away. You've never met Mitch's or your mother's father, but they have one. Don't you, Mitch?"

"But . . . you're not my father," Allison repeated.

Her voice was stronger, more insistent. It was filling with the distress of confusion and doubt.

"I know it doesn't look that way, Allison. You'll have to talk to your mother and grandmother." Graham glanced from her face to Mitchell's. "But I don't think they'll lie to you."

"I don't even look like you!" she said with childish logic.

"You do. More than you realize."

Allison suddenly began to cry. "No . . . no . . ."

she sobbed, drawing the attention of several people around them.

"Okay, that's enough. You could have waited, Graham."

"Would you?" he asked simply.

Mitchell put his arm around Allison's heaving shoulders. She turned her tear-streaked face to gaze once more at Graham through her tears.

Graham wanted to touch her, but instead put his hands in his pockets. "I'm sorry you had to find out this way, Allison. But I want you to know . . . I'm *very* glad you're my daughter. I . . . hope you'll let me get to know you."

"No . . ." Allison blurted out, breaking away from Mitchell. "No!" She turned and pushed her way through the crowd toward the exit.

"You're getting to be very good at this," Gayla said to David as the taping crew finished packing their equipment. The interviewer, from a well-known black cable program, stood to the side talking into her cellular phone. They were waiting to thank the reporter and to say goodbye.

David shrugged, smoothing a hand wearily over his head and across the back of his neck. "I'm still not comfortable about this."

"Don't you want to be famous?" Gayla asked.

"No. Just give me the money."

Gayla smiled at him. His sense of humor was always a bit self-deprecating, but she found that attractive. Unlike most artists, his ego did not require constant attention. He didn't like talking about himself at all, although he didn't shy away from questions about his background. And he made no apologies. She had grown used to the light beard, and wondered if, in some way, David was using it to alter his appearance. Not because he was hiding, but because of the different man he had grown into.

"Thank you for hanging around," David said to Gayla.

He was perched on the edge of a stool, which had been placed strategically so that while he sat being interviewed the camera could take in the background, some of the gallery where his work hung.

"That's okay. I didn't mind. Besides, I wanted to make sure you didn't get asked any inappropriate questions."

"I appreciate that you didn't mind. Maybe when we're finished . . . why don't we go get something to eat? Or maybe . . . that's out of line, considering."

Gayla felt the shift immediately. It was like a wave washing gently over her. Cleansing. Refreshing. She realized it was a much more significant suggestion than just getting something to eat. Gayla looked at David and saw that his expression was watchful. As if he was waiting for her to shoot down the idea.

"Sure, that would be nice. We never have a chance to sit and talk about anything but the show."

Gayla finished her conversation with the interviewer, exchanging business cards and checking about the possible air date for the taping. When they were gone, Gayla returned to her office to retrieve her purse. David remained in the gallery.

Alone, he wandered through his exhibit, looking at it with different eyes than he'd used when creating it. He thought it was good work because it accomplished his goal: to portray the tough existence in a lower-class black community. But now that he'd made his statement, now that he'd presented his images to the world . . . he was ready to move on.

"Where would you like to go?"

David turned and walked to meet Gayla as she stood just outside the gallery. "I don't know. To tell you the truth I didn't expect you to say yes."

"Why?" she asked, as they slowly headed toward the exit. "Because of the relationship we used to have? I think we both need to forget about that and focus on the here and now. I'm not that same girl and you're not that same boy. If I am, shoot me."

He grinned. "I found a place I like on West Nineteenth Street . . ."

Gayla was about to consent to his choice when, through the gallery doors, she caught sight of her daughter approaching.

"There's Allison," she said. "They're earlier than I thought they'd be," she murmured to herself.

"No problem. Maybe we'll get together some other time."

"Well, let's see what's going on before we change our plans."

Allison rushed at the door with more force than was necessary. Mitchell was behind her. Gayla began to smile as her daughter came in and she glanced questioningly at Mitchell's expression.

"You're back. Didn't you want—"

Gayla stopped when she saw Allison's face. It was infused with anger, and she seemed on the verge of exploding.

"What's the matter? What happened?" she asked, looking swiftly from her brother to her daughter.

"Can we go home?" Allison asked in a sharp tone.

"I was about go out with David, Allison. I didn't expect you back so soon."

"With him?" she asked, incredulous.

Gayla frowned. "Yes, with David. Allison, what is the . . ."

Allison marched up to David, and finally the glistening in her eyes turned to tears. Her eyes squeezed almost closed as her face contorted into fury.

"Why don't you leave my mother alone!"

"Allison! What is wrong with you?"

"Just leave her alone!" Allison screamed, nearly hysterical, before starting to cry in earnest. She ran into the first gallery, which was empty, and could be heard sobbing.

Gayla, stunned at what she was seeing, turned to her brother. "For God's sake, Mitchell, what happened?"

She began walking off to comfort Allison, but Mitchell held out a hand to stop her. "Maybe you'd better let me talk to her for a minute."

Gayla tried to push his arm away. "Tell me what's going on. I want to know . . ."

"We ran into Graham Whelan."

Gayla was nearly speechless. "Graham . . ."

"He knows, Gay. He knows about Allison. He was there and talked to her . . . and introduced himself. He told her who he was . . ."

"Oh, my God," she uttered in a thin voice, turning a stricken face to first her brother and then David.

She reached out blindly as her world began to tilt.

David quietly regarded Gayla as she sat with her head bowed, her forehead supported by her hand. There was not much he could have said in the last half hour that would have helped, other than to offer to stay with her. He had agreed with Mitch that for a little while Mitch should be the one to try and console Allison.

And he had been left to console Gayla.

She'd resisted at first, straining against his attempts to reason with her that Allison needed some time alone, and so did she. And like that summer when he'd found her crying, Gayla had permitted him to hold her for only a moment before pulling herself together to consider her daughter's pain and outrage. But it had been long enough.

Another shift had taken place.

"Why didn't you ever tell her?" David asked Gayla.

She shook her head, her face hidden. "I couldn't."

"Why? Didn't you think that exactly what happened today could happen sooner or later? She'd come face to face with her father?"

"No, I didn't." Gayla raised her head. Her eyes and nose were red from crying. "I didn't think of any of that. I was . . . scared. Ashamed. I was mad and disappointed."

David thought better of adding to the list. Her regret and fear at that moment were palpable. "And she never asked?"

Gayla looked at him, her eyes filled with distress. "No, she didn't. Once she said she wished she had a father. Once she told her grandmother that she didn't look like anyone in the family. But she never asked."

David sat forward, reaching out to touch her arm. They were in Gayla's office. "Look, right now Allison is probably in shock. If she's figured out who Graham is, she's got a whole lot to deal with, Gay. But it's going to be okay."

"You don't know that."

"Yes, I do. She's a strong little girl. She comes from good stock and a family that she knows loves her. Right now she's angry with you . . . but she's not going to hate you." He saw more than fleeting denial in her eyes. "I know. Where do I get off trying to tell you, right? Matt Nelson told me once we all have choices. Either learn to forgive or give up."

She gave her full attention to David. Her crying had dried up and she crushed the tissue in her hand. "Who's Matt Nelson?"

"A friend. A . . . kind of father figure. He's a retired judge who basically kicked my ass when I got out of line, but gave me advice and a helping hand when I was ready to turn my life around. He's acted as my parole officer, taking on the responsibility of keeping an eye on me."

"Really? Well, I could use advice right now."

"You know what to do. Give Allison some time. And then tell her the truth."

Gayla nodded and wearily stood up from the desk. "I have to go get her." She opened her purse and took out a small mirror. "I look terrible . . ." she complained.

David stood up, too. "Not to me. Allison's not going to notice."

Gayla gave him a grateful glance. Then she faced him. "Thank you, David. I appreciate your . . . understanding."

He grimaced. "Didn't think I had it in me, right?"

"Yes, I did. I've seen it in action before, remember? I do."

Gayla spontaneously placed her hand on his shoulder and leaned forward to kiss him on the cheek. She lingered for mere seconds and was surprised at how soft the layer of hair felt against her lips. How warm and firm his skin was. And his scent . . .

Another shift.

They stared transfixed at each other. And completely gave up the past. She realized that his hand was resting lightly on her waist.

"Why doesn't Allison like you, David? From the start she's been so . . . so hard on you."

He arched a brow. "I told you she's a smart little girl. She knows about my past with your family. She's not happy about it . . . like you and Mitchell used to be. A little jealous, maybe. I think Allison is unsure about me, and she's a little threatened . . . because she knows how I feel about you."

She blinked. "How you . . . feel?"

He nodded, concentrating on her reaction. "Yeah. How I feel."

Gayla was drawn to him. Not physically because he wasn't touching her now. But it was almost magnetic. Something forced from her head and tugged from her heart, not exactly against her will . . . but unexpected and a revelation.

David lowered his head toward her, and she stood while his mouth returned the favor of her kiss. But to her lips. It was very brief, but very expressive and clear. She didn't resist. And she was too stunned to respond.

David smiled gently into her startled eyes. But taking her arm he urged Gayla out the door of her office. "Go see about Allison," was all he said to her.

Gayla was *not* convinced this was a good idea, or the way to handle the situation. It was a beautiful day, but she couldn't enjoy it. Everything seemed gloomy in relation to the current chill between herself and Allison. Twenty-four hours had not changed anything and Allison still refused to say much to her. She robotically did what she was told, but otherwise had disengaged herself from her family, protectively withdrawing into herself.

"I don't know how much more of this I can take," Gayla said quietly to her mother.

"You can stand as much as your daughter can stand," Sylvia said calmly next to her.

They trailed behind Allison, keeping at a distance as she meandered listlessly through Central Park. Sylvia was of the opinion that Allison's natural vitality would get her quickly over her shock of discovering who her natural father was. Once she opened up, they could all talk through her history . . . and tell her about her father. But Sylvia knew there was no point in trying to push the girl.

"Has she said anything to you?" Gayla asked her mother.

"No. Not about her father. I think Ali is still in denial. She'll come around. Mark my words."

Gayla sighed. "Yeah, but when? *Before* Christmas this year . . . or after she's graduated high school?"

Sylvia chuckled but didn't think a real answer was required. Ahead of them Allison stopped to watch several talented in-line skaters with their street routines. After a mere fifteen seconds she lost interest and moved on.

"This is driving me crazy," Gayla muttered.

"Now you know how I felt."

"What do you mean?"

"When you got pregnant and wouldn't say a word about who, when or where. Not that I didn't figure it out eventually."

Gayla moaned at her mother's revelation.

"There was nothing I could do to make you tell me, Gayla. I don't know why you felt you couldn't. I would have understood, been there for you. Lord, child . . . it's not as if you're the only one on God's earth who ever made a bad decision. But I'd hoped you would have learned from it. I don't know what you really felt for Graham or what he felt for you beyond puppy love and a summer fling. But Allison is here, the real deal, and you should have remembered that sometimes history returns to bite you in the butt!"

Gayla had to laugh. Her mother had never shown anger at her for getting pregnant and having a child before she'd finished school. She'd never lectured her or held it against her . . . the way she'd continued to hold her anger against Graham. And what for? Out of pride . . . or punishment? His? Or her own?

Gayla looked around her. It really was a beautiful day. As a child she had loved going to the Whelans' large bright apartment on Central Park West overlooking the park. It was like going on a trip and visiting a foreign country. The inhabitants were not like her, her mother or brother. They had white skin and eyes that were gray and blue and hair that was long. The children were bigger and could do things that she knew nothing about and had never heard of. She had met Graham and Reilly and their sister Sarah, who was Mitch's age. They had spent a lot of time together. And she had adored Graham. No . . . she had been in love with him.

He had protected her from the other white kids in the park who wanted to know what she was doing outside of Harlem. He used to share those giant salted pretzels with her, and let her take some of his books home to read. Gayla remembered that she did things downtown at the Whelans' that she couldn't do at home. She had found out how big the world was outside of Harlem. She was curious to explore it. And she'd wanted to do it all.

But . . . was she in some way crucifying both herself and Allison because she couldn't have Graham? She watched her daughter, knowing, somewhere in the back of her mind, that the truth had been bound to come out, one way or another. Now she only had to accept it, and help Allison to accept it.

"Allison . . ." Gayla called out. For a while it looked like Allison was going to ignore her. But she stopped, turned halfway around and glared.

"What?" Allison asked rudely.

"I don't feel like walking all the way to China. I think we should stop and sit for while."

"I don't want to talk about it," Alison said, turning away.

"Allison." Sylvia tried next. Her granddaughter pouted at her as well, but it was clear she wasn't going to be as totally impertinent. "You might remember that I'm not as young as you. My feet hurt."

Gayla was both impatient with and amused by her mother's blatant con. But it worked. Allison turned around and, staring at the ground, made her way back. It was not lost on Gayla that she chose to stand next to her grandmother and not herself.

"Thank you, sweetheart, for indulging an old lady." Sylvia, exaggerating, perhaps, her aching feet, sat on a nearby bench. Her daughter and granddaughter followed suit, one on either side of her. They were silent for a moment.

"Did your mother ever tell you about your grandfather?" Sylvia suddenly turned to Allison and asked.

Gayla felt her stomach tense at once. She waited for Allison to sprint up and again announce her unwillingness to discuss her family, but she didn't.

"He lives in Alaska."

Curiosity was written all over Allison's face as she glanced at her grandmother, but she stubbornly refused to voice it.

"Gayla and Mitch have not seen their father in more than twenty years. You know why? Because my pride was hurt. And I was too stubborn and too selfish to realize they had a right to know about him . . . and he needed to know about them.

"In a way, your mother went through the same thing you are, Ali. There were all these things she didn't know . . . because I couldn't bring myself to tell her or Mitchell. That wasn't fair."

"No, it wasn't," Allison murmured in agreement.

"I just thought . . . what do they need to know about someone who isn't even in their lives? Just like your mother might have said to herself about your own father: Graham Whelan."

Gayla tried to lean forward to see Allison's response. She was still pouting, but she was listening.

"Now, everybody has a father . . ."

"That's what he said."

Sylvia glanced at her. "Who?"

"That man. Graham. My . . . my father."

Gayla closed her eyes and felt herself very close to tears. She bit her lip and sat still and silent.

Sylvia reached for Allison's hand. She held it and cupped it protectively with the other. "Does that mean you believe now that he is your father?"

It was a long time before the answer came.

"I guess so," Allison's voice was barely audible. Her chin was tucked in against her chest.

Sylvia squeezed and patted the hand she held. "Your mother has a lot of explaining to do. She has a lot she has to tell you, Ali. But you first have to be willing to listen. That's being fair, too."

Allison sat forward and peeked around her grandmother to her mother. Gayla made no signals to her, no overtures. This was her daughter's call. After a moment Allison sat back again. She didn't say anything. Sylvia didn't push.

"He's a very nice man, Allison," Gayla finally ventured. "Graham is so anxious to know you."

"He has a daughter," Allison whispered.

"He has *two* daughters. He called and told me that Holly is wildly excited that she has a big sister."

"She's not going to look anything like me."

"And you're not going to look like her. Isn't that great? That means you're both unique."

"Well . . ." Sylvia said, taking control and wisely deciding to end the discussion there. She stood up and patted Allison's shoulder. "My feet feel much better. Thank you, Ali, for letting me rest a bit. Want to walk some more?"

"I'd rather get a soda and a pretzel."

"Go ahead. I'll catch up and pay for it . . ."

Allison almost skipped away.

Gayla reached for her mother's hand and squeezed it fervently. She didn't have to say thank you.

Gayla sat back as her plate was removed from the table. She turned down the selection of desserts, and placed her coffee cup in front of her. All the time she was aware of Bill's close scrutiny across the table. He played with the sugar packets in the service container, and Gayla knew that he was as anxious as she was. Now that the distraction of dinner was over, they were left with Bill's questions to be answered.

"How's Allison?" he began first.

Gayla winced. Bill's interest was genuine but a painful reminder. "She's still very angry with me. But we're talking. I guess that's the good news. It's going to take time."

David had told her that.

"Mind if I ask how she feels about the fact that her natural father is white?"

Gayla sighed. "I don't know yet. She seems to be more upset that I didn't tell her anything for all these years. In a funny way, she would have been just as happy not knowing she had a father who was real and out there somewhere in the world. Having seen him, meeting him the way she did . . . it . . . it changed too much for her too fast." She gave him a considering glance. "What do you think about it?"

"If you were concerned about what I think, you

would have mentioned this some time ago. Since you didn't, I can only conclude that you didn't want me to know, or you were worried about my reaction, or you believed it was a non-issue."

She grimaced at him. "That's a very lawyer-type answer. It evades the question."

He shrugged. "Maybe I'm not prepared with anything else right now. I'll just say I was surprised that Allison didn't resemble you a great deal. I never considered that she might be biracial. But Ali's going to be fine. So are you."

"I hope so."

"So, where does that leave me?"

She looked at him. "You mean, will I marry you?"

Bill regarded her calmly. "I already know the answer to that. Now I only need to find out if it's no for now . . . or no, you don't know. Or no, as in the end."

Gayla briefly closed her eyes. Too many options. David . . .

"I'm in love with you, Gay. I think you're a fantastic woman. We'd be good for each other. We'd have great kids, and Allison would have brothers and sisters, hopefully. What about you? What do you want?"

Now she had no choice. Her stomach roiled, and she was sorry she'd agreed to dinner. All day Gayla had felt the telltale signs of pain in her arms and joints. The stress and too much running around were pushing her toward another crisis. And the truth was, Bill's proposal had been the last thing on her mind. But even before that . . .

Gayla looked at Bill, clear on all his many good points. She had yet to encounter anything to make her cautious. Except that, in the bluntest terms, he didn't light her fire. He was safe. Gayla shook her head.

"Bill . . . I don't know what to say. I . . . I think we'd be very good for each other, too. But I don't think I'm in love with you."

"You mean, not in the adolescent way where you can't sleep at night because you're thinking about me? And you can't imagine a little boy who looks like me, and . . . you can't see us old together and baby-sitting our grandkids?"

She wondered if there was any way she could give him hope. "No . . . I can't. I'm sorry."

He stirred his coffee. "Is it someone else? Not Allison's father, for God's sake."

She didn't respond to the sneer in his voice and she avoided being specific about his first question.

"I think I've known for a while I wasn't in love with you. Maybe I was hoping there'd be a sudden flash or something. I'm sorry," Gayla said helplessly. "I hope this doesn't mean we can't be friends. Or that you won't continue on the board for the gallery."

Bill shook his head. "I have to tell you, Gay, I haven't made that leap of faith yet."

Guilt made her reach across to hold his hand.

"But . . . there's no fool like a fool in love. I'm not going to count myself out yet."

CHAPTER FIFTEEN

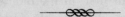

Through the glass entrance of the gallery, Kel saw the reflection of the young girl approaching and he smiled. She was right on time. In the few weeks he'd been watching her she'd never veered from her routine. She was very young, budding on being a teenager. For now she was kind of long-legged and thin. Still unconscious of her body, she moved with the carelessness of a youth who doesn't think anyone is paying any attention to her. The shoulder straps of her knapsack pulled the sweater taut over her narrow torso. He could just detect the swelling of adolescent breasts. Awkward little mounds rising under her top. She was a pretty little thing. He could see her in another three or four years. The potential stroked his imagination. But for now his plan was very simple.

When she was at a comfortable distance from the door, he stepped out into her path, as if by coincidence. Far enough away to be seen, but close enough for her to see his expression and not be threatened. He smiled at her as she became aware of him.

"Hi. I was hoping to catch you at the corner, Allison, but it's just as well that I waited here. Teddy said you'd be here soon."

Allison slowed her steps, looking suspiciously at him. She was maneuvering to walk around the man, but he made no attempt to block her path, just talk to her.

Kel chuckled softly, moving with her. "You don't remember me. I'm Kel Monroe. David Alan Kinney's friend. We met one day after David's show opened. It was a Saturday, and you had to sit around and wait for your mother because she had to get some work done. Remember that?"

Allison nodded, as he knew she would. He'd gotten enough information from Dak, and had seen enough himself to speak mostly the truth. He reached into his pocket and took out a business card. He held it so Allison could see the gallery logo and her mother's name, but he didn't give it to her.

"I was told to wait for you. Your mother said you get here on Wednesdays between three-thirty and four-fifteen, depending on traffic and the school bus. She and Dak had a meeting this afternoon with Bill Coleman. I know you know Bill."

Allison nodded again, but was less skittish. "My mother's not here?" She glanced past him toward the gallery, but they were just far enough away that she couldn't see inside.

"No. That's why I'm here. She had to leave a while ago and knew she wouldn't be here when you came in. So I'm the messenger and the chauffeur. I'm supposed to bring you to Mr. Coleman's office at . . ."

He squinted at the handwritten information on the back of the card, reading aloud an address. Kel smiled at her and took a chance. "Do you need to use the bathroom or anything before we get started? My car is right over there."

Allison glanced at her mother's business card and again at Kel. She followed his pointing finger and saw the black Town Car. Once more she tried to see into the interior of the gallery. "Well . . ."

"Teddy's right inside if you want to talk to him, but . . ." He looked at his watch. "I know your mother wants you to catch up with her. I told her to go ahead to the meeting. Dak was going to wait for you, but I said I would. Oh, by the way, Teddy said this was yours."

Allison readily accepted the library book. She recognized it. One she'd left n her mother's office and kept forgetting to return to the library. "It's overdue," she said in resignation.

Kel chuckled, gently coaxing her toward the car. "It must be a good story."

Allison shrugged as she accompanied him to the car. He opened the passenger door and held it for her politely as she got into the front seat. "It was okay. I just keep forgetting to take it back."

Kel closed her in.

Allison realized that someone else was in the backseat. A man she didn't recognize. Kel was already sliding into the driver's seat and starting the engine. She looked back at the man, but he watched her so carefully that it made her uncomfortable. She tried to think as she settled stiffly in her seat. She looked at the gallery again, and finally her instincts kicked in and apprehension made her heart race.

"I think I should go inside and call my mother if she's at Bill's office." She tried the door, but it was locked. She fumbled for the mechanism to unlock it and couldn't find one. "Could . . . could you wait a minute? I want to call my mother. Just to make sure," Allison said in a small uncertain voice.

The car pulled into traffic and headed west toward the next avenue. Kel grinned as he looked in the rearview mirror at the man in the backseat. "Sure. I want you to call her. After we get to where we're going."

Allison shrank back against the door as it dawned on her that something was wrong. "Where's my mother?" she asked.

Kel shrugged. "In her office, far as I know."

"But you said . . ."

Kel's voice grew stern. "You know, your mother is going to be real mad at you. Didn't she tell you to be careful of strange men?"

Allison stared out the windshield, blinking rapidly. She didn't know where they were headed. She couldn't find the lock for the door. And even if she could, the car was moving too fast. She looked at Kel Monroe. "Where are you taking me? What . . . what are you going to do to me?"

"Nothing, I hope. I don't want to hurt you, Allison. You'll be okay as long as Dak doesn't try to fuck with me." Kel looked at her sideways. "The brother changed up on me. He forgets I saved his ass once."

"But that doesn't have anything to do with me," she said, close to tears, her voice quavering.

"Yeah, I know," Kel agreed. "Ain't it a damned shame?"

"Teddy, is Allison down there with you? She should have let me know she was here. It's after four already."

"No, Miss Patton, she's not here yet. I was just wondering myself where she could be."

Gayla frowned and checked the time. "She hasn't gotten here yet? But it's almost four-thirty."

"I know, but I been watching for her. Nobody's come in 'cept for gallery visitors."

Gayla only felt mild concern as she listened to Teddy and tried to remember if Allison had told her she might be a little late for any reason. But their morning conversation had been clear about what her daughter was to do after school.

"Well, let me call the school and see if there was any delay. But please let me know the minute she walks through the door."

Gayla's anxiety went up a notch when she was informed by Allison's school secretary that the school bus had departed on time and Allison had been on board. But the driver had not returned from the route yet, and they could offer no other explanation for her lateness. Her concern grew to monster proportions as five o'clock approached without a word from her daughter. By five-fifteen Gayla was frantic. She tried to fashion a story that perhaps Allison had gone to her grandmother's, or even to Mitch. But she knew that if she called her mother or brother they would both say they had not seen her. Then there would be three people worried instead of one. Gayla thought of calling Bill, but she couldn't think of a plausible reason for Allison to have gone to his office. What on earth for? For a wild moment Gayla imagined that her daughter had actually contacted her father, Graham Whelan. But Gayla herself had no way to reach Graham . . . except through his parents, or maybe even Sylvia.

Tension began to twist itself into a headache for Gayla. She saw an ever-widening circle of involvement as she tried to figure out where her child might be . . . and with whom. She was about to give in and call her mother when the phone in her office rang. Gayla fairly pounced upon it, fighting to keep her voice calm while every fiber of her being struggled not to believe the worst.

"Hello?" she said, her heart beating fast.

"It's me, Mommy."

Gayla closed her eyes, biting her lips against tears. She could hear the confusion and fear in Allison's voice. "Allison . . ." she managed to get out, half in relief and half as a confirmation. "Honey, where are you? Are you okay?"

Allison softly began to cry and didn't answer.

"Allison? Allison, please say something . . ." Gayla whispered, on the verge of tears herself.

"I'm okay. But this man says that it's David Kinney's fault that I had to come with him."

"What man? Who is it, Allison? Maybe I can talk with him . . ." She stopped as she heard muffled voices and what she interpreted as the handing off of a phone to someone else. Gayla knew it had to be cellular. Technology had made criminal lives a lot easier. "Hello? Hel—"

"Your daughter's going to be okay. Don't worry."

Gayla frowned. The voice sounded familiar. "Who is this? What do you want with my daughter?"

"She's just insurance. Nothing is going to happen to her as long as I get what I want."

"What is it you want? Who is this?"

The voice chuckled. "A friend of a friend. As a matter of fact, if you talk to Dak he can explain everything . . ."

"Dak . . ." Gayla uttered, feeling the tightening in her chest restrict her breathing.

"Yeah. You know, you really brought the brother *down*. Talk to him. I bet he'll do anything for you. Whatever it takes to get your daughter back. By the way . . . she's very attractive."

Gayla bit her lip so as not to make sound to accompany the sudden fall of tears. "Don't . . . don't hurt my daughter. I'll do anything you want."

He chuckled again. "If I had time, I'd take you up on that. It's all up to you and Dak. He knows what the deal is. You want Allison back, you work it out with him."

Before she could say another word the line went dead.

The call that David received was less polite and more specific. He had not heard from Kel in nearly two days but wasn't particularly surprised to hear from him now. Except for the purpose which even he would not have thought the Kel Monroe he'd known most of his life capable of.

"You have something that belongs to me, man. I have to have it back," Kel stated.

"No problem," David responded. "I told you when you first came to the apartment I didn't want your money. I still have the envelope. I haven't spent—"

"Fuck the envelope, Dak. That money is chump change. I'm talking about the rest of my things. You switched up on me, man. You found the other box and now you actin' like you don't know nothing."

David had to overcome more than his ignorance of what Kel had tried to pull off in the short time they were together. A lot of years of trust had vanished with his revelation. "You got heart, Kel. I don't know what other box you're talking about. You can still have the money back. After that . . . we're finished."

Kel chortled. "You think you can wolf me? Listen up, bro. You ain't in no position to make the rules. You have nothing to bargain with. I can turn the whole deal out with one word."

David, knowing Kel, was suddenly apprehensive as to what aces Kel held. "I'm listening."

"Allison."

"Allison . . ." David repeated softly. And then Kel's meaning gripped him, and his muscles tensed. He couldn't be cool anymore. He couldn't even think straight. David suddenly visualized a frightened thirteen-year-old, and a man who, when thwarted, could get ugly and mean. David tried to think if he'd ever known Kelvin Monroe to hurt a child. Nothing came to mind . . . but that didn't mean he wasn't capable of it.

"This is very simple, Dak. I don't want the kid. I want what belongs to me. I want my box back. *And* the money. Give me my stuff and we're straight."

David narrowed his eyes. "Are we? You shouldn't have used me to start with. Holding the box might just be insurance. I can't trust you, man. Now I know why."

"Well, it goes both ways, bro. Now you know why I have Allison with me."

"I get your meaning. Just tell me what you want me to do. If you have a beef and want to kick some-one's ass, do me. It's me you really want to take down, right?"

"I never thought it would come to this, but . . . that's the way it goes," Kel said without regret. "You only get one chance at this, so get it right. I keep the kid until after I see the box and what's inside."

David felt his stomach muscles cramp. His mouth was dry. "No deal," he said flatly, not revealing any of his anxiety. "It's an even exchange. We hand off at the same time. You can trust me on this. I'm not going to risk Allison's life for anything you have."

"Okay. We do it your way . . ."

David listened carefully, hoping for some weakness in Kel's plans. There wasn't any. He chose an early morning hour because it would be quiet. David knew that Kel figured that any other presence but his own would be easily detected. And finally, Kel was only going to call with the exact location a mere fifteen minutes before David had to be there. This, presumably, to not allow any extra time in which police might be called in.

David assured Kel he had nothing to worry about and then they hung up. David continued to sit another ten minutes while he tried to figure out his options. There were only one or two . . . and they were too dangerous to risk a thirteen-year-old's life on. He could call the police right now, or Matt Nelson, who already knew about Kel's reappearance in his life. He had one other possibility, and it still made him sick to think about the many ways this last choice could go wrong. He could try to take Kel himself.

David thought of the third box he'd found after their fight and after Kel had left the apartment. Instincts had told him to hold onto it. But now look what it had led to.

He hadn't opened the box to see what was inside. Now he did. David found more drugs and nearly one hundred and fifty thousand dollars in cash.

David hoped it was enough to get him and Allison through the next twelve hours.

David had to figure out how to leave the building without being seen, assuming that Kel was having his movements watched. He had his own plans to set in place. He was just about to exit his apartment when the intercom sounded.

"It's Mitchell Patton. Can I come up?"

David frowned. "Mitchell? Look, I'm sorry. I'm on my way out. I have something—"

"It'll only take a minute. It's important. I think you'll want to see me."

David reluctantly gave in and buzzed him into the building. He kept checking the time, trying to calculate how fast he could get Mitchell to leave.

David was standing right behind the door when the bell was rung. He opened it quickly. Standing in the threshold were Mitchell . . . and Gayla. He saw the stark terror in her eyes. It was clear she'd been crying. Before David could say anything, he watched as Gayla's expression quickly changed to rage and despair. And then suddenly she launched herself toward him, her arms up and fists flailing at him.

"Where's my daughter? Where's my daughter?"

David was taken completely off guard by Gayla's attack. For an instant he let her go at him, putting up his forearms to protect his head and face. He absorbed her blows, not surprised by the strength of them. "Gayla . . ." David managed.

"What have you done with my daughter?"

Gayla's screams made David feel as though his

skin was being peeled slowly away from the muscle beneath. He gritted his teeth, and her pain stabbed him in his chest.

"Come on, Gay. Take it easy . . ." Mitchell said, trying to grab her by the shoulders and pull her away.

"No . . . let . . . her go . . ." David got out as she continued her furious barrage.

Gayla was beside herself. But her anger was quickly spent until her blows just glanced off David's arms. It was then that he reached out to encircle her, trapping her arms to the side. She struggled, thrashing about as tears streamed down her face and her sobs left her nearly breathless. Finally, she slumped helplessly against David, her head dropping to his chest.

He had to take her full weight. Together they slipped to the floor just inside his apartment door. Now he could try to comfort her. David could feel that she wanted to strike out again, to continue her fight. But Gayla simply didn't have the strength. He gathered her tightly to him.

"My baby . . . my baby . . ." Gayla wailed. She clutched David's jacket with her fists.

"It's not me, Gay. I swear to God I had nothing to do with taking Allison . . ." He glanced up at Mitchell as he spoke. David could see that Mitchell, at least, believed him. "I just got a call from Kel. He's . . . *was* an old friend of mine," David admitted. He bent his mouth close to Gayla's face as he held her. His fingers massaged through her hair into her scalp, soothing and tender. "Kel won't hurt her, Gayla. He's only using her in exchange for something that belongs to him. He gets what he wants, and he lets Allison go."

"But what if he doesn't? Oh, my God . . . what if he doesn't?"

David could barely talk because Gayla's anguish was tearing at his insides. There wasn't much he could tell her.

He was in no position to make promises he wasn't sure he could keep.

CHAPTER SIXTEEN

⬦⬦⬦⬦⬦

David didn't see anything particularly unusual outside his windows. The parked cars didn't appear to have anyone just sitting and waiting, and all the occupied cars didn't stay long; they were just dropping off or picking up people. Most of the neighborhood businesses had closed for the night. David checked the time, tilting his wrist toward the dim illumination from the streetlights. It was a few minutes before 3:00 A.M.

The cat meowed and David automatically bent to lift the animal in his arms to keep him quiet. He tickled King Tut's ears.

"I never thought you capable of loving anything, anyone."

The soft, drowsy voice seemed to float and drift to him in the dark. David turned from the window and stared across the room to the barely discernible figure stretched out on the sofa.

"I didn't think you ever gave much thought to me at all," he said.

"Now and then." Gayla sighed. "Now . . . a lot." She sat up slowly.

David came to stand over her. He sat down on a corner of the coffee table, facing her. "King Tut gives me unconditional love, and I learned how to love back. But I have to give a lot of credit to Sylvia, and . . . a few other people I cared about," he said evasively.

Her arm came out of the dark to pet the cat on the top of his head. David put him back on the floor. "Did it work?"

David's chuckle was soundless. "Better than I could imagine. I think I needed Tut more than he needs me. He keeps me around just to feed him."

Although she was now sitting up, she was suddenly very quiet.

"Gayla . . . I'm sorry. I didn't . . ."

"It's okay. I . . . I know this is not really your fault."

"I should have made Kel leave after the first week. By then I think I knew that . . . he and I weren't the same. We didn't have anything in common anymore."

"You were being a loyal friend," Gayla countered. "I guess it's not your fault if Kel didn't deserve it."

"None of which helps us right now."

"No, it doesn't."

"As soon as the call comes, I'll leaving. I'll be back in an hour with Allison."

David heard a small strangled sound and knew that Gayla was trying not to cry. She had literally cried herself to exhaustion a few hours ago. He shifted position from the table to sit next to her on the sofa. She let him put his arms around her to hold her again, desperately needing comforting and reassurance.

"David, I'm scared. I can't even think how I'd live if anything happens to Allison."

"Hey . . . come on," he began. "It's not going to come to that. Kel isn't stupid. He knows if anything goes wrong, he's done for. There's no way out, no more second chances."

She was quiet for a moment, her head against his shoulder. "You said you've known him all your life. Then how come he's doing something like this?"

David thought about that. "I don't know. I always saw Kel as this guy who couldn't see until next week. Everything was about today; how much and how fast."

"David? Do you think . . . if anything goes wrong . . ."

"It won't. It's going to be fine."

She turned her head to try and see his face. "But if something . . ."

David pulled back so that he was facing her squarely. He touched her face. Bent forward to kiss her lightly to make her stop talking and thinking. "Then I lose everything I've always wanted," he whispered earnestly. "But I'm not going to let that happen. You have to trust me, Gay. It's not going to happen."

Quietly, she began to cry again.

The door buzzer went off a few minutes later, and David let Mitchell back into the building and the apartment.

"See anything strange?" David asked him.

"No, not really." He glanced at his sister, who sat blowing her nose and trying to get some control over her emotions. Mitchell exchanged looks with David. "You ready?"

"Just about."

David checked the time again. While Mitchell and Gayla talked quietly, David got his things together. He was not going to take any ID with him, and he was dressed in dark, concealing clothing. He had a small pocket flashlight and a small knife. He spent a few minutes listening to the low voices of Gayla and Mitchell. They had agreed not to say anything to Sylvia unless absolutely necessary. David stood in his room, considering the Tech 9 pistol. He thought of all the reasons why he should just wrap it again in the felt cloth and return it to the bottom of his bureau. They all outweighed any benefits to having it, but when the phone suddenly rang with the call David knew he'd been waiting for all evening, he slipped the gun into the back waistband of his pants where it was concealed by his jacket.

David picked up the phone on the second ring. Kel gave him the location of a pay phone and told David to expect the call from there with his final instructions. David turned to Gayla, who stood anxiously as he told her it was time.

"I'm coming, too."

He shook his head, already holding her back as he signaled to Mitchell. "You know you can't. Kel was clear. He doesn't want to see anyone but me approaching."

"No, I'm going . . ."

Gayla held onto David, her arms circling him. He

tried to pry her hands loose, but not before she'd felt the hard metal protruding from his back.

"This . . . this is a gun. David, you can't take a gun . . ."

David gently but firmly prevented Gayla from grabbing the gun and removing it. Mitchell stepped forward to hold onto his sister as David moved to the door.

"David, please . . . *please!*" she shouted after him.

"I'll be back," he said. "Mitchell knows what to do if you don't get a call from me in an hour."

David was mindful of the time he'd been given. He'd made the call from the designated phone booth and was told where to go. He'd arrived two blocks away, and carefully explored to find out the direction of street traffic, building entrances that were still open, alleys, courtyards . . . anyplace where concealment was possible. Satisfied that Kel wasn't going to change the game plan, David slowly walked to the rendezvous point of Hudson and Charlton streets. He was to wait in front of a closed branch of the post office. There was virtually no traffic, and the street was dim enough that any activity would not really be noticed.

David stood back in the shadows. He made sure to keep his hands out of his pockets. He spotted a black car driving toward him, but it continued north, turning on Houston toward the West Side Highway and the Holland Tunnel approach. A minute later another car followed the same route.

It was five minutes past the meeting time when David realized that a car had pulled up just off the corner where he stood. It had its headlights off and didn't turn off its engine. David waited, unsure if someone would signal him, or if he should walk to the car on his own, or even if this was the right car. The yellow park lights were turned on, and the back door of the car slowly opened. David, after taking a final look around the street, walked to the car. He stood there not sure what to expect. Another car going westbound passed the stopped car and continued across the intersection into the next street.

From the backseat of the car in front of David, Kel stepped out. He looked closely at David, his expression alert. He bent to say something to the person who'd been sitting next to him in the backseat and then he stood aside so that David could get a glimpse inside.

David watched Kel's every move. He knew that it was too late for additional conversation. He was there solely to get Allison back. After that, any connection he had with Kelvin Monroe would end forever. He saw Allison's head, her dark bright eyes and her mouth as she gnawed on her lip. He could do nothing more than to assess that she was physically okay—she seemed more tired than frightened—and try to get her away from Kel and the car as fast as possible.

"David . . ." Allison tried to reach out to him.

David put up a hand to warn her to stay still. "Everything's okay, Ali. I'm here to take you home."

Kel held onto Allison's arm and beckoned to David with his free hand. David, holding the box comfortably under his arm, carefully took hold of it in both hands, and held it out in front of his chest, toward Kel. Kel silently urged him forward. David passed the box to Kel, placing it in his outstretched hand. All the while they maintained direct eye contact. David was fully aware of Allison's relieved reaction at seeing him, and he hoped that she would say nothing more to distract Kel until the deal was completed.

The motor of the car was still running, but the windows were tinted a protective black, and David could not tell how many people were in the car. Kel pushed Allison to sit back inside, and she whimpered in protest but followed Kel's instructions.

Finally, David spoke. "I don't know what's in the box, Kel, but it's exactly the way you left it. I didn't look inside."

Kel opened it. "Not that I don't trust you, bro. But you understand that the kid goes nowhere until I check it out myself."

"You'll never be able to get rid of that junk, Kel."

He grinned. "I thought you said you didn't look."

"I'm guessing what you have in there is from a couple of the robberies I read about in the papers."

Satisfied with the contents, Kel closed the box. "This is one of those times when what you don't know can't hurt you, Dak. I see you returned the money."

"I told you I didn't want it. Allison, get out of the car . . ." David said, loud enough for the girl to hear.

Kel reached out and again pushed her back. "Wait a minute . . ."

"You got what you wanted. The girl's mother is waiting for her."

Kel narrowed his eyes, considering. He took a swift scan around the street. "But there's nobody to worry about me . . . except me. So . . . I think I'll just hold on to my security for a little longer . . ."

"Let the girl go. I kept my word," David announced.

Kel nodded. "I guess you did. That don't mean anybody else will. Did you call anyone since I talked with you?"

"No. I swear I haven't."

"Sorry, Dak. I don't think I can trust you anymore. The girl stays with me . . ."

Suddenly, the box Kel held went flying out of his hand. His body seemed to twist and buckle awkwardly as he was pushed from behind. David watched dumbfounded, as Allison scrambled from the backseat. She struggled to get around Kel and break free.

"Allison, don't . . ." David cautioned, but saw that she might succeed. He hurried forward to help her.

The box thudded to the ground and the contents spilled from the opening, some of the white packages bursting open. From inside the car someone shouted.

"Get in! Get the fuck in! Let's *move!*"

"Let me go!" Allison screamed and twisted as Kel grabbed her arm to prevent her from escaping.

Suddenly there was activity all around them, and

men running in their direction. They had guns drawn. David grabbed Kel's wrist with one hand and clawed his throat with the other, cutting off his air. Kel released Allison and she stumbled away. Out of his peripheral vision David saw two men in SWAT gear pull her to safety.

David heard the commands to freeze, but couldn't as he felt Kel begin to fight him. The car suddenly screeched away from the curb, shooting out into the street and away from the police. But it careened broadside into a car driving across its path. Glass splintered and shattered, and metal caved in under the impact as the getaway car sent the other into a short spin.

Kel got his wrist free and quickly pulled out an automatic from the inside of his coat. David released Kel's throat and used the force of his hands clasped together to try and knock the gun loose. He only succeeded in pushing Kel off balance. David reached for his own gun. He hooked Kel around the back of his ankle with a foot, and Kel went down backwards on the ground. The two of them ignored the calls to stop. Kel retaliated by quickly twisting to the side and grabbing David's leg to bring him down as well. David's hand hit the ground and his gun fell out.

David was aware of Allison crying. He heard the police shouting, and a siren. His adrenaline pumped hard, and he remembered something frighteningly familiar as the police closed in with their weapons trained on him and Kel. David still ignored them, struggling with Kel over his gun. He got the gun free only after applying his arm with some force again across Kel's throat, obstructing his breathing. David pulled the gun from Kel's hands and turned it on him. The next time he was commanded to drop the weapon and lay face-down on the ground, David complied. He tossed the gun aside, and stretched out in the street on his stomach as directed. He couldn't see if Kel did the same. Suddenly he was surrounded by cops, and his hands pulled behind his back and cuffed.

It was over.

David didn't struggle. Didn't try to defend himself as he was surrounded and roughly searched for other weapons. He craned his neck and head and caught a glimpse of Allison. She was being led to an official Police Department vehicle and questioned. He could see her trying to watch what was happening to him. He could hear Kel cursing a blue streak at the arresting officers. He was relieved that his risk to contact Matt had paid off in the timing of events and his meeting with Kel. But it could all still have gone wrong. The appearance of the police probably saved at least one life. He was grateful that one was Allison's.

It was over.

David methodically went through the short list of people he knew, trying to imagine their response to this latest in his history of official detention. But this time it had been deliberate. He also realized that it was probably the end of his second chance.

David was Mirandized and taken into custody with Kel.

It was all over. . . .

CHAPTER SEVENTEEN

❈❈❈

David quickly remembered every single reason why he'd hoped never to be locked down again. Not the least of which was the overwhelming sense that he was discarded refuse. He had finally proven to himself that that wasn't true. Yet here he was, back in the joint.

He sat in a deceptively comfortable office. It was only a kind of middle passage, a holding pen between the before and after . . . freedom and incarceration. He was still unsure which it would be. David felt oddly calm, knowing that no matter what the final decision, he had proven to himself his own self-worth. He had dared to reach out for love . . . and had found it waiting there for him.

The door to the office opened, and the gray-uniformed guard on the other side let an aging black man into the room, closing and locking the door behind him again.

David stood up as Matthew Nathaniel Nelson came into the outer office, where brief and often emotional meetings took place. Matt slowly smiled at David before reaching out to embrace him.

David looked down into the face of the older man who had been a creative blend of father, psychologist, minister and drill sergeant in his life. He smiled at Matt as he pulled forward one of the two roomy leather wing chairs in front of the big desk.

Matt studied him with amusement and affection in his brown bespectacled eyes.

"Now, is that a beard you're growing, or are you too lazy to shave . . . or is it some fad that I'm too old to have noticed?"

David rubbed his chin. "I hear that some women find it sexy."

Matt nodded as he laid his worn leather attaché case across his knees and opened it to extract a thick folder of legal documents. "Would some women include the mother of that young girl you rescued?"

David grew reflective. "I don't know if I saved her from anything. Kel would have let her go as soon as he thought he was safe."

"Maybe. Obviously you didn't trust waiting to find out."

"Have you heard anything from him?"

Matt shook his head, "Nothing different from what I've already told you. He's not giving up any names and he didn't implicate you in his crimes. Do you want to know the outcome of my meeting with the judge?"

"I'm not hopeful that it's good. Too many strikes against me."

"My boy, you underestimate my persuasive powers."

"No. You overestimate any sympathy for me. Look, I have a track record. I've been here before. Isn't this where you tell me they're going to throw away the key?"

"I am very happy to tell you it's a good thing I'm on your side. It's clear I believe in you a lot more than you do. I've managed to get all the charges against you dropped, except the illegal gun possession. I can get that reduced to time served . . . these past three days . . . and community service."

David stared at the man as he looked through the folder, and extracted one sheet. He held it out and David took it.

"It's the judge's orders to release you. You're free to go."

David read the paper carefully, but he didn't change his expression. "Thank you, Matt," he murmured. "Sometimes . . . I'm not sure I'm worth all the trouble I put you through."

Matt Nelson reached out and clapped his hand on David's shoulder. "Then it's a good thing I don't depend on you to make that decision. You've always been too hard on yourself, David. You have more strength of character than you give yourself credit for. You're one of my biggest successes. Of course, as I've often said, you didn't belong behind bars anyway. There was nothing wrong with you that a little TLC couldn't cure. Apparently you're getting that."

David shook his head ruefully. "Kel fell out when he saw Tut. Told me I needed a good woman."

"Glad you listened to him."

David's head came up, his expression alert. "What do you mean?"

Matt stood up. "I think it's time I retire. Quit while I'm ahead. You're going to be fine. Got a place to live . . ."

"Upstate. The place here is not mine."

"You'll find someplace else. You have a job . . ."

"My contract wasn't renewed for next year . . ."

"I'm talking about a position being offered. Gayla told me about it. It's a sure thing. And you have people who care about you." Matt got up from his chair and slowly made his way to the door, on which he knocked loudly.

"What . . . what are you up to?"

"Just wait a minute . . ." The door to the chamber opened. After a brief whispered conversation the guard walked away and Matt turned back to David. "You can go."

David approached the door. He was more reluctant to leave than he could let on. But he walked to the door anyway. David looked out into the hall . . . and found about a half-dozen faces staring back expectantly at him. He knew them all.

The first person David saw was Sylvia, because she gasped and hurled herself into his arms with a stranglehold hug. Right behind her were Mitchell and Gayla. She was as far as his gaze traveled. He was afraid to take his eyes off her. It was only when Sylvia stepped back to give others a chance to say hello, and Gayla had boldly stepped forward right into his outstretched arms, that David began to believe that Matt Nelson might be right after all. And when he kissed Gayla, for all the world like a dying man who'd just been granted a reprieve, David began to believe that maybe he could go home again.

"This is crazy. You know that, don't you?" David said in a hoarse voice.

"What's crazy?" Gayla asked. Her voice was lazy and quiet.

"Gay, I have no prospects. You couldn't have made a worse decision than to think you want to be with me."

Gayla sighed and pushed her back tighter against his chest. She ran her toes along the hard, hair-sprinkled calves. She closed her eyes dreamily and threaded her fingers with his. It was like she couldn't get close enough.

Making love had taken them to a new level of awareness. It had ended the stalemate, bridged a gap in time. It had worn down resistance and taken the edge off and only whetted their appetite. But most important, it had finally brought Gayla and David to a resolution of their feelings, long skewed by youth and inexperience.

"It's not as if I didn't have other proposals. It's not as if I didn't think I was in love before."

"What makes you so sure you're in love now?" David asked, kissing her shoulder and the side of her neck.

Gayla sighed and writhed against the bold explora-tion of his hand. "When I saw you again at the gallery, my first thought was I couldn't believe you were back. The second was how handsome you are. And the third . . . well, the third was how could I prove to you that I wasn't the same little know-it-all bitch I was when I was fourteen or fifteen." She heard David chortle at her self-evaluation.

David turned her so that Gayla was lying flat on the bed. He bent and teased at her mouth with his lips. He let his hand stroke her stomach, trailing his fingers provocatively across her breasts and rib cage, exploring the soft skin of her breasts and the puckered nipple.

"I admit it. But that didn't stop me from wishing you'd look at me the same way you did Graham Whelan. It didn't make me hate you. But I didn't like you making me feel like I wasn't good enough. I didn't like you comparing me to Graham."

"Then I don't understand what you saw in me that made you hold on to memories of me all these years."

"I think first of all was that you weren't afraid of me. You made me feel like . . . I had to earn your respect and love. You were the first woman who was really honest with me. And I wanted you to look at me the way you did at Graham."

She groaned softly. "Please don't mention Graham."

"Why not? You were in love with him. That doesn't bother me anymore."

"Yes, I was in love with him. I certainly thought I

was. But by the time I realized I wasn't . . . I found myself the mother of his child."

"And he was married."

"That hurt a lot. I was so stupid to think he was only seeing me, and that I was so special to him."

"You know what I think? I think he always regretted not asking you to marry him."

"Well, now I'm glad he didn't. Except for Allison, of course. Sometimes I'm very sorry that she didn't grow up having a father she knew and could have a relationship with."

"You didn't. I didn't."

She let him kiss her. His touch was still filled with the wonder of both discovery and expectations. A dream deferred. His hands were surprisingly gentle and skilled. Gayla loved that David took his time making love to her. And although the buildup and anticipation made them both breathless and hot with desire, so far it had only shown that age and experience and daydreams and love had everything to do with the depth of feelings for each other. Their first time really together had been in David's apartment, and it had felt like a tryst. Their mutual attraction coupled with the wait of so many years made the night wonderful and perfect.

Gayla wasn't surprised by her mother's lack of surprise at finding out that she and David had a thing going on. It was Allison's mature observation, after her dramatic rescue, that she'd guessed David really wanted to date her mother, that made Gayla see in turn that David had been right. Her daughter had instinctively known what David was feeling. Which only made Gayla feel pretty clueless and slow on the uptake. Everyone seemed to know how David felt about her . . . but her.

"What do you think of Allison?" she asked David.

He began to position her on the bed, to kiss her mouth and throat and breasts. To explore through the curly pubic hair to the soft mound and wet center of her body; to hold her with a tenderness that felt real and strong and enduring.

"I think you're very lucky," David whispered, gazing into her eyes as he urged her to open her legs wider. "And I'm a little jealous."

"Why?"

He levered his body above hers, feeling the telltale pulsing in his penis as he thrust into her. "Because she's not ours . . ."

Gayla held tightly onto David, gladdened by his confession.

It was a thought.

It could be remedied.

David walked along the platform of the station. He glanced over his shoulder to the parking lot and saw Gayla standing next to his car. He gave her a reassuring smile, which he hoped she could see across the distance. She must have, because she smiled in return. He turned his attention to Allison as she walked slowly next to him, contemplating the shadow of her footsteps.

"Are you nervous?" he asked her.

She shrugged. "A little, I guess."

"I bet he's nervous, too."

"I guess," she repeated.

"It's not that your father didn't care, Allison. He didn't know about you, either. You just need time to get to know each other."

"Yeah, but he already has a daughter. And she . . . she's more like he is."

David glanced down at her. "You mean . . . she's white?" Allison silently nodded. "I don't think that matters. Don't forget, he loved your mother. It may not have lasted, but it's true. You know, I'd give almost anything to be in your shoes. At least you get a chance to meet your dad. You now have a stepsister. You have *two* families." She didn't respond and David wondered if he should just keep his mouth shut and not try to explain something he didn't know much about.

"David? If you and my mother get married, you'd be my stepfather, right?"

He tried not to show his reaction to Allison's question. It was the first time she'd actually acknowledged that that's where he and Gayla were likely headed. "That's right. Does it bother you?"

"I don't thnk so. Not anymore. I like you."

"Thank you, Allison. That means a lot to me."

"But then if you have kids, does that mean that they will be Holly's stepsister, too? Or stepbrother? Is it half-brother?" she asked, wrinkling her brow.

David grinned at her. "We'll get it straight before you have to worry about it."

They heard the toot of a car horn, and Allison's name being called. David followed Allison's gaze to a car pulled up just outside the Metro-North Station in Fairfield. A little girl was running to meet Allison, and Graham stood with the car door open on the driver's side of the hunter-green Trooper. The two girls were already in conversation, falling comfortably into a bonding that had more to do with their gender and age than anything else. But watching Holly and Allison, Graham could see that any adjustments in the family structure of the Pattons and Whelans were going to be smoother than he'd first imagined.

Graham acknowledged David's presence with a broad smile and a wave. David walked to meet him until the two men could shake hands. David had a thought then, that this Graham Whelan was different from the privileged guy he'd known at seventeen. Judging by Graham's affability David guessed that Graham was probably having a similar assessment of him.

"Good to see you, David," Graham greeted him.

"Is it?" David responded cautiously.

"Yeah, it is. I feel like I've known you or about you all of my life. And yet . . . I don't know you well at all. We should do something about that."

Allison and Holly's giggling drew their attention. David considered Graham's observation. It was fair. "I guess we will," he finally answered.

"Where's Gayla?" Graham asked.

David wasn't surprised. For a fleeting instant he

felt the old insecurity rise up, only to quickly give way to the awareness that he and Gayla were in love with each other. They both knew they couldn't change the past, but they could build and improve on it.

"Here I am," came back the clear reply.

David and Graham turned to find that Gayla had approached from the parking lot. David watched her closely and she sent him a warm and reassuring smile. But then she gave her attention to Graham, and he to her.

David stepped back out of the way.

Gayla could see that there was a lot about Graham Whelan physically that had not changed in almost fifteen years. She hadn't noticed that afternoon he'd surprised her by showing up at her apartment. She'd only wanted him to go away, motivated by a surprising surge of hurt and anger . . . and an instinct to shield Allison. At best it had been a pointless wish. And a selfish one.

Her apprehension and uncertainty faded when she realized that she didn't need to judge Graham, herself or David based on the past. However things had turned out, Gayla believed now they were for the best. She and Graham had loved each other once, and the proof was in Allison. That was all that mattered.

It seemed for a moment that neither could say anything. They grinned and stared until Graham awkwardly lifted his arms and Gayla walked into them. They embraced gently, silently. Briefly, to bridge the gap of time and circumstances. Graham released her, grinning ruefully.

"This is a lot different from when I saw you a few weeks ago."

"You took me by surprise," she said.

Graham stared at her. "You were angry."

"And scared."

He pursed his mouth. "So was I."

"Guilty conscience," Gayla said astutely.

He nodded. "I thought up all kinds of things you'd say or do to me. It was pretty rough. After you walked away, I felt awful."

Gayla hesitated, faltering, "I have to admit, Graham, I hoped I'd never see you again."

"That's fair. I wasn't exactly . . . honorable about us, was I?"

"Maybe not. But I . . . I was wrong, too. I should have told you about Allison. You had a right to know. So did she."

"A lot of lost years, Gay . . ." he said thoughtfully.

"I'm sorry."

"Just don't be mad. It wouldn't do to have my daughter's mother ticked off at me. Makes for bad family relations."

His acknowledgment made Gayla feel peculiar. She'd never cast herself in that role before and it opened up a new vista for her. She *was* part of the Whelan family now, and Graham forever a part of hers. She glanced at Allison and Holly. They seemed to be getting along without explanations, apologies, excuses or guidance from the adults around them.

And despite Allison's doubts that she would not be accepted, or that she and Holly would have nothing in common, Gayla could see similarities between them that dispelled them all.

She looked at David, who stood close enough to make Gayla feel loved and needed, but just far enough away to let her and Graham have their reunion, so they could forgive and move on.

"Mom is beside herself." Graham chuckled. "She can't wait until we're all together at some dinner so she can claim Allison. She's very anxious to meet her other grandchild."

"I guess that means your parents aren't upset."

Graham's brows rose. "No. Why should they be? What for?"

Gayla sighed inwardly. What for, indeed.

"Gayla . . . I don't think there's much point in beating ourselves up over how things could have turned out between us if I hadn't gotten married and you hadn't gotten pregnant. But the way I look at it, we lucked out anyway."

"Did you feel that way all these years?"

"Honestly? Not until I found out about Allison."

"Is that why you came to see me, out of the blue?"

"Yes, it was." Graham nodded. "I felt that something wasn't quite right. I had a talk with Sylvia and I began to figure it out. She was reluctant to talk about Ali. She wouldn't say exactly when she was born. I was pretty dumb not to realize before. But I wasn't angry, Gay. I was grateful."

Gayla stared at him, resisting the urge to second-guess all those years. What if she'd told Graham right away she was pregnant? What if she'd given Allison a chance to bond with her father, with the Whelans?

"I guess . . . maybe there was a part of me that felt . . . you might reject her. You might . . ."

"She's my firstborn, Gayla. *Our* firstborn. I want to thank you for that. She's . . ." He struggled for words. "She's awesome!"

Awesome . . .

Gayla was surprised and pleased. She laughed at the expression that was part of Graham's background and experience, not hers.

Allison was going to have quite a family.

It occurred to David as he watched Gayla and Graham, and Holly and Allison, just how lucky he was. He was finally about to arrive at that complicated arrangement of relationships made up of surprises, skeletons, different colors and sizes; of steps and halves and firsts and seconds and long-lost and married into . . . and called a family.